The Dreamcloth

The Dreamcloth

Joanne Fedler

By the same author:

25 Essential Things you should do before getting married,
sixtyminute books, 2003.

Ideological Virgins and Other Myths: six principles for legal revisioning,
with Ilze Olckers, Law Race and Gender Unit, UCT and Justice College,
2001

First published in 2005 by Jacana Media (Pty) Ltd.
10 Orange Street
Sunnyside, 2092
Johannesburg
South Africa

© Joanne Fedler, 2005

All rights reserved.

ISBN 1-77009-101-7

Cover design by Michiel Botha

Set in Bembo 12/15

Printed by Pinetown Printers

See a complete list of Jacana titles at www.jacana.co.za

This book is dedicated to those I love.
Home is where you are.
All else is exile.

Thanks

To my grandfather Solomon Fedler, for the treasure of his life-story *Shalechet*; to my father, Dov, who takes from my loneliness, though the distance is torture; to my mother Dorrine, my best correspondent, for her generosity in always crossing oceans to take care of me; to my sisters Carolyn and Laura for sustaining my spirit; to Violet Matlapeng for wooden-spoon discipline and mielie-pap; to Joan Orkin (a rare gem of a teacher) for her adoring confidence in me when I was just a little pipsqueak; to Thandi Ngayi for taking care of my babies so that I could write, *ngiyabonga Mma*.

To Hedgebrook Women's Writer's Colony in Seattle, USA, for an island of precious weeks in the care of kind women; to Adrian LeBlanc for nudges in the right direction; to Sandra Miller, for steadfast counsel and too much fun; to the late Lionel Abrahams, and the participants of his workshops for a safe space; to Nella Freund, Anne Schuster, and my dear friends Catherine Stewart and Ilze Olckers, for reading the first shitty draft and not holding back; to my aunty Rae Abramowitz and Rose Zwi, for help with Yiddish translations.

To Maggie Davey, for making it happen (bless you); to my editor Alex Dodd, for saving Henri's life, and other radical acts of narrative courage; to Chris Cocks, for always returning my emails.

To my Zed, for standing by my side in my life's journey. Without your support, I'd still be dreaming about *The Dreamcloth*. I'm sorry gratitude isn't a currency. I'd love to have bought you that boat.

And to Jesse and Aidan, for reminding me, 'It's enough writing, can we go to the beach now?'

Joanne Fedler

Part 1

He Wishes for the Cloths of Heaven

Had I the heavens' embroidered cloths,
Enwrought with golden and silver light,
The blue and the dim and dark cloths
Of night and light and the half-light,
I would spread the cloths under your feet:
But I, being poor, have only my dreams;
I have spread my dreams under your feet;
Tread softly because you tread on my dreams.

WB Yeats

***

I have dreamed a dream and I do not know what it is.

Musaf Service for Rosh Hashana

***

God save us from having one shirt, one eye and one child.

Yiddish proverb

S uddenly everything became shrill—even the silence—
and she knew with the clarity of physical pain that
planets had shifted.

Mia—naked beneath the apron splashed with the maroon and
amber of a hand-painted chilli—was cooking red lentils with
garam masala, the taste she always craved after an orgasm with
Juan, when she stopped mid-stir, shook her head to unsettle
the shrillness and sneezed three times in quick succession.
Death? It felt tremulously close to it. Whose? She breathed in
deeply to nudge the premonition into a corner. Not her
mother, no. Fran would never die so heartily. Not Henri.
Definitely not. The shadows shuffled, releasing a splinter of
light that travelled a long way to some distant past place.
Christ, it had to do with *him*. Asher.

She shuddered now—almost two decades since last she had
seen him—even in thinking his name. Her body, racing to
keep up with the mystics of intuition, emitted a furious rush
of sweat. She wiped her upper lip, her forehead and curved her
body over the steam from the pot. Lacing her sticky fingers in
her hair, dark but for the sheath of her white birthmark, she
cupped her hands over her skull to hold her ghost still. It
wrestled free. *Settle*, she thought, *just settle down. I'm trying to
figure it out.*

Here she was, at the chilling hour of 2am, in Sarajevo after
passionate lovemaking with—don't get her wrong—a lovely
man, but a stranger nonetheless. Bosnia had been her home for
almost five months now, the place she ran to when 'ethnic
cleansing' became a new phrase in the English language, and

where she had slammed her face up against stories salvaged from the bodies of broken girls and women. She had only intended to write a few pieces for the Bosnia-Herzegovina Information Centre, to slap the world into recognition. But here her heart had stopped, grown swollen and spacious, and she could not leave. Not yet.

He stuck a bottle inside me. He jumped on my belly. The bottle broke inside me.

Mia's eyes had come to rest on the interpreter's face. Perhaps something had got lodged in the translation. Mia moved her gaze cautiously to the eyes of the young Muslim girl.

*"Ne razumijem,"** Mia ventured softly.

The interpreter did not repeat the words again. Turning to Mia, she said, "You heard."

He bit my neck until I was covered with blood.

He slashed my skin in the shape of a crucifix if I refused to have sex.

Mia listened and wrote, fumbling for words to fix to happenings language struggled to hold. And still the women streamed in through the doors each day to tell someone behind a desk their stories of detention at a sports hall, a high school and a construction workers' barracks in Foca, the southeast Bosnian city overrun by Serb forces. *He raped me. They raped me. They raped me again.*

Mia's mouth had been dry, her fingers cramped. It had been three hours of testimony. She had needed the toilet at some point, but had not dared break the fragile thread of the girl's voice. She was only twelve, her mother huddling close to her side. *Seventh grade. A virgin. Eight months. Don't know how many times. Torture. Gang rape.*

Each day, for a hundred and forty six days, she had remained stoic for the re-telling, yesterday by a fifty-nine year old

_____
* 'I do not understand,' in Bosnian.

grandmother with a missing front tooth, this morning by a twenty-five year old pregnant woman with a stutter, at noon by a teenager with pimples the size of boils between her cheek and nostril. If you say a word over and over too many times, it unfits itself. Estranges from its mooring. She had played these word games as a child. Nervous Breakdown. Nerv. Ous. Brea. Kdown. Ner. Vous. Br. Ache. Down.

The mug had shaken in her trembling hand, when she returned from the bathroom. She needed caffeine. There was no sugar. She would have to drink it bitter. The brown coffee granules had fizzed as she poured hot water over them, when Djammera, one of the Bosnian journalists, laid her hand on Mia's shoulder and introduced her to Juan Rodriguez. Mia raised her eyes to meet his. UN representative. The pain of the world was their shared aphrodisiac.

"He's the new UN delegate," Djammera had mentioned later as they drank a beer at dusk on the steps outside. "An expert on gender war crimes. Did lots of work on torture in the jails of Argentina." Not that Mia had asked. Not specifically.

He was quiet, used words sparingly, but when he did, his eyes narrowed, as he spoke of *the unspoken societal absolution of war-spawned rape and the patriarchy of international bodies run by men who do not see the misogyny in their failure to take this human rights violation seriously.* Unlike most of them there, taking testimonies and tending to the human shrapnel, he believed (or perhaps she needed him to believe) that they could stop the madness. She had dug her fingernails into his back three days later in a multiple orgasm that wrenched a cry from both their throats and subsided into a quiet tenderness. The pain of the world was an aphrodisiac for both of them.

Now, five months into this affair, she took the wooden spoon and stirred the spluttering lentils as her hair gestured softly over her face. Why now? What did Asher want? Hadn't he died some horrible death yet? The smell of garlic and toasted curry leaves—what a passionate mingling—made her nostrils quiver. Sex always left her with a craving for one or other taste—a post-coital urgency that demanded immediate attention, like a full bladder, a sneeze, revenge.

It was as if each lover hammered a furious longing for flavour into her. She would always leave the scene of passion with ungracious haste and head for a kitchen, a delicatessen, a herb garden. There she would be drawn to suck on the bark of a cinnamon stick or bite into the nub of raw ginger or a full jalapeno, hungering for their sting, some close to the lips, others deeper in the throat. She had chewed cardamom pods and garlic cloves (without undressing their papery petticoats) whole. Bouquets of basil leaves had been torn from their stems; filigrees of honeycomb bitten full. Intimacy always left her bereft.

The lentils were almost done. She sniffed deeply into the steam. But something was missing—the texture of tannin, the density of flesh. Lifting the wooden spoon, she watched the creamy brew drip and lifted the spoon to her mouth. From the bedroom, Juan groaned in post-coital slumber. She felt the wetness of their lovemaking trace its way down her inner thigh as the past whirled in every blood cell. The shrillness began to subside. She turned off the stove. The lentils puffed less breathlessly. Eventually they emitted intermittent sighs. Mia wiped her face with the back of her hand, and found it wet. It was time to leave.

She had, in all her twenty-nine years, been devoutly allegiant to her childhood promise to herself, always to be the beloved, never the besotted. Love was not worth anything if the balance was not in your favour. That she knew for sure. She had to be the one to walk away. She had refused *one more night?* More times than she could remember, though sometimes the ligaments of her resolve strained in the leaving. She never said sorry or I never meant to hurt you. Her backpack always swung

Joanne Fedler

easily onto her shoulders, and her coloured head cloth was faded with use. She reminded each of her lovers that she was a gypsy. Still, some held on tightly with 'fuck off I never want to see you again'. Others let go more lightly. Now she stirred the lentils that had stopped huffing and puffing altogether and her heart raced as she wondered how her lover, blissing in the moist laundry of their love, would release her. Anger was not his emotion of refuge, he might even wish her well.

And as the hairs began to settle at the nape of her neck, and the fragility of all she had loved and lost was stirred into the depths of the red lentils, which are generous in that way, the alarm of the phone's ring ripped the air. It took seconds for her to pad silently across the kitchen floor and lift the receiver. Ordinarily at this ungodly hour she might expect to hear Henri's Afrikaans "*Meisie!**" on the other end. But when she heard the rumble of a voice thick with its Israeli accent: "Issat you Mia?" she laughed out loud for the magic of intuition and its cryptic ways. And just the possibility of revenge.

"It's me, Asher."

It was, after all, the taste of blood she was craving.

* Afrikaans for 'girl.'

Apartment 7/12 Rehov Zion, Tel Aviv,
February 1994

Israel has a crackle and edge to it as if there is a charge of God's electricity flowing through its veins. She had been there once before as a girl of fifteen for three whole months with other young Jewish teenagers soaking up Zionist propaganda. Israel Needs You. The Law of Return. Next year in Jerusalem. *Hava' nagilah*, and all that. The bustle of the Old City, the smell of singed cumin, the dark eyes of gun-bearing men and the grace of a sea that does not permit sinking had each enchanted her. But she had had to guard her virginity like a bull terrier. Desperate young men who did not speak English stalked her. It was as if Asher was everywhere.

Now she was returning at his request to nurse him, for death has a call that is hard to refuse. How he had tracked her down, she never asked. But a spy has his ways and means, she supposed.

She found him alone in a small flat in Tel-Aviv, a frail chicken of a man. "Not in bad shape for a sixty-nine year old?" he had smiled. Death's stench, a sweet rottenness, caught her in the throat and reminded her that dying is a sensory ending. She sat at his side. She lifted him on and off bedpans, wiped his body, offered him painkillers, combed his white hair, rolled his cigarillos, lit them, caught the ash, snubbed them out when they got low. She even managed a smile when he reached out to touch her face, and smiled, saying, "If not for dying…" and left it at that. Even with mortality circling his bones, he raged against the fading of his masculine power that had left her weak with an unknown longing as a child.

When he slept, she wrestled with her longing to smother him with his own pillow. But death was kindly attending to outstanding debts. And, when the ghost woke up at insane hours, she wrote furiously, using up three full diaries, the blank sides of all his tobacco paper and a handful of paper serviettes. When the writing subsided, she took out her Swiss Army knife and carved little figures from bits of cork she picked up off the streets, small branches she broke from passing trees. In the cup of her hand, she chiselled blind angels, some winged, others wingless. Sometimes in pity for those unable to fly away, she searched for triangles of paper or tinfoil she found around his apartment and gave them wings. They stood in a little row on the window ledge next to his bed.

"Fly away Peter, fly away Paul," she mused. "Come back Peter, come back Paul." Come back… such a mournful phrase, it sickened her with grief.

Sometimes she imagined it was her father and not him she was nursing to the grave. Even in his decaying state, he still aroused that ache from her girlhood, brought to life by his promise that she held secrets that life would answer for her.

"I 'ave nobody else," he whispered to her as she sat at his bedside. She nodded and held his neck so he could sip water.

"And I am afraid to die alone."

"You should be—you've got lots to answer for up there."

He smiled weakly. "Up there? Ha! You know where I go."

"Don't believe in hell," she said softly.

"Not a matter of belief—that's where I go, so we say goodbye for real now…"

"Goodbye… Oh, so this time round you think a goodbye might be in order," she mumbled. She curbed herself, mindful of compassion for the dying. She had been too close to death too many times.

He lay silently, eyes shut, resigned to her verbal accusations.

There was a long moment of silence.

"I did not kill your father," he said meekly.

"Do not start on that now…"

"Okay, okay…"

She fiddled with her white birthmark, twirling the hairs in her fingers. It was a while before she said, "You may as well have put a knife through his heart. Just take that to the grave, will you?"

His eyes shot open wide, gleaming with the remains of anger. "'is 'eart broke from you too."

Mia stood up, walked to the window, and slammed her fist on its ledge. She bit her lower lip until the pain forced her to stop. "I was just a child, Asher… You stole me, you stole from him—from all of us." She turned to face him now. "Don't you fucking blame me for his death… You hurt all the wrong people."

"I 'ave always looked after you—to this day. I didn't 'urt you. I provided for you. I gave you all I ad."

"What do you mean you didn't hurt me? My father committed suicide for Chrissake!"

"That was 'is choice."

"He thought he had nothing to live for…"

"Life is tough, we all suffer 'orrible things."

"You have no remorse… You're disgusting."

Asher laughed weakly. "Enough…" he said, putting his hands up. "Enough."

Sometimes around six in the evening, when he slept, she would let herself out and walk to the café on *Rehov** Altman, and buy a *shwarma*, asking for the reddest, rawest meat and a beer. Israeli men smoked around her, but she pulled her shawl closer, uninviting of their smoke.

"Where you from?" they drawled in heavy accents when she did not respond to their "*Mayayfo ut?*" †

---

* 'street,' in Hebrew.
† 'Where are you from?' in Hebrew.

"*Ein makom,*"* she sometimes answered, but never stayed to cast wider word circles with them. Sometimes she let them look at her without minding, letting them see only her body— her breasts, mouth, big nose, dark ringlets of hair, generous thighs—letting the curves and corners of her body distract them as they wondered what the texture of her pleasure might be. From behind. On her knees. Hard. More. Handcuffed. On top. She drew comfort from the persistence of their gaze, incapable of imagining the texture of her pain; whether they would get swallowed into it and never come out again; if nights terrify her because of their darkness or the nightmares they bring; and whether it is the hand of a ghost that has given her a lock of silver white hair. She sometimes even felt a rush of warmth for these disillusioned strangers blind to the deep life in her that their olive-toned jack-in-the-box crotches could never reach. And she scoured the market places unable to rid herself of the longing for the taste of lamb, so freshly slaughtered, she could taste the fear in its pink flesh.

On day twenty-seven after her arrival, Asher died. On day twenty-three, he had given her the dreamcloth. She was out of breath from the seven flights of stairs she had to climb to his apartment, and was fumbling for the key to unlock the door, when panic flooded her. She rushed in to find Asher on the floor in the lounge in a foetal position, clutching a faded velvet blue *talit*† bag.

"What are you doing?" she shouted.

"What I must."

"For Chrissake, Asher, stay in bed," she said sharply. "Die with dignity."

"Dignity? Phaah," he said. She knelt down next to him.

* 'No place,' in Hebrew.
† Jewish prayer shawl.

"This is for you, *motek*,"* and he handed her the *talit* bag.

Now her heart was furious, and before she even opened the bag to dip her trembling fingers into its velvet belly, she knew, because her ghost knew, that her dreamcloth was found.

Clutching it in her hands, she paced the room. And from the deepest place, where nothing had come to rest, not in as many years as it had taken to lose all that meant so much, the yearning engulfed her. She felt a warm wetness that was safe like holding arms, but it was just tears and her face streaked with the cleanness of fresh crying before the gasp in her body broke out.

"I can't take it to the grave," he said, his voice barely a whisper.

She held the dreamcloth to her face, buried her cheeks in its soft folds, as remembering broke over her in shudders.

"Touch the finger of a dead man," he used to smile, holding out his index finger, yellowed with cigarillo smoke, to touch the tip of her little index finger. Then taking her other hand he would make her rub up and down so that she touched his finger and her finger all at once. It was a half-feeling, something not quite alive, and when he did it with her, her father had watched them from the corners of his red-veined eyes, afraid.

"Oh Daaaaddddy, daaaadddy," escaped from her lips as she cradled her head in her hands, her arms on her knees, her knees on the floor, and rocked, while Asher watched.

Inside her the gypsy ghost wailed and her own body felt clammy like a finger touched that is half one's own and half someone else's.

"You asshole," she blurted out. "God bless your fucked-up soul for giving this back."

* 'Sweetie,' in Hebrew.

Apart from the Rabbi and Mottie the gravedigger, a nineteen year old with a brain frozen at the age of six and soft brown eyes, she was the only one at his graveside. When the ritual was over, holding the cloth in her fingers, she spat on his grave three times before she booked a one-way ticket to Johannesburg, South Africa.

★★★

In this life, air travel is the closest we can get to heaven, Mia mused, though the air stewardess—with her lip-lined smile and neat hair, bothering her with a tray of neat food prepared unlovingly—reminded her otherwise. But, food aside, she could sink into her reverie in a controlled air pressured capsule, until it landed in a faraway place, a new time zone—she, several hours older or younger, depending on how many invisible lines of longitude they had crossed. Mia closed her eyes, eyelashes to cheeks, and felt the gypsy inside her uncross its legs, stretch out, and make as if she would sleep for a time.

Air made her unstable, unsure of what to trust, but to be able to cut through it at hundreds of kilometres an hour had given her Beijing's Tiananmen Square in the aftermath of the massacre, the jubilance and rubble in the fall of the Berlin Wall, the poverty and distress of Somalians as public order collapsed around them. And finally, Bosnia. In seven years, she had been drawn from one disaster to the next, witnessing, listening, writing fiercely, documenting other people's pain.

"Can't you find some happy things to write about?" Fran's voice had crackled into her ear—could it have been two whole years ago? Shit, she ought to have called her since then—on her birthday or the anniversary of her dad's death, at least. She was a shit daughter. At least that was something both

Joanne Fedler

she and Fran could agree on. "Can't talk anymore, run out of money," she'd answered, returning the receiver to its cradle. Rich coming from Fran—she wouldn't know happiness if it moved in next door.

She was a journalist. That's what journalists did. Pain took up more place in the world than happiness. It deserved attention. What should she be writing about? Hollywood celebrity weddings? Rags to riches fairytales? Cancer survivors? *The purpose of life is not to be happy, but to matter, to have it make a difference that you lived at all.* She could still recall the quote word-perfectly, and how she and Grace had each penned it into their journals when they were girls. Well, she *was* making a difference. The challenge was to stay sane.

In each place, she made her flying figures. Some from driftwood, bequests from the ocean, others from scrap metal she found in the gutters. Not one figure was identical to any other, as if infinity lent itself to this task she had begun in a childhood many lifetimes ago. Some were voluptuous, bosomed, bellied females with tiny wing buds, others were long-bearded skeletal males with penises as long as their outstretched wings, others were blunted, androgynous, with coppery spiked feathers, arching towards the sun. She always left them behind, a token that she once was there.

From a seat at a small window, life can be explained: the world is small, turbulence is inevitable and you carry your ghosts wherever you go. By boat, water takes forever to cross, and you can only arrive at places whose edges rest on the ocean's lip. But her gypsy ghost had crossed oceans before and knew the motions of passage. Just the sounds were unfamiliar. Air hums; water knocks.

The knee in the seat next to her touched hers for the fifth time in the last while. She moved hers away, fumbled in the pocket of the seat in front of her for her diary covered in purple satin and studded with turquoise sequins and tiny drops of mirror, and turned to the window. She opened the pen nestled in the book's interior seam and wrote: '*In mid-air some thousands of feet above the earth. From: Israel. To: Jo'burg, South Africa.*' She stopped. The ghost did not want to write. She pushed the nib of her pen on the page, insistent now. C'mon, help me out here. The ink seeped out of the nib onto the page making a blot. She had already traversed all the conversation terrain with her travelling companion and politeness had now given way to weariness.

Jabulani Khanyile, an immaculately dressed returning exile from London, heady with hopeful nostalgia, had shared his opinions about sanctions, the referendum, Boipatong, Buthelezi, De Klerk, Chris Hani's assassination (he had wiped his tears with the back of his hand), and his hero and inspiration, Nelson Rolihlala Mandela. He told her of his arrest in the Eighties for his work in the unions, his escape to Botswana, from there to London, and how the cold makes the longing to return all the more unbearable. Was she also returning for the election? She had nodded, and said 'Partly'. 'Did she think the Afrikaner would let the ANC come into power without a civil war?' She didn't know. He thought, wiping his lips, that there would be violence. Bloodshed. His eyes never strayed from her face. Bloodshed, he repeated.

She had listened patiently, ventured opinions sparingly. She couldn't remember when his hunger to talk politics had eased into 'Have you ever slept with a black man?' accompanied by his knee-touching itch against her sari skirt.

"That, Jabulani, is none of your business," she had said.

"Too scared?" he laughed, pouring his third gin into the plastic glass filled with ice and tonic.

"You've got to be kidding," she said, and in that, his friendliness got an edge to it that was laced with 'white bitch'.

She had taken the opportunity and turned to her silence. It was tedious to be forever escaping. Running from. What was it about men that they couldn't just be still, allow the approach, give way to a softness that comes from patience? Her black lovers, peppering her past, exempted her from a black man's fury against an unflirtable Settler Woman.

Settler Woman was Blokes' pet name for her: a joke, see, to soften the 'one settler one bullet' chant that had chilled her when she first heard it from a toyi-toying Pan African Congress crowd on campus in early Wits days. On his tongue's journey from the palette behind her ear to her navel those words would come out in a harsh whisper.

"Settle on me, my settler woman," he'd say, pulling her thighs onto his toasted ginger-brown torso. And she would descend, a cascade of long dark hair, with its white lock, into the impaling cradle of his lust.

That was the kind of settling she was good at. The magic she worked with her groin let her ground all her lovers where she left them. But leave them she always did. Just when the sweetness became its sweetest; the longing its most intense. Heartbreaker, cock-tease, commitment-phobe—she'd been called them all, some in rage by burly lovers, some with gentleness, by those who knew her secret or at least suspected. She wondered if gypsies ever gave up the ghost and decided to buy the house, get the pet, plant the tree or take the oath. Sometimes the ache to stay, to feel what lay beyond the corner of tomorrow, left her unable to write for days on end.

Perhaps her Jewish blood was made of nomadic DNA and she carried leaving inside her like a genetic deformity. Or maybe it was that gypsy ghost who stalked her, always pushing her onwards to the next unbearable tragedy. She slipped her fingers inside her cerise blouse, between the buttons. Inside her bra, around the left breast nestled the dreamcloth. Now it lay like a skin across her nipple, a shield over her heart, folded twice upon itself.

She yawned. Jabulani was still sulking, adjusting his headphones and squinting his eyes at the screen where Forest Whittaker spoke mutely in *The Crying Game*.

Juan's eyes had moistened, "Go, go home," he had said

gently, running his fingers through her hair, and she thought of him fondly now. Lentils had been his flavour, but right now she was beginning to crave something that could only be described as… as (could it be?) raw potatoes?

Pointing at her journal, Jabulani said, "Egoli, not Jo'burg."

"I'm sorry," she said.

"Johannesburg is now called Egoli. It's a Sotho word, meaning 'City of Gold.'"

Mia nodded. "I like that."

Her hand moved back to the page. She crossed out Jo'burg, South Africa in one neat line and wrote 'Home'.

aheym tsu kummen:

to come home:
return to the place where one was born;
find one's way back to the starting place; be understood

At the southern tip of Africa, the warm Indian ocean and the cold Atlantic ocean meet. You might expect a dramatic clash of waters. You would be disappointed. From a tower, you might think that Africa is the centre of the universe and Cape Point the fraught seam, holding the earth together. But this, like so much of what we witness, is just an illusion—Africa is the end of the world, or so it felt like to Maya, huddled in her shawl, dank with a month of unwashed days. And then some learned man might nudge her, to 'let you know, should you be interested', that Cape Point is not where the two oceans meet, rather Cape 'Agulhas' is, some degrees of longitude east. Longitude? What did she know from longitude? People around her, weary from weeks at sea had nodded, '*Tah-keh*?*' If matters of geography meant anything to one, and one had the heart for the future, one might have found comfort in such facts and perhaps repeated them to a neighbour, breastfeeding her child in the folds of her garments.

It is these same waters she crossed that the first Dutch ships to arrive on South African shores must have sailed in 1652— long before any Jew, escaping whatever *pogrom* or *golem* haunted his past or future, looked south. With three ships, the *Goede Hoop*, the *Ryger* and the *Dromedaris*, the first white men docked at the Cape of Good Hope, a name that would lift one's spirits, if one's spirit had not been broken. For the sake of

* 'Really?' in Yiddish.

pepper, they first came here. The Turks—those Anti-Semitic dogs—had blocked Europe's overland trade path, so what could not be done by wheel was done by water. The Cape was the halfway point between the Netherlands and Indonesia, the 'spice oasis' (wasn't that a phrase to please a poet?). There sailors, bleeding and thirsting for anything that grew on a tree or from the soil, rested and buried their friends whose journeys ended far from home. Scurvy they called it. A person is not meant to be at sea for so long, isn't that so? Especially one like herself, who until that cursed passage to Africa, had never stepped foot outside Kovno.

Greediness grows. It starts with pepper, but it gets a taste for more. Soon, those with a hunger for, how do they name it?, 'colonization' (not to do with matters of the relieving of one's bowels, one should excuse the possible confusion) became greedy for land. Perhaps the dark-skinned natives who inhabited the place deserved what they got—they did not fight for what was theirs. They welcomed the white men who, in their foreign tongue spoke of their hosts behind their backs as the sons of Ham—'dull, stupid, odorous black stinking dogs'. As for Maya, she felt sorry for them.

Word got out—Africa, like a helpless woman on her marriage bed, was there for the taking. The Germans and French followed, grabbing whatever they could by raiding and battling with the people who had always lived on the land. Men did what they have always done—what they could not take in peace, they took by force. A *pogrom* is a *pogrom* no matter whether in Europe or Africa.

In 1795 the British came to separate these landed Dutchmen, 'the Boers', and the blacks. The British, with their tight-lips and pale skins, were shocked by the nakedness—in public—of these 'hewers of wood and drawers of water', (as for Maya, she was enthralled by their shamelessness, a fascination that grew into a full-bodied envy). British gentlemen put their fingers to the soil, hoping to turn a desert into an oasis—but

Joanne Fedler

what is held by force, can only offer its barrenness. Harsh weather and locusts, they blamed it on. So they scorched the earth, took black slaves and hid their flags behind their backs, offering Bibles in their outstretched hands. Hypocrisy you should expect from such Jew-haters.

Then madness—white men turned on each other, fighting over the land in a tug-of-war, not like the communal celebrations of strength they would sometimes have in the town-square in Kovno. They burnt crops. Destroyed families. Killed and killed and killed—each other, and the black man. The English beat the Boers in a bloody war. And as with all victories, hatred and revenge grew from the blood-watered earth.

Elsewhere, Jews, like Maya (and her husband Yankel, three years earlier), throughout Europe feared genocide. They murmured prayers in secret, married out of the faith and held fast to the promise that it is they who were God's chosen people. Those less certain boarded ships and looked to the south for shelter from extinction. They arrived, tattered and poor, but after a good wash, white in a place where that was all that mattered. And it is the place they began, in thick Eastern European accents to call 'home', if their hearts had not been left behind.

What does a Jew know from home? Some call them the Chosen People, but God surely does not love a nation he condemns to such nomadic circumstances. Was Kovno home? That wretched poverty, that icy shtetl? Maya stood under the *chuppah** at the age of eighteen with a stranger at her side. People sang '*yismach chatan im kalah*'—may the bridegroom rejoice in his bride. What of the bride? His rejoicing reviled her. She was not made the way God made Eve, from the rib of Adam, but of some other substance. Being his wife, she was in exile from herself.

* the marriage covering held by four poles to symbolize the house the couple will make together.

No, only in one place did she find home. A place hidden from all the eyes of neighbours with their itching tongues. Only with her by her side, was home the wooden doorframe they crossed each day, into their private world, the threshold from which all roads led and to which they all returned.

Home was where she kept her secrets, treasures and things unknown.

Home smelled of the chicken fat on the stove warming potatoes and yesterday's beetroot soup that stained her hands to a magical colour.

Even oceans away from it, she carried home inside her, just beneath her skin. She bled more easily far from home.

Without the love that kept her alive, this earth, this body, this life was not home.

Emmarentia—it was a friendly name, one Fran took to with inexplicable fondness. Not that it was pretentious. But it had the air of mystique, unlike its neighbouring suburb, 'Greenside', insipid, uninspired. 'Emmarentia' was named after someone and therefore lent itself to historical inquiry. Who was she? Who loved her? Did she die happy? 48 Komatie Road was an unimpressive face-brick double-storey in this lush suburb, which was designated a white's only area by the Group Areas Act of 1950. It was several jacaranda-lined streets up from the Emmarentia Dam, also named after the elusive ghost in whose honour it was built. It was the fourth house Fran entered with her husband of eight and a half weeks, Issey, on the bright-eyed mission of purchasing a 'family home'. From the threshhold, Fran silently determined that this was the doorway through which she would be carried out in a coffin.

Fran posthumously befriended the unknown Emmarentia Botha, the wife of Louw Geldenhys, the first white farmer to lay claim to this particular piece of land after the Great Trek. This leafy suburb was once part of 'Braamfontein', an enormous farm stretching from Victory Park, around to Rosebank in the north and Killarney just south of it, down to Commissioner Street in the heart of the city of Johannesburg, over to Mayfair and Coronationville in the south-west, and up to the base of the Northcliff ridge.

Though renowned for his equal treatment of Afrikaners and Englishmen, Geldenhys will, in all likelihood, rather be remembered as that 'bastard who kept Greenside booze-free' (in Issey's words). To this day, you need to travel beyond the borders of the suburb to find a bottlestore. Geldenhys did not want alcohol supplied to black men on the mines. God knows they were wild enough without it.

Sitting on her *stoep** with *A History of Emmarentia* propped on her knee (which she would renew seven times over the next three months from the Emmarentia Public Library), Fran educated herself about Geldenhys's life: his return from the Anglo-Boer war, his offering of work to the many landless Boers and his penchant for commissioning only white men to construct the dam wall, by hewing great blocks of stone from the Melville Koppie, that now holds back fifty vertical feet of water. Consequently, the Emmarentia Dam, at the lower end of his farm, is one of the few man-made constructions in Johannesburg built entirely without the sinew and sweat of exploited black men.

Emmarentia, who was a fervent gardener, planted five palm trees in a circle in front of the main farmhouse in Greenhill Road, which still stands in its original form. Reading about her, Fran almost imagined she had a friend, for she was not easily able to engage in the intimate task of actually making them.

By their first summer in 48 Komatie, Fran, in a rupture of inspiration, threw herself into the transformation of her garden. Like an Israelite spurred to whip a wasteland into an eden, she, in her green-fingered, rose-patterned gardening gloves from Pick 'n' Pay (on special for one rand fifty), weeded, pruned, mulched and planted, perspiration glimmering on her brow and the grass staining the kneecaps of her trousers, heady with an emotion bordering on joy. But it wasn't joy—such excesses eluded her. It was contentment. Unthreatening, unenviable. But hers alone to savour.

* 'balcony' or 'verandah' in Afrikaans.

Joanne Fedler

Each morning, folded in her royal blue silk dressing gown, sipping her Earl Grey tea, she took in the wonder of what she had made beautiful all by herself. Not a snowdrop whitened nor a fern frond uncurled that Fran did not notice. Each tiny stretch of every bud brought her satisfaction. September brought promise and the gush of jasmine breath in the hedges, though a warm August might outwit the jasmine into an early appearance. October and November brought a rush of colour to the flowerbeds, like 'hundreds and thousands' scattered everywhere. But it was the pleasing hum of bees—those blessed little martyrs—that reassured her as they got on with their business.

Fran's favourites were the roses: *Baronne Prevost* of tender pink, *Blush Noisette* with its hints of lilac, *Boule de Neige* of Camellia-like whiteness, *Dainty Bess* of the peachy whisper and *Don Juan* in its flaming red blazer. She envied their proud beauty, vulnerable, unapologetic. For this reason she protected the most beautiful of all, never picking them, but allowing them to die a natural death unsevered from their stems. Her garden, described as 'a dazzling testimony to Nature's palette of cerises, ambers, fuschias and pale pinks' would, by the height of apartheid, see her photographed holding a teacup in her left hand, alongside her rose beds in one of South Africa's leading home and garden magazines. She secretly attributed this honour to Emmarentia, her muse.

On her numerous domestic errands she always chose the route down Greenhill Road. This road runs in front of Geldenhys's original farmhouse, still standing in its inaugural majesty. In passing, Fran would brake and take her eyes off the road momentarily, hoping to snatch a peek of the homestead beyond the verdant growth of the exterior. But this she would do only for a second or two—no more—for the road has a slight kink in it due to Emmarentia's insistence when the suburb was being laid out that a huge oak tree, earmarked for felling to accommodate the road, be spared.

Despite its Afrikaner heritage, Emmarentia is now a suburb inhabited mostly by Jews, who migrated from Mayfair when families wanted to be close to 'good schools', and Mayfair started becoming 'a little too Indian'. On every right hand doorpost, or to avoid exaggeration, every three in four, a *mezzuzah** is attached with the Hebrew letter *'shin'*, the first letter of God's name embossed or engraved on its slim body. 48 Komatie Road had its *mezzuzah* affixed the day after its newly-weds moved in, in a ceremony involving Rabbi Goldenbaum, *Zaide†* Yankel (Issey's father), Issey and Shmooley (Issey's brother), who apologized for his lateness – the *mezzuzah* had already been appended. There had been an accident on the corner of Muirfield and Barry Hertzog and he had stopped to see if he could help, but no-one was killed, thank God. Whiskey and chopped herring were served in celebration, though Rabbi Goldenbaum brought his own cup and declined the herring.

And 48 Komatie Road was where, a few years later, Sarafina Senemela was passing on her way up to Barry Hertzog Avenue to catch a bus into town, Zolisa strapped to her back, when a black and white terrier snapped at her through the grid of the gate. She swore back at it, *"Aai, voetsek!***"* but the dog, snarling and yapping, squeezed its way through the gap between the gate and the fence, and bit her full on the ankle.

A passing steel-grey Mercedes, with Mrs Yudelowitz who lived in number 85 at its wheel, screeched to a halt to help. Sarafina, in a high-pitched scream, intermittently shoo-ed the dog, and kicked at it with her unbitten ankle as it barked wildly at her and the baby. Zolisa, only six months old, hooded and overdressed, woken from peaceful slumber,

* small amulet attached to the doorpost of every Jewish house, containing a
  Hebrew prayer.
† grandfather, in Yiddish.
** 'Go away, get lost,' in Afrikaans.

howled in misery, and the commotion drew the attention of the neighbours. Mrs Yudelowitz tried to grab hold of the dog's collar, but he sprang free, bolting into the middle of the road, just in time to get caught under the wheels of Rabbi Goldenbaum's passing car, which was on its way to number 62 Clovelly to visit Moshi Blumberg, who had just had a triple bypass.

By the time Fran had waddled down the driveway, her seven months pregnant belly leading the way, her guard dog was dead, the Rabbi was late for his visitation of the sickly, Mrs Yudelowitz was clutching a shrieking Zolisa, and Sarafina was collapsed in a heap on the pavement, hyperventilating from shock. Once Zulig had been covered with the hand towel from the downstairs guest toilet room and the RSPCA had been called to come and collect his body, Fran, bloated with hormones, and overcome with guilt at the attack by Zulig, not only took Sarafina to get a tetanus shot at her GP, but gave her an old blanket from the cupboard in the spare room and pressed a twenty rand note into her hand.

Three weeks later, Sarafina, with seven terrier teeth marks on her right ankle, rang the doorbell again, this time without Zolisa, and asked Fran for a job.

Beyond the sunny north-facing lounge and dining room, through the kitchen with its paisley floor tiles, out the laundry room door, beyond the washing line, in the yard behind the main house of 48 Komatie Road, is the maid's room: a full four metres by three metres when empty of furniture. Even on the hottest summer's day, its inhabitants would be spared the indignities of perspiration, for its walls retain the cold with miserly precision. Not only is it built at the furthest possible point from the sun, but it squats in the shadow of the house. Sarafina blinked many times as she stood in its doorway for the first time, her eyes squinting to get used to the darkness. From the opposite wall, a shoebox of light ungenerously gave something of the outside to the inside. Fran flicked the switch for the light, but it didn't go on. "Sorry, old globe," she murmured. "I'll get the master to change it as soon as he gets home."

In the weeks that passed, Sarafina raised the bed on stilts of bricks she had taken from the renovations that were going on at number 43 up the road. The madam cleared a patch in the back garden for her to grow her mielies, ("But no *dagga*,* you hear me?"). Sarafina also managed to siphon four full cups of sugar from the grocery cupboard, which she put in a Tupperware and kept under her bed, waiting to send it home to her mother in Natal at the first opportunity.

She was still lactating when the madam's child was born some six weeks after she started at 48 Komatie. And it was just as well. For the madam did not want to feed the child and the child only cried when it was with the madam. Sarafina would strap the baby to her back, walk down to the Emmarentia Dam, and under the shade of the willow trees, behind the shrubbery in a secluded spot, and with a blanket covering the baby's head of hair that was pitch black except for a small spot of white strands, she would feed that baby from the maroon ache of her nipples and softly implore the ancestral spirits that held onto the child to be kind, for they were not pleasing to her.

That unremarkable day in 1965, at summer's end when the leaves formed crinkled huddles at the curb, heralded many endings. Summer was gone for the year and autumn bulbs would need to be planted and tended soon, Fran had mentally noted on the way to the hospital in the lull between

* marijuana.

Joanne Fedler

contraction number one hundred and eighty three and one hundred and eighty four. The crowning of Mia's head at her mother's tearing vulva brought an end to the months of pregnant agony Fran had endured, hoping that this one would live. And dragging not only the afterbirth but Fran's entire uterus with her, like a fish caught in a net, Mia brought an end to Fran's fertility.

The madness of emergency took over and Issey waited again, doors keeping him out, panic holding him in a pinch of fate—which way will it go? "Will she make it? What if... oh God... please..." Somewhere in the belly of the waiting he was handed a bundle by a kindly sister and, when he looked down, the squashed little bulb of a face wailed up at him. Issey clasped the parcel of wriggling life to his unshaven cheek, and whispered, "You survived, you survived." He sank to his knees in the hospital corridor, mouthing silent thanks for the survivor, and begging all at once for Fran, beseeching God not to muddle beginnings and endings. *"Shema Yisroel, Adonai Elohainu, Adonai Echad,"** he murmured over and over.

Fran lived, but something finally had been wrung from her. When her eyes opened from the drugged nightmare of tangled birth and death, only to find her stomach empty of all that lives and could have lived, elation and despair mingled, mottling celebration into a numb acquiescence to the capricious vicissitudes of life.

She lay in the Lady Dudley Nursing Home for fifteen days, unable to respond to the cry of her newborn child. She asked for pills to dry up her milk. She read *Mrs Dalloway* twice and ate Cadbury's Nuts 'n' Raisins chocolate, spitting out the raisins and the nuts into her bedpan. Like a Jew leaving Egypt, she had been pushed and bullied into a landscape of hardship from which there was no turning back, no choice besides the

---

* first line of the daily Jewish prayer, 'Hear oh Israel, the Lord is our God, the Lord is one.'

compulsory wandering; no certainty of survival. She had long dreamed of motherhood, a promised land flowing with milk and honey. Instead, motherhood had passed over her like the Angel of Death.

During those fifteen days, when Mia was without a motherly caress, Issey became all Mia knew of touch, smell and comfort. He alternated his vigil between Fran's bedside and the nursery, where he stroked, changed and bottle-fed Mia. On the third day after her birth he noticed what could only be described as a fingerprint on her skull—a pale oval dent on the centre line of her head. It looked like a birthmark and yet the deliberation of its shape made it seem as if it had been crafted there by a human hand, rather than by nature.

On the sixteenth day Fran said she was ready to see her. Issey gingerly placed Mia, swaddled in receiving blankets with little pink blossoms, in Fran's hands; his heart stretched in hope. Fran opened the blankets and, with careful indifference, examined the blotchy chicken murmuring and undulating with newborn tremors. It was only when she removed the cap she had knitted some weeks earlier from a pattern in *Living and Loving* from her head and saw the indent on her skull that a wave of forgiveness swept across the sands of her longing for a different ending. It was the mark of a furious birth. Branded like a Jew with a number. So there could be no forgetting. And forgiveness soon heralded the resigned dutifulness children mistake for love.

As the dark downy hair began to cover Mia's head, the birthmark grew its own hair, different not only in colour but in texture to the rest. While Mia's childish locks curled thick and tough and black, the hair from the birthmark grew white, not blonde, for there is gold in blonde, and these hairs glittered silver, rather than gold.

Zaide Yankel claimed that it was a sign that she was chosen for something.

"Chosen for what, Pop?" Issey asked.

"The Jewish people were chosen to be a light unto other nations, to be an example, to carry the morality of humanity. But also, to suffer. This child is chosen for somethink none of us will understand. She is touched by the finger of the Almighty. We can only pray that she will not have to suffer."

Granny Olive, Fran's mother, lifted her gaze from Barbara Cartland's latest novel, peered above the rim of her reading glasses and simply expressed her gratitude that the offending piece of hair could easily be dyed to match the rest when she was older.

And Sarafina who was not asked for her opinion, while brushing Mia's soft tresses one afternoon, stopped in midbrush, and said, *"Aikona wena"*. She shook her head, stood back, shook her head again and muttered, reminding herself to get some *muti* * for this *umnta'mlungu*,† for the ancestors were not pleased.

Every *Erev Yom Kippur*** Issey lit a *Yorzheidt*†† candle in memory of his stillborn firstborn, whose small skull looked as if it had been crushed in an act of deliberate anger. He breathed for a few hours, gasping for air. Mark, he would have been, after Issey's mother Maya. Fran had held him, watched the life slip from him in small breaths. Inside her, he had lived, kicked with the certainty of his existence. Then, severed from her, he spluttered, suffered and died. Fran held on to him for three days, little wisps of lullabies peeping from her dry lips, finally parting with his cold still body as sleep claimed her.

And then—at last—there was Mia. She was going to make it all right. For Issey, for Fran, for his father, Zaide Yankel—she was his offering.

* African traditional medicine.
† white child, in Zulu.
** evening before the Jewish fast on the Day of Atonement.
†† a candle lit in memory of those who have died.

But Mia would not be offered.

From the moment she was placed in Zaide Yankel's arms, Mia began a howl, the likes of which Zaide Yankel claimed he had only ever heard in Kovno when an animal ready for slaughter had had its neck cut, but the *shochet*,* due to poor eyesight, an unsteady hand or ill-health, had missed the crucial jugular. It was a sound that instilled in Zaide Yankel a horror for the past he had made such efforts to leave behind.

Through the crying, which had begun on the day of her birth and hardly ceased, Issey nurtured patience. Gripe water, Mozart and even the odd dose of whiskey in her bottle could not calm her. Colic they called it, but Issey suspected a deeper angst. Fran worried little, left the night feeds to Issey, the day feeds to Sarafina and busied herself with her roses and gardenias. Issey, however, anguished through the stupor of the unslept.

He blew raspberries on her belly-button; pulled faces for her—crossing his eyes and contorting his tongue; and he tickled the bare soles of her feet. But Mia cried still. Though he was not to know—how could he?—that on nights when the moon was full and ripe in the sky, so luminescent that it shone through the small crack between the closed curtains in her nursery, her sobbing subsided. But without words with which to say it, she wailed and bellowed. On such nights, Issey would wrap her in his thick overcoat, and carry her downstairs to his art studio, where he overturned his aluminium tub that held old paintbrushes—too frayed to use, but with which he could not bear to part—and put her into it.

"God, but you're a pain in the arse," he would say through a smile. "A parent needs some *nachas*†—just a little, just a drop."

* Jewish ritual slaughterer.
† 'nachas' is a Yiddish word for proud enjoyment, usually that parents derive from their children.

When exhaustion gave way to delirium, he would leave her fretting and wailing—but only for a minute or two—while he stood in the dark night sucking on a joint. Christ, it was that or whiskey...

One Jo'burg winter's night towards the end of July Issey held Mia in his arms as she buckled her body against his. As Issey looked down at her, love and irritation intermingling, a horrible memory returned to him: words from a play he had seen when he was no more than a boy—at the Civic Theatre with his father and brother, each with their own piece of liquorice. Shakespeare, Macbeth, yes, Lady Macbeth. Something about dashing toothless gums against a wall. It had seemed so monstrous, so inhuman, and yet...

In such a state of semi-memory, semi-delirium, he murmured in reverie, "My life is dreary, she does not stop". He said, 'I am a-weary, a-weary, I would that I were dead'—that's not Shakespeare, Tennyson, I think."

He inhaled deeply. How amazing the hairs on his knuckles looked—each individual one curling out of his skin like worms. 'The worms crawl in and the worms crawl out, they crawl in thin and they crawl out stout,' his mind wandered. He did not know how long his musings continued, perhaps just moments, perhaps a full fifteen minutes, but suddenly, he became aware of silence. He looked down at Mia. Her eyes had visibly darkened—and Issey knew every nuance of shade—as if some old place had called her to its shadows.

"What did I say? What did I say?" He tried to remember what his last words were—it had been a thousand thoughts since he last spoke. 'My life is dreary, I would that I were dead...' Tennyson! Did you like that?"

Mia's eyes fixed on his, imploring, expectant.

"I can give you more—wait," and he strode, this silent creature in his arms, into the study, and with a heart that thundered with the adrenaline of discovery, he scanned, rummaged through the bookshelf, saying, "One moment

Miala, don't start crying on me now. I'm getting there."

He finally found the dusty doorstop weight of *The Oxford Book of English Verse*. Back in the lounge, now cradling Mia in his arms, he opened the book to the contents page. Tennyson, Tennyson, why wasn't it alphabetical? Crikey, it was by date. When did Tennyson live? Okay, after Edgar Allan Poe, and thank god, *Mariana* was the first poem, page 698. Issey flicked to the page and began, his eyes straying from word to face, tracing the spiral of stillness.

> *With blackest moss the flower-plots*
> *Were thickly crusted, one and all*
> *The rusted nails fell from the knots*
> *That held the pear to the gable wall...*

'Mmmm,' she murmured.

> *The broken sheds look'd sad and strange;*
> *Unlifted was the clinking latch;*
> *Weeded and worn the ancient thatch*
> *Upon the lonely moated grange*

Mia's body relaxed, like a bag of sand against Issey's chest.

> *She only said, 'My life is dreary*
> *He cometh not,' she said;*
> *She said, 'I am aweary, aweary*
> *I would that I were dead...'*

Stanza by stanza, until all seven were faithfully completed, Issey read and then looked down to find Mia folded into slumber. A cold electric emotion flickered through his blood like the tail of a goldfish. "My God— she's just like Ma," he breathed. "Just like the old lady."

He would not wake Fran. This was his stumbled-upon

discovery and he wanted it all to himself, at least until morning. Sarafina, on her way past the lounge, taking morning coffee upstairs, found the two of them, father and daughter, asleep in the Eaziboy, she cradled into the crook of his arm (*einah** with pins and needles when he snapped awake), the *Oxford Book of English Verse* open on his knee.

Between August and Christmas, Issey had worked his way through the *Oxford Book of English Verse*, not skipping a line. It was as if the words themselves held breezes and the calmness of underwater, for they never failed to lull Mia into sleep or to rest her frenzied cries. Alongside her crib, on the bookshelf, in place of *My First ABC* and Dr Seuss's *The Hat in the Cat*, a modest library of poetry books began to gather.

Mia's first word, which she uttered at the age of ten months and five days, was, not "Mama" or "Dada", or any such endearment, but "dead". She said it a few times before Issey finally gave up hoping that what she really meant to say was, "Dad". Issey recognized it as the refrain in *Mariana*, the first poem he had ever read to her, the one that had stopped the crying. Her second word was "fire", which Issey took to have come from Blake's *Songs of Experience*.

"You should someday read her your mama's poems," Zaide Yankel had suggested to Issey. "Not all the love poems which she wrote for me, because, it is —how shall I say, not becomink for a son to read such words from his mama, but some of her earlier poems."

"Pop, aren't they all in Yiddish?"

"Most certainly."

"Mia won't understand them then."

The old man looked at his son and shook his head. "You

* Afrikaans slang for 'ouch.'

think a child understands what you read her—Blake and Wordsworth? It is not the words themselves, but the spirit of the poet that she loves."

★★★

He was just an old man in an overcoat at the front door on a Friday night, for his son, bless him, always invited him for a *Shabbat* meal—where else would an old man go, all alone, orphaned, widowed? Tucked under his armpit was a large brown envelope and the early edition of *The Star*. It is important to know what is going on in the world, and then to have a laugh at the cartoons, maybe try the crossword. What else does an old man have to do with his time? He rang the doorbell, shifted the newspaper from his left armpit to his right armpit, and then rang it again. Fran opened the door. "Come in," she beckoned. "God, where is that girl? I called her to open the door—they never come when you call them."

"Pardon?" he said, leaning in towards her.

"It's the girl—she never comes when I call her. Just come in," she replied hurriedly.

The old man gestured for help to remove his overcoat. Fran took the newspaper and envelope from under his armpit and tossed them onto the chair in the hall. "Issey's not home yet," she said.

"Never mind, I have a newspaper. Don't mind me, I'll wait," he said, shuffling out of the armholes.

Fran placed the overcoat on the hook in the hall.

"You see Verwoerd was assassinated?" Zaide Yankel pointed with his crooked sickle of a finger to the paper, its headline, 'Verwoerd stabbed to death in the House of Assembly'.

"I heard on the radio this morning. Should we laugh or cry?"

"Good riddance to an anti-Semitic dog," he said, speckled with righteousness. Fran, who still had to dress for *Shabbat*, could not stay to chat.

"What's in the envelope?"

"Issey's mother's poems, may her soul rest in peace. All in Yiddish. The originals."

"Really? That's nice. Make yourself comfortable, I'm just finishing upstairs. I'll be down shortly. Sarafinaaaa, can you offer Zaide something to drink?"

Fran disappeared up the stairwell. The old man bent to pick up the newspaper and shuffled to the lounge, where he paused before bending at the knees and rocking back into the armchair.

Ordinarily, the sound of her Zaide's voice caused a fit of inconsolable crying. So why was this night different from all other nights? On this night, Mia crawled down the hall towards his voice, and into the lounge. She toddled up to the chair where the large brown envelope lay, placed her dimpled hands on the sheath of its body and, for a while, did not move. But then she pulled it down into her lap and held it to her chest. Her Zaide, engrossed in the evening newspaper, was scouring for details of the prime minister's assassination, expletives in Yiddish escaping his lips at odd intervals. Fran was plucking her eyebrows at her dressing table upstairs. Sarafina was stirring the soup in the kitchen. So nobody was near enough to hear Mia's voice, as she held the envelope to her heart, saying, "Mine".

Downtown Johannesburg,
July, 1969

On an otherwise uneventful car journey (Sarafina needed to be dropped off at the rank in town to catch a taxi to Durban to attend her nephew's funeral) Issey, one hand on the steering wheel, the other holding a half-smoked Peter Stuyvesant, swallowed several times to dislodge a feeling he could not at first identify. His father's words, like a letter in a bottle, tossed out but returned by insistent waves, echoed in his head. *'Chosen for something. Touched by the finger of the Almighty. We should pray. She should not have to suffer.'*

Perhaps there was a perfectly acceptable explanation. He took three long drags from his cigarette before tossing it out the window and checking in the rear-view mirror to catch her eye, but Mia was sitting with her nose pressed up against the glass, staring.

Fina had sat alongside Mia the whole way at the back, clutching her handbag, with a green beret on her head, which didn't cover all the wiry black hair that grew out of it. She was dressed in one of Fran's old dresses, which gaped between the buttons, revealing the vest she wore underneath. She smelled of Lifeboy and snuff, and was scrubbed clean for her long journey home.

"You'll come back, Fina?" Mia had asked her, leaning out of the window.

"Ja, where will I go? I have nowhere else to go," Fina told her.

"Fly away Peter, fly away Paul, come back Peter, come back Paul."

"Ja, I come back," Fina had said.

They had watched as she dragged her heavy bag to the boot of the taxi and lifted it in by herself. There were some men standing around, smoking, talking loudly as they pulled up, but who had grown silent while the car stood idling. They greeted Sarafina and one of them sidled over to help her with her bags. Clutching her four Checkers packets filled with the two hundred scones she had baked for the funeral, she had smoothed down her dress and returned their greeting. Two women were already in the taxi, a meal laid out on a towel on their laps, eating *pap** and chicken's feet with their fingers. They greeted Fina, and shifted over so that she could get in.

"See me once, see me no more," Mia had said.

Issey looked at her in the mirror.

"What did you say?"

"See me once, see me no more," Mia repeated. "There on the taxi."

Issey glanced at the taxi Sarafina had just boarded. Yes, the sign in the window read, 'See me once see me no more'.

And that is when the lump lodged in his throat.

He swung around to look at her.

"Can we go?" Fran muttered impatiently.

Issey switched on the car.

"She'll come back, hey Dad?" Mia asked.

"She bloody better," Fran muttered.

"She will," Issey assured. He cleared his throat. The lump stayed firm.

As they swung onto Nugget Street, a rather bizarre sight met their eyes. Just legs and feet with high-heeled pink shoes protruding from the upstairs window of the building on the corner of Nugget Street. They were kicking in the air like twisted spider's legs.

* a thick porridge made of maize meal.

Joanne Fedler

"They're just dolls," Issey said, slowing down so that Mia could get a proper look. As the station wagon drew to a slow crawl alongside the building, two street children scuttled from the gutter where they had been squatting over a pile of stones and cocked their heads to the side, holding their palms open. One of the boys pushed his face right up against the back window to meet Mia's eyes. He held his hand out. His baby finger was only half a finger, the top point of it tapered to an unfinished circumcised stub.

"Change mem, small change?" the one with no shoes said. His toes were gnarled with the grit of the pavements.

"Not real ladies, just dummies, like in John Orrs windows. No need to be scared," Issey continued.

The dummy Mia had seen in the window at John Orrs the last time had had no arms. Mia had stopped and pressed her nose up against the cold glass window, letting her breath make frosted bubbles under her eyes. It was like a big Barbie doll with no fingers, hands or elbows. That smooth space between its legs, its face turned away, its gaze cast down. A man with a tear in the bum of his jeans and an earring in his ear was holding an arm in his hands and struggling to fit a long black glove over the stiff fingers. He had turned to face Mia's gaze and using the arm, had waved hello to her. She had backed away, walking into a lady passing behind her holding a maypole of four dogs on leashes.

"For Heaven's sake, child, don't you watch where you're going?" she had snapped.

Mia had nearly stepped on the poodle. It nipped at her and gave out a yelp, running in circles, winding the leashes around the poodle lady's feet and confusing the other dogs.

It wasn't until much later when she got home that her ankle had started to sting and Fina had to put mercurochrome and a plaster where the dog had nicked the flesh from above her socks with the sunflowers. Until then, Mia had thought dogs only bit blacks. That's what Fina had told her.

As Issey pulled away and the street children, tired of asking and itchy with grime, returned to their stone game in the gutter, Mia said, "Pink Ponies. Real Live Ladies."

Issey clutched the steering wheel until the whites of his knuckles showed through.

"Fran, do you get what just happened?" he whispered harshly.

"They're everywhere," Fran said. "You see them wherever you go, just milling about, looking for trouble."

"Not the streetkids," he said, "but what she just did." He nodded towards the back of the car.

"What?" Fran asked.

"She can read."

"Can she?"

"She just read those flashing words inside the rectangle with the pink globes. 'Pink Ponies. Real Live Ladies.'"

Fran shrugged.

"Is it normal for a four year old to be able to read?" Issey asked.

"I have no idea," Fran said.

"But did you teach her?" Issey asked.

"Me? You must be joking."

"So how…?"

"You can see their brooks," Mia said.

"Who knows?" Fran said.

"Mom, you can see their brooks," Mia repeated.

"Don't you think it matters?" Issey asked.

"Not really," Fran said. "Whose brooks?"

"The dummies. Their pink brooks are sticking out."

"That's not very ladylike, is it?" Fran sniffed.

As the building disappeared from sight, Issey sneezed. And with the jolt to his body, the lump in his throat dissolved and became a liquid feeling that sank from his chest to his belly. It was then that he identified the sheer nervousness of premonition stirring inside him. *Chosen for something.* Chosen for what? Did God mean to bless or curse the Jewish people when he chose them? He couldn't be sure.

That night the dream came back. And even the light turned on didn't make it go away. The needle in her hand, her hand full of blood… She sat up in her bed, her body icy with sweat.

"Dream, dream go away, come again another day…" she whispered. Who would chase it far away? She tiptoed out the door and down the passage. The rumble of his snore gave her courage. Maybe he would wake up because he knew she was scared. Dads knew these things. And then he would let her hold the cloth. Just feel it between her fingers. She would just stand by the door and wait.

Stand stand stand.

Phut-phut-phut-phut-phut.

She would just go and stand over him and see if he was really sleeping.

Wait wait wait.

Issey, dad, Issey, it's me. I'll just touch your big old shoulder and whisper wake up.

Touch touch touch. But Dad was deep in a sleep she could not pull him from.

Maybe she would just open the drawer next to his bed and feel deep inside for the soft velvet of that old *talit** bag. The drawer squeaked open. She held her breath. Her hand reached for the bag and her fingers closed on its form.

"Who's there?" Fran mumbled in semi-sleep.

* Jewish prayer shawl.

It's only me. Her hand scuttled out of the drawer and behind her back.

Fran's eyes accustomed themselves from dream to darkness and it was her girl, a forlorn figure in the shadows of night's unfinished business.

"Wassamatter?"

I was trying to wake dad.

"Answer me."

Mia wished a mother's dream would pull her back.

Big Bad Dream.

"I had a bad dream."

Fran sighed. "My God, it's three am," she groaned as the luminescent digits of her radio clock took their ghostly shape. "Go wee and go back to bed."

But Mom, I'm scared all on my own. Sleep doesn't want me back. Holding is what wants me, mom, holding. Mom, Mom, don't send me back there.

"I need to wash my hands."

"Your hands? Why?"

Mia walked around the bed to her mother's side and held her hands out to her. "The blood."

"There's no blood, Mia. It was just a dream," Fran said. "Go wee and go back to bed. The dream is gone."

Mia stood at her mother's bedside. Her mother could not see. And her father was asleep. And her yearning was for that velvet bag at the back of her father's drawer. Only it could shake the horror of all that was terribly wrong with the world.

In the morning, while making Mia's bed, Sarafina clicked her tongue when she found a raw potato nestling under her pillow, before slipping it into the large pocket of her apron.

Victory Park, Jo'burg,
November, 1971

I f you happened to be driving through Victory Park late on
a Sunday afternoon on the way home from the Delta, and
you weren't thinking about very much, and you took that
road that isn't really steep, but somehow makes the rest of
Johannesburg lie before you as if it were in a valley, you will
see a ship. At least that's what Issey told her. You had to imagine
that the Hillbrow Tower was the ship's funnel and the General
Hospital's beacon with the red cross was the ship's horn, and
the little square windows all along its side were actually little
round portholes. And that the city sprawling below was murky
ocean water lapping at its sides. Each time they turned the
corner into Lynton Avenue, and drove past the houses with the
high walls and guard dogs and nannies napping and playing
*faafi** in the shade of the jacaranda trees, Issey would say, "See
the Ocean Liner sunk in Jo'burg?"

And Mia would tear her eyes away from the window, which
framed each passing house, and say, "Ja, I see it". She said this
even though she never could, because otherwise Issey—who
apart from being her dad, was also the best portrait artist South
Africa had ever had, though nobody but Mia and Issey knew
it yet—would slow down and talk that ship up, the way he'd
done every time before that. Sometimes he would even stop

* illegal lottery.

the station wagon and make Mia get out of the car. He would take off his brown hat that smelled of Old Spice aftershave and Peter Stuyvesant cigarettes, and lodge it under his armpit. With one hand on her shoulder and the other stretching beyond to the concrete landscape cushioned by the green and purple of jacarandas, he would say, "Use that crazy imagination kiddo, to see something ordinary for once." And then he would say, "Follow my fingers," and Mia—who knew that she should stretch her eyes to the busy city and muster a ship so she could take from him the loneliness of seeing it by himself—couldn't shift her eyes from the tip of her father's index finger, for his hands, large and delicate, stirred a wonder in her. And she would nod, and say, "Mmmm, I see it," and nestle against his leg, waiting softly for his telling to be over. Then his hand would drop to his side and take hold of his hat, and he would become silent like a little boy uncertain of the way. But the ship did not appear with repetition, nor with the bigness of how much she wanted it to.

"Your Zaide came to South Africa on a ship that looked just like that a long time ago," Issey said.

Mia said nothing for a while. She looked up at her dad and nestled her head against his hip. "Why did he come?"

"It was bad for Jews there in Lithuania. Lots of Anti-Semitism."

Mia watched him. "What's ansi temitism?"

Issey put his large hand on Mia's head. "It's not something a child should know about. It's a sickness, a *goyish** madness when people hate Jews."

"Who, us?"

Issey sighed. "Ja, Jews like us."

"Why do they hate us?"

"You ask difficult questions, my girlie. Good questions."

* non-Jewish, in Hebrew.

Joanne Fedler

Issey ruffled the hair on the head of his only child. "Jews are special. We are God's chosen people, so that makes others jealous."

Mia was silent for a time. She looked out again at the landscape. Where was the Ocean Liner?

"Why did God choose us?"

"Ha!" Issey laughed. "To be Jewish, to be God's people. That's why he gave us The Torah—and the Ten Commandments. That was how God showed who he loved the best."

He squeezed her shoulder with his big beautiful hands. Mia's fingers curled around a lock of hair and she twisted and twisted.

"God doesn't love the blacks."

"Nonsense, Mia. God loves everyone."

The hair around her finger was twisted into a tight coil. She fell quiet.

"That's what Sarafina says."

"That's rubbish. God loves everybody. But especially the Jews."

Mia looked up at her father. She squinted at him from the corners of her eyes.

"Is Zaide Jewish?"

"Of course, how do you think we got to be Jewish?" Issey laughed. "We come from a line of *tzaddikim**. And Zaide's father, Chaim Moshe, put Zaide, his only son, on a boat. And he sent him to a place where he had heard the sun always shines. Zaide Yankel left his dad and all his sisters and *Bobba*†
Maya behind. And when he made enough money, he sent for Bobba Maya, but apart from her, he never saw any of his family again. Imagine that!"

---

* Hebrew for 'very righteous men.'
† grandmother, in Yiddish.

Mia imagined.

"And if it wasn't for that, you Miala, would be a pale little Lithuanian, wearing a *doekie** on your head picking potatoes every day of your life in the icy snow."

Mia laughed.

"But instead, you live in the most beautiful country in the world. You are blessed. You should be grateful to your Zaide. Thank him one day."

Mia just nodded and gazed out at the city spread before her, eyes half-closed against the fading sunlight, but she would not thank her Zaide, not then and not ever, because she knew only two things for certain: that she loved her daddy and she hated Zaide Yankel.

The first time she was put in Zaide Yankel's arms, only days old, she exploded into a fit of screeching so horrible it was as if his very touch was scorching numbers into her baby's flesh. The incident so distressed Zaide Yankel that he wept for the first time since his young wife had died inexplicably thirty-five years before, and collapsed into a gargle of Yiddish curses about how much a man was expected to suffer in his lifetime. Widowed as a young man with two small sons, only a few years after his arrival in South Africa, Zaide Yankel had been unable to relove (though not for want of offers, he always reminded them), so great, he claimed, was his love for his beloved departed wife.

Mia's cries caused Issey's guilt to shoot up inside him like Jack's beanstalk. Though Zaide Yankel would have shaken his head and spat three times in denial, Issey knew that his own childhood needs of comfort and tenderness had drained his Mama Maya of her last remaining shreds of love, which Zaide Yankel coveted and of which he believed he was the rightful recipient. When Mama Maya died, he, his brother Shmooley and his father nursed their own loss as if it were the ultimate

---

* diminutive of the Afrikaans word, 'doek' which means head covering.

Joanne Fedler

loss, each devising rituals of remembrance he believed was the truest to her memory. Zaide Yankel, with fervent discipline, learned every one of her poems by heart, letting half-lines, naked phrases and, sometimes, full verses pass his lips; sometimes in a whisper, other times in a bellow, whenever the shadow of her memory passed over him. For her poetry moved the human spirit to such depths, that legend had it one of her poems had caused one of their neighbours who happened to read it to commit suicide. Such was her talent.

Each Saturday night, as the *Shabbos** went out and the spices had been sniffed, the *Havdola*[†] candles waved and the wine sipped, as soon as the stars appeared in the violet sky, Yankel would shuffle to the rolltop desk and remove an old chocolate box with a picture of a young woman, in the silken pale garb of the wealthy and English, on its lid. Then, by the light of the dining room globe, he would, in meditative devotion, edit his wife's poetry collection, adding grammar, form, capital letters and headings to the handwritten scrawl of the paper mass. "Don't bother me," he would warn the boys. "I am with your mama now."

Shmooley, two years Issey's senior, collected small dying things—insects without legs, lizards with lost tails, and flies all flyed out, buzzing in one spot waiting to expire—and kept them in an old Pecks Anchovette bottle. He was the self-appointed witness to the passage from life to death. He loved a tragedy, not so much for what it was, but for the power it gave him to relate it, and thus instil dread in those to whose ears he first brought its announcement. Because of his friendship with tragedy, he felt a certain flexibility with the truth, and took the opportunity to invent more horrific and gory details to enhance the drama of its impact.

* the Jewish Sabbath.
[†] the ceremony at the end of the Sabbath to separate the Sabbath from the weekday.

Issey, on the day of Mama Maya's death, scrambled into the room where she lay and rested his head on her belly. He left the room clutching the little cloth his mother had pressed into his fingers before her death. In the darkness of his youth, he would open it to its full shape, touching sequin, button, the patch of velvet, the fringe of lace, the corner of satin, reading its beauty through his fingertips. He knew that there was nothing, not anything at all, that meant more to his mama than the little square of patchwork detail she had bequeathed to him. And so he loved her blindly through it and let her love him back.

They passed the years, a house of grieving men, muted resentment holding them close, each lost in a place of too little love. Mama Maya's ghost came to visit each Friday night, when the white *Shabbos* tablecloth, which held nothing but a *challah** (given kindly by Mrs Cohen in number 35, who always baked an extra one for the 'house of men'), Malamed's sweet wine and a few drumsticks Zaide Yankel bought from Seymour Maisels, the kosher butcher, was laid out. Like the spirit of Elijah the Prophet, for whom a place is laid at every Passover table, her place at the bottom end of the table gaped wide and hollow. Zaide Yankel insisted on singing *Ashet Chayil†* addressing the lap of the empty chair, and reminding his boys that their mama was, indeed, a woman of valour. He talked her up for them, holding them to her watchful eye: "Don't slouch in your plate, Isselah. What would your Mama say?" or "Would your Mama let you eat with those dirty hands?"

Mama Maya was bigger and grander in death than in life. She moved amongst them, weaving memory into habit, remembrance into routine. Her death left a hole in the universe, unfillable, unbridgeable. Issey did not dare to stand at its edge to peek in lest he fall and never stop. So he skirted it,

---

* braided bread for the Sabbath.

† 'a woman of valour,' a psalm to the woman of the house said on the Sabbath by the man of the house.

held it at bay, a vicarious mourner through his father's superior loss. He watched and grieved. Waited and ached. Soon the ache for his mama mingled with the ache for his lonely father, who was caught in a corner of time that only made sense through Mama Maya's poems about love. Issey sat out the years, waiting for the day when he could make something big enough to fill the cavern in their lives.

But from that first catastrophic moment when he watched his daughter spit and struggle in his father's arms, his heart sank like a doomed Ocean Liner.

Issey believed that Mia's antipathy to her Zaide, though hurtful and inexplicable, would not last. She was a gifted child, far advanced for her years. She spoke her first words at ten months and could rhyme by the age of two. By four she was reading, without anyone ever showing her the ABC. Such a natural with language, perhaps she too would be a poet like his mother? In her, he saw a passion passed on from one generation to the next. And so he never grew impatient standing alongside an idling old Chevrolet, arms outstretched to the city, willing his daughter to see what he could see.

But although Mia looked out and squinted her eyes, the grey city never seemed like water on which anything could float. Float like Noah's Ark which, Issey told her, saved the only Jew in the world worth saving since the world was once so evil that God decided to destroy it all and start again.

And then, one afternoon, perhaps in late November, she sat curled up in the backseat of the Chevrolet, all played out and stringy-haired from the sun and wind and grass. The Sunday feeling soaked through her bones and she leaned her head against the cool glass of the backseat window and became only eyes, feeling the hard armrest of the door pushing up against her side.

Issey and Fran's voices saying, "…for the life of me…" and "…come to think of it…" became far away, a mumble of words. The world passed by outside. The sun was going down and the houses slipped by one by one, each telling her something: patios with plants that prickle meant that children didn't play there. Mommies played ring-a-ring-a-rosies under shady trees and chuckled as babies 'all-fall-down'. There were fences around swimming pools, so mothers didn't worry about children going too near the edge. White marble dogs were never touched or visited by children and stood lonely, as old people sat around a table dipping Marie biscuits into milky tea. Orange dresses on washing lines meant a party, yesterday or tomorrow. Some houses had curtains drawn, even in the day, in rooms in which nobody lived anymore. And those were the saddest houses of all.

She longed to lift the roofs off all the passing houses so she could peek inside them and know all at once the secrets of corners and dark cupboards. And it was in the midst of this longing, before she remembered that they were coming down ship's hill, that it suddenly sprang out at her like a hologram. A shimmering shape of a long ship set in the city's lap. It caused Mia to suck her breath inwards and hold it there until it trickled out in a small shudder. Perhaps it was the evening sky smudged with shadows, with the city lights dotting the base of the hospital, that gave her that moment of closeness with her father for which she had wished. The little windows of the hospital beamed yellow portholes like a row of beads along the belly of an Ocean Liner.

And when Issey said, "See the ship sunk in Jo'burg," and Fran just sighed, Mia murmured an "Mmmm," that came from her deepest parts. She lodged her head between the two front seats so that the streak of pure white hair, like a stolen lock that grew from the dead centre of her otherwise ebony hairline, prickled with the thrill of 'at last'. And seeing this, she wondered why God hadn't decided to let Zaide Yankel, in a grey overcoat, smelling of herring and clutching a small suitcase, drown with all the evil in the world.

***

Uncle Shmooley was the bearer of bad tidings. He had just turned four when, on his way to the bathroom, he passed his parent's bedroom and found his mother dead in his father's arms. He had proceeded to the bathroom, urinated into the toilet bowl without lifting the seat or washing his hands, and then marched out through the back door to call the neighbours who had phoned the *Chevrah Kadisha.**

After the funeral he had been praised by the Rabbi, his father and the neighbours for being such a pillar of strength to his father. It was more attention than he had ever received in his life. It was Issey, the baby with a talent with a pencil, who usually attracted such praise. Shmooley learned loyalty to things that went wrong and consequently developed a morbid sense of humour, a fascination with all that is unwell, unhappy and struck in misery.

Despite his immersion in the world of the sick and departed, he was a cheerful fellow. He worked full time at Westpark cemetery, and in this way was able to know, before anyone else in the community, the name, personal details and circumstances surrounding the death of every Jew who died in Johannesburg, whether by fire, gunshot or complications during surgery.

Uncle Shmooley, Aunt Selma and the cousins came every second Friday for a *Shabbos* dinner. On these evenings the smell of *gribbenis*† and chopped liver from the kitchen lured Mia down to watch as Sarafina fed the liver through the mincer. Then she pushed bread into its gaping cold mouth to get rid of the bits wedged in corners and around its steel intestinal bends before she minced the herring.

* the Jewish burial service.
† the fat cut off the chicken fried with onion.

As evening gathered, Fran called Mia to come and watch her light the Friday night candles. Standing on a chair alongside Fran, Mia watched, each time as if it were the first, as her mother struck a match, held it still for a moment, before dotting the wick of one, then the other candle, and blowing out the match. Cupping her hands, she made circles—once, twice, three times—over the burning heads of the twin shafts of candlestick, and brought them up to cover her eyes. A sense of something quiet and ancient held them gently in the faint glow of candlelight.

"*Baruch atah adonai elohainu melech ha'olam asher kidishanu bemitzvotav vitzivanu lehadlik nayr shell Shabbat,*"* her mother recited.

"Amen," Mia replied.

Sarafina ran Mia's bath and rubbed her back with a soaped up *lappie.*† Then she pressed a towel around her shoulders and dried every inch of her. On a Friday night Mia was allowed to choose 'an outfit' to welcome the bride, the *Shabbat*. Then Sarafina brushed Mia's hair, sometimes tying it back with a ribbon. By the time Zaide Yankel rang the bell or tapped hard with his walking stick on the front door, Mia was dressed and ready to greet all visitors, welcome or not. When he arrived, Fran would kiss him on the cheek while Mia, from obedience and enforced politeness, murmered from a distance, "Hello Zaide". The old man sometimes lifted his hat at her, or raised a hand in her direction, and said, "Good *Shabbos*".

Then Uncle Shmooley arrived with Aunty Selma, whom he had courted one December by spitting watermelon pips at her as they sat on Muizenburg beach, and the cousins in tow. Mia scampered to meet him and jumped on his lap, waiting for

* the Friday night prayer for lighting *Shabbat* candles.
† Afrikaans slang for 'facecloth.'

him to make his fingers pop and crackle by pulling them as he told her the latest bad news.

"Did you hear about Mrs Smuskowitz?"

Mia shook her head.

"She had a tumour that was removed from her bowel only two years ago—doctors gave her a clean bill of health. Three days ago, she complained of diarrhoea. We buried her this morning."

"Shmooley, cut that out," Issey said. "I'm going to send you the therapist's bills. Can I get you a Scotch?"

But Uncle Shmooley always delayed, "In a moment, *Boet.**
Have you heard this one? Why don't coloureds marry blacks?"

Issey shrugged, "Put me out of my misery."

"They're scared their kids will be too lazy to steal!"

And then everyone laughed, (even Fran) so that it felt like happiness and Mia cherished Uncle Shmooley for making things smile that never did.

Soon Fran called them to the table and Issey asked Zaide Yankel to make the *brocha*† and each time, like a rehearsed dialogue, Zaide Yankel refused and reminded Issey that he, as the head of the household, should make the *brocha*. And only when Issey and Fran and Shmooley and Selma begged him, telling him that no-one could make the Friday night blessings like he could, would he hold both his hands up, and say, "Alright, alright." Then he poured sweet purple wine into a silver chalice with Hebrew letters engraved on its body and, with one hand on his head to hold down his *yarmulka*** and the other holding the goblet, spilling wine as he shook, he would make a *brocha*, while Mia and her cousin Trevor pinched each other under the tablecloth.

"You should listen to the *brocha*—one day, you will have to

* 'brother,' in Afrikaans.
† 'blessing' in Hebrew.
** Jewish male head covering.

make it," Zaide Yankel said to Trevor.

"We learnt it already at school," Trevor said. Trevor, who was the youngest of Shmooley's three children, and the only boy, ('Third time lucky,' Uncle Shmooley always joked) was going to King Solomon Primary, the only Jewish day school in Johannesburg.

"Costs us a fortune, but hell, it's worth it," Shmooley said. His daughters, Dale and Karen, were at Emmarentia Public School.

"What about you, Selma?" Fran asked, holding a dish out for her.

"Oh, don't worry about me, I've brought a boiled egg and some crackers. I'll just have some salad."

Mia had never seen anyone eat as little as Aunt Selma did and that's why she couldn't understand how come Aunt Selma was so fat. Issey and Fran didn't call her fat, they said she had a 'weight problem', but Mia once asked Sarafina and she agreed that Aunt Selma was just plain fat. If you could hold all her chins back, and see just her face, it was a face that was pretty, but it was always sweaty, and sweaty makes pretty a bit yucky. When Aunt Selma kissed you hello, she left a wet spot on your cheek. Mia didn't mind being kissed by Aunt Selma and she would let the wet dry by itself, without wiping it away.

Aunt Selma did not speak a lot, but when she spoke, she talked about 'calories'. From Aunt Selma, Mia learned that cheesecake was like maths. It had a number and you could only eat so many numbers. Aunt Selma had a little scale, which she carried in her bag, on which to weigh food. Sometimes she just had milkshake for dinner and would watch, her deep-set eyes watery with desire, as the others ate. There were lots of names for why she was so fat. One was 'Thyroid', another was 'Slow Metabolism'. Fina's name for it was 'Eats Too Much.'

Dale and Karen chewed gum and rolled their eyes when the adults spoke. When Aunt Selma said, "Eat some dinner" or "Please don't put your chewing gum on the side-plate", they said things like, "Shaddup, Ma" or "Who asked your opinion?" Sarafina said they needed a 'wooden spoon on their bum', but Uncle Shmooley said nothing, and Aunt Selma looked away, down into her fat lap, where her fat fingers, heavy with gold rings, played with the serviette and her fat eyes got blurry, and then she became quiet and lonely in her seat, the only one without a plate of *Shabbat* food in front of her.

"It is important for Jews to be amongst Jews," Zaide Yankel said, waving his index finger, curled as a sickle at his son, "so they can remind each other of what they forget."

"I'm not disputing that, but Pop, it's a really expensive school, and frankly, we don't know if we can afford it for next year."

"There is nothink more important for a Jew than an education. What else is there to spend money on?"

"A little bit of everything?" Fran asked.

"Ja, ja, everythink. But two potatoes."

"I didn't go to a Jewish day school, Pop, and I turned out okay," Issey said.

"That was many years ago. Now thinks are different. When you were a child, you were livink in the time of the Holocaust. It was easy to remember who you are. Now, these days, children forget. They are protected from history, because we have the state of Israel now and the Holocaust is somethink you learn about in a book. When children are born into luxury and safety, they expect it. Besides, you went to *Chader*."*

Mia looked up at her Zaide. Spit was collecting on the sides of his mouth. Once he began to eat, dribbling food onto the tablecloth and into his lap, she would feel her stomach turning inside out and the food on her plate would not look very delicious at all.

"Well, I went to a Christian school; I said 'Our Father who

* Hebrew lessons outside of school.

art in Heaven' every morning like the rest of them; I learned about Jesus; and it did me no harm," Fran said. "I married a Jew, I have a Jewish child, I light *Shabbos* candles on a Friday night," she said, "and I'm as good a Jew as anyone else. I think sending her to a private school is excessive and, with all due respect to Shmooley and Selma, will probably turn her into a spoilt brat."

"Look, as long as the girls can make chopped herring, they'll find a husband," said Uncle Shmooley. "But a boy has to have a *barmitzvah,* and he's got to know what's what. Do you know what happened to Mitzy Edelstein's middle son, Bradley? He got beaten up in the toilets by the other boys for being a Yid—a circumcized Jewboy who killed Jesus Christ. That was last week, at the girls' school. Mitzy enrolled Bradley at King Solomon the next day."

"Wanna see my love bite?" Karen leaned over and whispered in Mia's ear. Mia's eyes grew wide and she nodded.

"Come with me to the loo and I'll show you," Karen whispered.

"It's rude to whisper at the table," Fran said to Mia.

"We're just going to the loo," Karen said.

"And do you need her to wipe your bottom for you?" Fran said. "Mia, you stay here."

Karen sidled out of her chair and pursed her lips. When she got to the door, she turned and winked at Mia.

Sarafina entered the dining room, dressed in her white uniform, salad dressing perched on a tray, and murmured, "Evening Master."

"Hey Sarafina, what's cooking?" Uncle Shmooley said, and laughed at his own joke.

"My son, sometimes you speak without thinkink," Zaide Yankel said to Shmooley. "Boys, girls—what is the difference? We would all be on the same train to Auschwitz. It is important, as a Jewboy or a Jewgirl, to know what it means to be a Jew. How else have Jews survived? We survive by rememberink. And with this child," he said, curving his finger at Mia, "is somethink goink on. I don't know what it is, but it is somethink. Somethink of your mama," he said, turning to Issey. "I know it would have made your mama very happy for her grandchild to learn some Yiddishkeit. But—" and here he paused, took a bite of his chicken leg, chewed and said with a full mouth, "it is your decision, and I don't want to interfere."

And with that, a chicken *polke** in his hand, he clinched it. Fran ate silently, cursing the old man. And Mia, who peered at her cousin Trevor with frowning eyebrows, wondered about a circumcized Jewboy killing Jesus Christ. Wasn't that against the school rules?

*Yiddish for 'thigh', commonly used to refer to a chicken leg.

der kholem (n); tsu kholemen:

dream:
imaginary sense-impressions of unrealities;
indulge in fantasy;
allow oneself to believe;
abstraction of the mind, soul or spirit

She had not asked for it—this gift, this curse, like the monthly blood she woke to, reminding her that she carried dying inside her. She did not choose her love affairs. They had claimed her. In Kovno, choice was a luxury—is it not said that beggars cannot be choosers? Choice. What was choice? Live or die.

From where came this *meshugas*, this madness to scrounge for paper, such precious parchment, a pen, some ink, a candle by which to write? Just as a blind man does not question the darkness, but finds his way by feeling, so she did not pester with curiosity the ache under her ribs, the pressure in her fingertips, the urgency to hold nib to paper, the yearning for the greediness of paper for the ink. She longed to sit down at a table. Perhaps not even a table, perhaps just the humbleness of a chair, a bench, a place against which to press her lower back to take the responsibility from her legs, her tired feet.

From the folds of her garments, she would remove her treasure—a page, a rectangle of clean space on which nothing had been marked. Such an invitation, calling to her from her dreams, her chores, her sadnesses, was impossible to resist. Adultery. It was easy to understand, despite *Hashem's**

---

* one of God's names, in Hebrew, literally 'The Name.'

injunction *Thou Shalt Not*. Only those cravings that were stronger than common sense did He forbid.

From her pocket, she unsheathed the instrument of both her joy and her shame. A fountain pen belonging to her Zaide, a learned man of the book, which she had slipped into her blouse one *Shabbat* on her way to the outhouse. Only later had it dawned upon her that this was, in fact, theft, if one were a stickler for the letter of the law. And her silence when he had inquired as to its whereabouts was also in all likelihood a sin, a falsehood. But what were God's commandments other than obstacles to happiness?

From the shelf next to the bag of flour, she removed a small bottle of ink, by now so diluted from the adding of water to make it last, that its jet fluid had become a milky grey. With quickening pulse, she unscrewed the lid, placed it neatly beside the bottle and, if the day were ending, she might light a small wedge of candle she had sliced off those reserved for the next *Shabbos*, insert it into the brass candleholder—not the *Shabbos* candlesticks, for that would be a disrespect—and with a flurry, she would move her hand to the page.

And there, between her and the paper, words appeared, rendering a life within her—not the one she manifested in the company of others, but a hidden life that rumbled in the margins of her self. Here she wrote, 'and so I feel…' and 'then I thought' and perhaps 'if only…' speaking from that untouched unchecked voice in her that was not trying to please a father, a brother or a husband, not taking others' needs into account, not calculating, modifying or holding back.

Here alone was her sacred space, her place at the altar, the open *Aharon Hakodesh**, where she walked the unfootprinted paths of imaginings. Here gypsies, madwomen, angels and crones nattered endlessly to her their stories of things she had

* The Holy Ark in which the scrolls of the Torah are kept.

never seen, but had sometimes wished for. And only in this way and at this time did she feel a pulse in her blood, a heat from beneath her apron, a shaking of something—what word could possibly express such feeling?—a passion, perhaps. No, better, an exhilaration. Could that be the right word? Yes, an exhilaration, the whisper of a promise that something existed beyond the stingy pinch of her meagre life.

Perhaps you, a passing stranger with good intentions, might ask—it would be a fair question—why she wrote at all, when this page would be buried and hidden from the eyes of others. For she sought no acclaim, no honours for these hours. Just the hope that this time to write would come again. It was one of those things not so simple to explain, like how a man-made steel construction might soar like a bird or a voice many miles away might be heard from a radio. And she would not tell you, for how could she?

This was her secret. Her thing unknown. Her temptation and her condemnation. Here, alone, in this private world, she was not the good wife, the obedient daughter, the woman of valour with her price above rubies. She wrote not to please, not to account for herself, never to lift her own spirits. She wrote the way she dreamed. Because in silence and at night, the mind will dream. And the heart, once given words, will do the same. And there, in those moments she sanctified with her ritual of sitting, she allowed every longing to unfurl and breathe and stretch and pulse, until they were *golems* dancing around fires, writhing in ecstasy, wet and glorious and panting. Would you, a passing stranger, want your ears to hear such things? Would you not seek the counsel of the Rabbi to ask for a blessing to cure such peculiarities? You would be tempted; you are only human.

For some, braving battalions and surviving famine are great acts of courage. Even she would not dispute this. To be a Jew, a target for a *pogrom*, also took courage. But courage, like potatoes, comes in many shapes and sizes. To derobe, as she did, to allow her nakedness onto the page, that too took bravery. Only there, and for a moment, could she approach something clear and right. It was the fading of the mists, the lifting of the veils, the mercurial lucidity that comes from scripture. When she sat down in this way, she was not in search of seduction or romance. She had grown weary of waiting for her life to take her by surprise. It was a modest affair, just the search for a tiny voice, in the din of her cramped existence, which spoke in truth, and lied not at all, never saying, 'I don't mind' or 'it was a pleasure'. This voice, immune to bullying or command, like a father's instruction to fetch water or firewood, would answer when she sat down to write. When the voice appeared, she kept the beating thrill of her heart to itself, afraid to frighten it back into the shadows, terrified to ask of it too much.

There she sat, pen poised at the page's surface, until wick was consumed by candlewax or the sound of footsteps crushed the voice. She watched her hand move across the page, its letters sometimes neatly touching the lines, at other times crossing them, a swelling growing in her breast that never failed to cause her to weep. As long as she put ink to the page, her hidden life was not forgotten, not wiped out in a pogrom, not buried in an unmarked grave, despite the days and hours she had to live outside of the writing. She wrote for the comfort that she was more than the baker of the weekly *challah,* the collector of water, the carpenter's wife, Maya Kaslowski. She wrote so that she could return to that life. She wrote so that her life might go on.

Part 2

Come, my beloved,
let us go forth into the field…

There I will give you my love…

If I found you outside, I would kiss you;
Yes, and no one would despise me.
I would lead you, bringing you into my mother's house…

Set me as a seal on your heart,
As a seal on your arm,
For love is strong as death,
Jealousy as cruel as the grave…

The Song of Solomon

★★★

Three things cannot be hidden: love, coughing and poverty.

Yiddish proverb

Henri was there waiting at Jan Smuts International Arrivals in a blue plastic raincoat, with a banner that read, *'She returns. Halle-fuckin-looyah. But will she stay?'* She glowed from the crowd as if in spotlight. Mia's eyes fell on her instantly the way children behold their mothers, in an endless sea of faces. No older or gaunter, with her number two haircut and bra-less vest.

Henri yelped, folded the banner under her armpit, and scampered towards Mia as Mia ran towards her, backpack and arms full. Mia, dressed in a purple sari skirt and ajangle with silver bracelets up to her elbows, dropped her hand luggage and threw her backpack to the ground before grabbing Henri and hugging her skinny bones, while her friend just stroked her hair, saying, "*Meisie, meisie**… Seven years is a lifetime, but you're still a babe."

They unlocked, held elbows, and Mia, tracing Henri's nine-stitch scar above her left eye, whispered, "My eyes have missed your face."

Henri had been her only anchor in South Africa during her years of flitting from country to country, from bed to bed, scattering her body parts, looking for somewhere to leave her ghost. Mia had sent Henri a dyke postcard from every city her footsteps had known. Photographs of bare bottoms. Nipples as

* 'girl,' in Afrikaans.

taut as blueberries. Women kissing. Lips to lips. Lips to nipple. Nipple to nipple. And always on the back, a telephone number.

Henri did not write, 'being *mos* dyslexic and all'. She phoned. No menstrual cycle of 25 days would pass without the phone ringing at some preposterous hour when only tragedy or drunkenness could justify such disturbance. She called at the same time every month, on the day her period began, after her morning shower, before her first cup of coffee. Mia had become so accustomed to speaking to her in a state of half-dream that sometimes she might wake to the weight of a heatwave in Ethiopia or the chilly nip of a morning in Mongolia uncertain whether she had dreamed of Henri in the night or spoken to her in semi-sleep.

Mia had left a message on Henri's answering machine two nights earlier after her, 'If you need a lawyer urgently, call Lifeline, 788 2727, otherwise if this is a howzit, leave your message now': "SAA flight SA43, arriving 15 March, 11.40am, still tall, still dark, but a nosering."

"Yes!" Henri had yelled. "And it's about bloody time!"

In the battered green Volksie, the two of them sang in unharmonious duet to the crackly tape of Leonard Cohen's melancholy ballads, both transported back to those golden Wits days when they had skipped Faggot Wengrave's lectures on Trotsky to concoct rituals for cleansing, a new moon, a period that came on time, one that came late, for the evil in the nooks of the universe, or the smell of coriander. On days when the wind came up they had, with string and coloured paper ribbons, made prayer kites which they set loose on Melville koppie and watched as they took to the air and danced in the wind—before the two of them tumbled, out of breath, onto the dry winter grass, laughing so hard they retched.

The Volksie, in its geriatric years now, rattled along the highway, an aged hippie stripped of the *vooma* of youth, when they had sung at the top of their lungs into the teenage night about violins and blue raincoats and talknonstop, trying to unravel the secret coils of what Leonard had 'really meant'.

"Man, he's just a whiney old Jew," Henri had said.

"He was depressed," Mia had conceded. "The world's a sad place."

"Bullshit!" Henri had said. "It's beautiful, it's sunny and it's full of real coffee and oral sex, man. What's to be sad about?"

In lonely times far away from this place and this woman, Mia would come back time and time again to just this: the smell of the old Volksie, Henri's tattoo of Winnie Mandela on her left shoulder, and her fastidious love. Mia had fallen in love with her at nineteen because Henri could see ghosts. After asking Mia for a light as she stood in the canteen queue holding a soggy chicken pie and undrinkable coffee, Henri's second comment was, "You gotta get rid of that fuckin' spook *on-middel-lik,* * meisie."

Mia had grabbed her hand and kissed it.

From then on, they had moved as one. They had registered for the same courses in their BAs; sat together; eaten together; gotten drunk on tequilas in Rockey Street together; read Fanon, Marx and MacKinnon aloud to each other. Spoken until their teeth ached, punctuating conversation with cup after cup of *real* coffee.

'Henri' was an amputation of her christened name, 'Henrietta van Staden', (the 'etta van Staden' having been lost after six weeks of Politics I at Wits), she and Mia had melted into each other's lives over caffeine and outrage at Botha's States of Emergency and his preposterous Rubicon speech. They marched with banners— 'The tide of liberation will not

* 'immediately', in Afrikaans.

be stemmed'. They held their fists in the air and sang 'Nkosi Sikelela', just daring the police to disperse them with tear gas. They became members of the Student Activist Committee and went out every weekend to help black students with their matriculation exam preparation—or to help clean up another squatter camp.

"S'funny, you look so Jewish," Mia had joked at first. Henri's cinnamon complexion, black eyes and tightly-curled black hair set her apart from her blue-eyed, blonde-haired fairskinned siblings. Henri once told Mia that she was *seker** the product of her mother's secret garden.

"What's that?"

Henri raised her eyebrows at Mia. "Wacchu mean what's that? It's how women have survived this long under male patri-arrchy."

Henri had always imagined her mother, without her apron, de-curlered, with a spot of maroon lipstick and perhaps a scarf around her neck, skipping out the back door with a '*Ek's net by die Spar.*'† A wave, a swing of childbearing-weary hips, a squeak of the front gate, and she would vanish, leaving the six children—with Anneliza, all of thirteen, at the helm—to manage. '*Pas op dat die baba nie uit die crib klim nie, hoor?*'** she'd turn and say, already out the gate, turning back once more just to seal the ordinariness of the venture, and she'd be gone. And her dark-skinned lover would be waiting for her, behind a fence, in a shed, somewhere small and cramped and filled with a white *baas's*†† tools. There, her mother would smoulder into life at the touch of a man who worked his tongue down the length of her body and awoke moans and whispers from the back of her throat.

* 'surely,' or 'certainly' in Afrikaans.
† 'I'm just going to the Spar.'
** 'Watch out that the baby doesn't climb out of the crib, okay?'
†† 'boss,' in Afrikaans.

Joanne Fedler

This version of her conception delighted Henri better than the prospect that she was some throwback gene in her family's pool of raping landowners and that she had been conceived in one of her father's roguish bouts of drunken lust, always announced in front of the children who were banished '*Kamer toe*'.* Through doors they always heard his grunting and swearing. But her mother was always quiet as a corpse. Henri knew that during her conception her mother had moaned and arched when sperm met ovum, because there was life in her that left no trace in any of her brothers and sisters. When she finally left home at sixteen to live with Veronica, a saxophone player in an all-women band with a thick Kaapse Kleurling[†] accent, she told her father that, thanks to him, she would never fuck a white man in her life. Her father had rammed her face into the side of the fridge door, leaving a gash that needed nine stitches and became a mark of honour for Henri.

"Where'm I taking you?" Henri asked.

"My mom's place, 48 Komatie Road, Emmarentia. It's off Barry Hertzog Avenue."

Henri nodded.

"And then, can I crash with you for a while?"

"You got to ask?"

Mia ruffled her friend's hair, leaned over and smooched her on the cheek.

"I dig the nose ring the most," Henri smiled, "but how the fuck do you blow your nose?"

"Carefully," Mia laughed.

Mia leaned down and picked up a pamphlet on the floor of the Volksie. 'Your vote is your secret' was emblazoned across the front. "It's the first time for so many to make that cross, hey?"

---

* 'Go to your room.'
† Cape Coloured

"Ja, this voter education stuff is a mind-fuck. Inkatha are telling people that if they don't vote for them, they'll be killed. If you're an illiterate rural woman, you don't know any better. So we're teaching people that what they vote can't be found out by others."

Mia paged through the pamphlet. Her pulse quickened. The shadows and their secrets were approaching headlong. She wiped her forehead with the back of her hand. Just the adrenaline of being at home. Maybe the Highveld heat.

"How'd it go—in the Holy Land?" Henri asked.

"He died an agonizing death. Suffered 'til the end. It was a gift to witness… Shit, that's not a very evolved thing to say…" Mia's voice trailed off. In the silence that passed, she let herself move into places she had not visited for long. "It was sweet— as if I'd tortured him with my own two hands…"

Henri nodded. Was silent.

Mia looked out the window at the Jo'burg traffic. "Things feel different," she said. "I can feel the hope in the air… I just hope people aren't expecting to vote on the 27th and have homes and jobs on the 28th…" she said.

"Ja, it's a problem. Expectations are huge, but the ANC will deliver," Henri said. She had been a card-carrying member of the ANC in those years on campus when that was enough to be locked up and held in solitary confinement by the security police. Henri smiled. "Things are really going to move. And I don't mean maybe. It's a fuckin' miracle about to happen."

"You gotta swear so much?" Mia asked. "It's fucking unladylike."

"I'm sorry, I didn't realize I was in the company of any fucking ladies."

Mia smiled. "You know my dad was always a believer in miracles. Really. He would have been happy to see how things have turned out here. You would have liked him, Henri."

"Who, your old man?"

"Ja, he was switched on in a really deep way. We were

Joanne Fedler

close—once. For a while."

"Close?" Henri asked.

"Ja, didn't you know that?"

"Naah, you never speak of him."

Mia looked away, watched the passing houses whiz past in a blur.

"Don't I? Never?"

Henri shook her head.

Mia nodded and leaned her forehead against the car door, feeling the hot air against her brow. The landscape was not indifferent. A passing house gave her a nod, an old café a wave. She was not forgotten here. Her footprints had not been erased from Yeoville streets, Louis Botha Avenue, Killarney, the Zoo. We may leave places, but they stay, yearning. It is easier to be the one who leaves.

"Things were taken from him, you know. Things he couldn't be without. He thought I was taken from him. He was wrong. So wrong. Ja."

Henri took one hand off the steering wheel, her eyes off the road, to squeeze Mia's arm. Suddenly the numbness of not feeling began to wear off like lipstick towards the end of the day and the pain in Mia's chest was real.

Though years had nudged time and its particles of distance between them, the wonder of their togetherness still hissed like something trying to catch fire. They drove in silence back to the city of gold, that sat on the horizon, with its Ocean Liner in its lap, its streets lined with jacaranda trees, weeping purple petals, and every lamppost carrying an election poster.

"That's my fav'rite one." Henri slowed down and pointed to a grotesque cartoon of De Klerk on his knees grovelling at Mandela's feet, with *'Mandela se Klerk,'** written on it.

Mia grimaced.

* Mandela's clerk – a play on the Afrikaans word 'clerk' and De Klerk's name, implying that De Klerk was subordinate to Mandela.

"What's it feel like to be home?"

"Am I?"

"What?"

"Home."

Henri shrugged. "You asking me? What's it feel like anyway?"

"Haunting. Bloody terrifying."

"Spook's still with you." It was a statement, not a question. Henri could feel her, just as she always could—Mia's invisible Siamese twin, hovering, watching.

"Ja, she's there, but she got her cloth back."

"Fantastic…"

But she did not ask to see it.

This was the love Mia had missed. One that does not press or invite itself. Girl-love was so different to the carnal connection she had to men that was bodily, that stopped at precisely the moment of orgasm and never beyond. She had long ago stopped telling men her secrets because their greed reviled her. Professor Amis Brooks, a Harvard professor of law, a specialist in gender equality she had met in Ethiopia, had interviewed her for his new book on economic empowerment of rural women in African countries. He had invited her for a drink after an unforgettable day at the battered woman's shelter. Zenash, a 19-year-old woman, had died only hours before from shock and third degree burns. Having your boyfriend pour boiling water over you will do that to you.

After her third glass of red wine, Mia had looked into the professor's eyes and mistaken familiarity for intimacy. She began to speak, almost a confession. A previous lover had spanked her during sex. At the time it had been erotic, she had almost orgasmed from the thrill. But after today violence could never arouse her. When she looked up, Professor Brooks and all five of his law degrees were leering like a flasher.

"I'd love to see that bottom."

Repulsion rose in her like bile. Later, in the dark streets of Addis Ababa, outside St John's Church, with the cold tiles of its wall against the sheath of her back, she had heard herself say, "Fuck me," aching for the chilly bite of his groin-centred appreciation.

Secrets need a home, just like the heart. But men could be trusted with neither.

She did not recognize the house.

The seven-foot wall and godwasthatbarbedwire? hid all that was once familiar. Henri kept the Volksie running, waiting for her friend to move.

"When last did you speak to her?"

"About two years ago," Mia said.

"How's she?"

"Same cold faraway ice maiden," Mia said, stretching herself out the car and walking to the gooseneck intercom, where she pressed the buzzer for 'House', above the one labelled 'Maid's Room'. Moments later her mother's voice crackled over the intercom with, "Who is it?"

"The prodigal daughter," she said. Laughter did not follow. Silence did. Followed by a click and the huge gates with lethal punk steel spikes atop slid to the side, as passage to the past was granted.

Time had been good to Fran. She was taut and trim. The grey had been washed right out of her hair and she took surprises like a daughter home after seven years with grace and calm.

"Sweetheart," she exclaimed. "What a surprise." She opened her arms and hugged Mia.

Mia cradled her head on her mother's shoulder, hoping for a smell of something familiar, but Estee Lauder got there first.

"Gotta run," Henri called out. "Come back for you later, girlfriend."

"You aren't staying?" Fran asked.

"We'll see, Mom."

Fran summonsed a smile. "Come in and have a cup of tea. I want to hear every–thing."

Time passed had not released the unbearable fragility of decency that strung them together as mother and child. Fran could unplug her soul with an inadvertent gesture, a smile unforthcoming, a thing said so misplaced, and Mia felt the leak even then, her body weakening. There was no real forgiveness between them and even seven years apart had not dislodged the cube of frozen tears that caught in her throat when she had to be Fran's little girl.

Mia took a deep breath and crossed the threshhold into a home all grown up.

The house smelled of polish and dogs.

"When did you get dogs?" Mia asked. "You were always a cat person."

"Oh come on, I've had Kneidel and Shlemiel for ages, surely you remember?"

"No, Ma, you always hated dogs since that dog bit Sarafina—you said they smell and behave just like teenage boys."

Fran laughed. "Yes, yes, I did say that, didn't I? But we had a few break-ins, and the cops recommended a watchdog."

"Is this your watchdog?" Mia asked, shooing the poodle that jumped up against her sari. "Ma, if he tears this, I'll tie his legs together."

"Don't be so dramatic, Mia," Fran said, taking Kneidel by the collar, and shooing him outside. "He makes a huge noise when strangers come—he yaps his head off. And what is with that Indian outfit anyway?"

"It's called a sari, Mom," Mia said, wandering down the hall. The studio door was closed. She tried the round-bellied handle, which fitted much better in her large adult hands. She had always cupped the sphere in both small hands as a child, looking for her dad deep in the wonder he made with his painting fingers. The door was locked now.

"It's locked," Fran said from behind her, as if that explained why. Mia just nodded.

She turned off the hall and stood in the doorway of the lounge, looking out onto the garden. The furniture had been re-covered in a rose-patterned material. And there was a television cabinet she had never seen before. She walked around the lounge, touching the mantelpiece, the piano, the cabinets of books, letting the slow moment of being back there catch up with the shifting memories that undulated inside. She stopped at the portrait, which still had its place. 'Moonsmile', Issey had called it, Mia's young girlish face looking out, up, with an awe infused with unsurpassable sorrow. He had always considered it his masterpiece.

"And that thing in your nose? God, Mia..." she sighed. "Would you like something to drink? Some tea maybe?"

"A double scotch on the rocks, Ma. Thanks." Mia murmured.

"It's not *that* time of the day," Fran said. "Besides, since when do you drink whiskey?"

"Since I was eighteen, Ma. I need a drink—it's not easy for me this... Please," Mia said, raking her fingers through her hair.

Fran did not move or speak for a moment.

Mia touched her mother's arm, said, "Maybe you could do with a drink too—I'll get them. I remember where the drinks cabinet is," and she turned and left her mother rooted in silence and reeling with the newness of a strange daughter home.

Fran was standing in the same place when Mia returned and placed a tumbler with ice and Bells whiskey in her hand. "*Le'chaim*,*" Mia said, clinking her glass against Fran's. "Good to see you, Mom. How've you been?" and then she downed her drink.

Fran lifted the drink to her mouth, took a sip and then mumbled, "What am I doing? I don't drink whiskey."

"I'll have it," Mia said, taking the glass from her hand, and downing it too, relishing the heat of the liquid and the iciness of the cubes against her lips.

"Slowly, Mia," Fran said with less conviction.

"Mind if I look around?" Mia said turning away.

"Be my guest," said Fran. "I'll be out in the garden."

Mia walked out of the lounge towards the stairwell. The carpet was worn and faded from feet going this way and that over the years. Slowly, she began the climb. Seventeen. There were seventeen steps from the ground to the landing at the top. Sarafina had taught her to count in Zulu. '*Kunye, isibili, kuthatu, okune, isihlanu*†...' Mia remembered aloud as she climbed.

At the top of the stairs she looked in at her mother's room. It was neat and tidy. The two single beds that had always been pushed together were now apart with a bedside table separating them. A patchwork quilt covered the one bed. On the other were two neat stacks of clean laundry. Beside the bed was a column of *Garden Beautiful* magazines with intermittent luminous yellow post-its sticking out from various pages her mother had flagged for future gardening reference. There was no trace of her father left here, as if he had never shed a tear or groped for some kind of happiness in this place. Why didn't Fran just sell the house and buy a flat somewhere? Its

---

* 'To life,' in Hebrew.
† 'one, two, three, four, five' in Zulu.

emptiness was unbearable, a place perforated with memory pockets of unmet longing.

Back on the upstairs landing, Mia stopped at the entrance to her bedroom door. It was closed. Was it locked too? Mia tried the handle. It turned. She swallowed.

The room was unchanged from the day Mia had closed the door and moved into digs in Yeoville. She had been eighteen and twenty-six days old, and fatherless for less than forty-eight hours. The fluffy pink carpet, the stuffed animals and the pale pink curtains belonged to an ancient time. Along the bookshelves her flying figures congregated in the dust. My god, there was an army of them. Some were childishly constructed from plasticine, now hard with age. Others made of folded paper, lay on their sides. Things with wings had always forced their way into her fingertips, demanding creation. With wings, you could fly away, leave a place behind, make it small with distance. Mia sat down heavily on the bed. She sneezed from the dust. So unlike Fran to allow a festering like this. Everything here could be burnt in a huge bonfire. Nothing deserved to be saved.

Mia lay back on the bed and closed her eyes.

Suddenly, she sat upright and bent her head down between her knees to look under the bed. She fumbled with her hand under the bed. "Fuck, where is it?"

She got to her feet, and then crouched down onto the floor, tilting her head to the side so she could see the space between the bed and the carpet. There it was. She reached far under the bed, her silver bracelets jangling noisily, and grabbed hold of its side. Sliding it towards her, she finally grabbed hold of its handle and pulled it out. Her 'Just in Case'.

She flicked the knobs on either side of the handle that had grown slightly rusty and stiff. They snapped back. She opened the case. *'Beware the Jabberwock, my son,'* glared back at her from a page in her father's tormented script. It gave her the same tremors she had felt when first she'd seen it up on the fridge. She lifted it up. Beneath it, where she had left them was a thick wad of poems and stories in her childhood handwriting tied with a purple ribbon. Sarafina's snuff box. She opened it and sniffed. The hint of a pungent smell still lingered there. She closed it. Lolling at the edge of the suitcase were two stones. A round white one and a small blue-ish one. What had he called it? A tourmaline, that's right. She lifted it up and held it up to the light. It was still beautiful. Wasn't there a third? She lifted the wad of papers and found the purple one, with streaks of white in it. Amethyst. She held all three stones in the palm of her hand and then slipped them into the pocket of her blouse. It was just the matchbox left. She picked it up and rattled it. It was still in there. Out of nothing more than a sense of final indifference, she pushed the containing box out of its sheath. Even the cigarillo stump had outlasted him.

The mulberry tree was still standing, shorn of its canopy of leaves. "To help the grass grow under it," Fran explained to Mia, who had joined her mother in the garden. Mia pulled off a mulberry. "Those berries make a godawful mess," Fran said. Mia nodded again.

"Is Two Boy still working for you?" Mia asked.

"No, not for ages. Shame, he was stabbed to death by some *tsotsis** one Friday—they stole his month's salary. Just on the corner of Clovelly and Braeside. And after that I decided garden boys are too much trouble." She paused, wiped her forehead with the back of her hand. "I get a garden service in once a week and the rest I do. And Princess waters it every day for me."

* thieves, rascals in Zulu.

"Princess?"

"The maid."

Mia nodded. "What happened to Shyness?"

"We had to get rid of her. She was drinking and running a *shebeen** from the room—if I could have charged for the traffic that was going through here every day, I'd be a rich lady," Fran laughed.

"You should get her to dust and clean out my room. It's like a ghost's boudoir in there," Mia said.

"Yes, I will get to it. Maybe you should take whatever you want from it, and I'll just clear out the rest of the stuff."

"Ma, I did that years ago. There's nothing left in there that I want." With the three stones wrapped up in the dreamcloth in her backpack, that was true.

"Fine," Fran clipped.

Mia looked around. This garden whose spaces and nooks she knew so well was so over-manicured, dressed up like the girl-next-door-had-a-makeover. It no longer beckoned.

"So how do you feel about the election? Are you voting, Ma?"

"Ja, I'll vote DP again." Fran paused. Then added, "Not that it will make any difference. The ANC is going to come in."

"And?"

"And nothing. I like Nelson Mandela. He's a gentleman. I'd vote for him, but he's not the ANC."

"You like Nelson Mandela?" Mia asked.

"Yes, he's a hero."

"This is the same Nelson Mandela that I was forbidden to have a picture of when I was at Wits."

"Mia, that was a long time ago. It was dangerous in those days to be… involved."

Mia nodded.

* an informal drinking parlour, mostly illegal.

"And they're not all like him, you know—they're mostly uneducated and tribal…"

"Mom, that's just racist bullshit, and you should get over it. This is the new South Africa."

"I know just what kind of South Africa it is. I've been living here for the past seven years…" Fran quipped.

Mia grimaced, touché-ed into silence.

They walked around the rose bushes. The blooms were pendulous and heady with summer. Mia heard the buzzing of bees and backed away.

"Maybe things are going to be good here, Ma? What do you think?"

"It would make a change, Mia, wouldn't it?" she smiled.

Mia stood in the garden, closed her eyes against the sun and lifted her arms out. "Could do with a swim, this sari is starting to itch," and before Fran could hold her back, she had stripped naked in the garden, leaving a heap of clothing on the grass. As she dived into the pool, she felt the amniotic kindness of cool water against her skin.

When she came up for air, Fran and the pile of dirty clothes on the grass had disappeared. Mia swam a few lengths of breaststroke, then got out of the pool and lay belly down on the hot slasto to warm herself, her long hair plastered down her back like a mane.

When Fran came out again, she was carrying a towel over her shoulder and a tray of tea. In the centre of the tray was a small pewter vase containing two golden roses with orange centres slouching flirtatiously like girls hitching. She handed Mia the towel.

"It's not really the weather for tea," Fran said apologetically. "Should've offered you something cold," but she didn't.

"Beautiful roses," Mia said. Fran smiled.

Wrapped in her towel, at the outdoor plastic table, Mia

sipped tea with her mother. Long stretches of silence pulled between them like skeins of wool.

"What's it like to see your only child again?" Mia asked.

"Lovely," she said.

Mia laughed out loud and sipped some more.

"I'm a little surprised—that you didn't call to let me know... But that doesn't matter now that you're here."

Mia looked up at her mother.

"I'm not staying for long, Ma," she said.

"Of course you're not," Fran said, and turned to look at her roses. "And it's perfectly okay."

zikh tsu frayen:

to rejoice:
enjoy by possessing;
feel joy on account of (an event);
to be glad or greatly delighted;
to exult

Maya's eyes—the colours of labradorite, greys infused with splinters of fern-greens and tawny stone—first came to rest on the figure of the seamstress in the communal bathhouse and, to Maya, she felt as unexpected as a shaft of sunlight in those unkind winters of Kovno. It took courage to look neighbours in the eyes, for each wretched body was doubled over with the weight of weather and worry, stinking of sweat and urine.

It was her smell that first drew Maya to look her in the face. It was almost impossible to distinguish where smells began and ended, for everyone encumbered by her body was part of that great stench that was the air of the *shtetl.** But the seamstress, she had a smell of something held to the earth, like a potato or a beetroot still wet with brown clods of soil. It was a smell that caused Maya to salivate, quite beyond her control and much to her shame. She wanted to bury her nose in its softness.

In the communal bathhouse, poor and smelling of a week of cold and hard work, the women would bathe together, first in shyness, covering their heavy breasts and tangled groins, like Adam and Eve in the Garden of Eden when the taste of apple was still sweet on their lips. The widow must have felt Maya's

* 'village,' in Yiddish.

eyes sniffing her, but she did not scuttle from her gaze. Knowledge brings shame, as was written in the Torah, and they were full of it.

Never before had Maya so desired to lay eyes completely on another. And when the seamstress untied the grey cloths across her head that held a bulk in a neat cradle of hair, the glory of those tresses that came tumbling down called Maya to touch, smell, mesh her fingers into it. The seamstress raised her eyes to Maya, a sideways glance exposing her neck—a place to lay lips, fingers, and (if Maya could be forgiven for such immodesty), tongue.

Maya spoke first. Words were her companions. The seamstress was shy. Lonely. At twenty-three she had already buried a husband. The small boy she bore was skinny, weak. She sewed for a living—jackets, dresses, trousers. Anything people asked for. And such hands she had—hands familiar with the inside of garments, the underbelly of the cloth that touches skin, hands that had pressed into seams that hold bodies from the frost and hands that were patient with the simplicity of stitch by stitch.

They parted. Wished one another well until the next bath day. As Maya walked back home, the crunch of gravel underfoot, a stirring began in her loins— perhaps it was her umbilicus. She reached to her belly, but the sensation, almost bubbles under water, rose to her chest, the heat ascending the shaft of her throat, and before she could cover her mouth a sound escaped for which she had no word to describe. Laughter? Almost. A gasp? Not quite. She fumbled for language—any part of it—to attach to this sound, a stranger to her body. She felt as if she was hovering at the edge of something wide and deep and endless, and she wanted to throw herself into it.

She clasped her hands to her face, and looked up to see who was watching. The town was unchanged, but everything had altered. A beginning. She was at the beginning of something, a place that marked a 'before' and 'after' in a life wound up in endless circles of mundane sameness, and it felt, god forgive her, like joy. It was a vicious secret, more prized than a handful of *matbeyes** sufficient to purchase a freshly slaughtered chicken, maybe even already plucked. Maya guarded it like treasure.

The days could not wind down into darkness with speed kind enough for a week to pass. On that next washday, Maya dared to call her 'friend'. Two weeks passed before they told each other small things—the boy's name, whose hem needed fixing, the shape of the moon the *Shabbos* passed. Sometimes they even laughed. Maya, reached out to tuck the strands of loose hair under the seamstress's headcloth. She blushed in turn, lowering her eyes and rubbing her hands together. They kept place in line for one another at the bathhouse, standing close so Maya could breathe the fullness of fresh potatoes.

Once she whispered to Maya, while she scraped the black calluses off her feet, that when she had time, of which she had but moments to spare, she would sew the dreams she had into small cloths with the scraps of cotton and cloth she saved from orders. These she kept to unfold when the days were dark for months on end and she could not meet the emptiness of her child's eyes with a handful of porridge. Sometimes a person with a celebration might buy a length of material that had sea-green or sky-blue woven into it, not that she had ever seen a green sea or a blue sky. For a wedding, one could always be sure that a neckline of lace would be requested. Even the cover of the Torah had to be replaced, and if she were so lucky as to be called upon by the *Shamesh*†—or even the Rabbi—to make

* 'coins' in Yiddish.
† beadle in the synagogue.

it, that would give her two weeks in which she could caress an arm's length of maroon velvet, the colour of her monthly bleeding. And in such moments she would blush with rare pleasure, for she would match the order, but by some miraculous stretch of fit, a corner, or a finger length, or a diagonal, or the angles left from a square from which circles or curves were cut, remained. And from those tatters she braided a deeper world, her own secret Garden of Eden.

And Maya was so bold as to ask if she might see them. Not all, she said, just one, maybe.

Maya waited the week, counting down the days for the time to wash. And there she waited for Maya, greeted her, and said nothing of the cloths of her dreams. Maya was afraid to frighten her away with eagerness, so she bathed with her, told of the chair her husband carved that week, it's handsome legs, its back with angel wings. And she smiled low into her neck and spoke only words needed for the sharing of the bathing. And it was time almost to bid her farewell and may she prosper for another week, when she took Maya by the hand, and led her behind the bathhouse, where their shoes got soaked in mud, and where it smelled of human waste, but Maya's heart was swollen and trembling.

From the dark seam between her bosoms, she drew out a piece of cloth, no bigger than a small handkerchief, and held it flat in the palm of her hand. Maya did not know where to look first or longest—into her palm or her eyes, for in both she saw tricks of light and sleights of wonder, a glimmer of blue silk, a copper sequin, a moon of filigree lace, a rosebud of buttons, woven cobblestones of amber and jade. Maya was made to think of meadows in starlight and rainbows after thunder, things unseen by her eyes, but suggested by her heart. That cloth whispered stories, its promises made her weak with longing.

"Why, it's a poem!" Maya whispered.

And then as quick as she had shown it, she folded it back

into her breast, and put a finger to her mouth, and Maya nodded. Perhaps it was the secret threaded from her palm to Maya's eyes and back to her that changed the world that day when she first beheld such beauty wrought from nothing. For the first time, she wanted to share her poems.

They would meet earlier than the bath times, wash quickly, sometimes not at all, but would find a spot where people would not venture. There they would find a rock, a low wall, a discarded barrel, and Maya would speak her poems. Through them, the seamstress never spoke, nor would she wipe the tears that fell from her eyes. Sometimes they would part without farewells, just an unspoken something bigger than both of them that swept the world clean like the floods in the time of Noah.

"Where have you been, Maya, my love?" he would ask, lifting his chin from his chisel.

"At the bathhouse, Yankel, my husband."

"Such a long bath?"

"The lines get longer and longer, for many of the newly weds have had children, and they must go first."

And he would nod and say, "Welcome home." And after a while he would lift his head again and say, "Perhaps it would be better if you made the dinner before you left for the bathhouse on a Thursday. That way, none of us will go hungry."

Maya would stand over the *pripetshok** peeling potatoes. Only the pink marks on the white potatoes alerted her that she had cut her flesh in her haste. Her body only came alive with feeling at the bathhouse.

Maya stood in her scuffed shoes—ah shoes, these coverings on her feet could hardly be called shoes. Her feet were her shoes,

---

* stove.

her soles her leather against the gravel, the icy streets. Before her, ten paces or so away, was her house—the room that she shared with Yankel. Inside he would be waiting for her, removing his *tefillen*,* but all the while wondering what had happened to his wife and his breakfast.

Something in the struggling morning light made her linger in this way, and she turned her back on her house and looked around her. The dark streets were not yet stirring, for this hour was too early even for early risers. From some windows the pale flicker of candlelight winked, as serious husbands readied themselves to leave for work. Nothing she saw was made to make hearts soar, yet something in her soared. She did not feel this heavy commandment of the dawn upon her—to *Shacharit*,† to bathe, to work, to fix, to make. The something in her lifted high above these serious buildings, with their serious people. She looked around. Could anyone see her? How could she be so girlish when others were so serious? She berated herself, 'Stop this nonsense, Maya.' But the nonsense soaked her to the bone like a herring in salt water. And before she could stop herself, remind herself that she was a married woman with food to prepare for her husband, her feet, her insolent rogue barely-shod feet, twirled her around and around, and then her arms spread out and she spun and spun like a *dreidel*** on *Channukah*,†† giggles of laughter and tears of delight gushing out of every unplugged part of herself, when others on that morning were so serious.

---

* phylactories, made of small black boxes with black straps, worn on the left arm and the head.
† Jewish morning prayers.
** Hebrew for 'spinning top.'
†† the Jewish festival of lights, when children spin spinning tops with Hebrew letters on their sides, representing the phrase, 'A great miracle happened there,' referring to the oil that burned in the Temple for eight days when there was only enough for one day.

Joanne Fedler

Maya closed her gloved palm over the handle, pushed down on it to open the door, but her hand slipped at first. It opened when she braced the handle with her other hand. She glided into the darkness, and turned for a final gaze outside to the place where her spinning feet had scuffed the frost, bunching it in places, leaving gravel bare in others, as if a strange-footed beast had fluffed its wings there and beat the ground. She shut the door behind her and shivered, for the inside was only barely warmer than the outside. She breathed into her cupped hands and felt the tip of her nose ache with the thawing. She covered her big nose with her hands, waiting to see whether fingers or nose would offer warmth to the other first.

The room was quiet. She could not make out whether Yankel was still asleep in the bed. The *pripetshok* stood untended, the coal bucket slouched dutifully half-full against it and, for a moment, she felt the shame in her rise at the way the morning did not bear her presence or attention. Would Yankel be angry? Hurt? He never showed emotion, never raised his voice, godforbid never his hand. He simply reminded her of her duties, and she would apologize and promise to be more mindful.

She moved to the pripetshok, opened its door and, as she bent to fill it with coal, her arm clumsily knocked over the bucket. It clattered to the floor, sending the coal scuttling to all corners of the room. She bent to pick it up—each block icy, not sharing the secret of how something so cold—in the presence of a humble match—might offer warmth. She filled the *pripetshok* in this way, one block at a time.

From the shadowed corner of the room, Yankel moved silently towards her, his *tefillen* on his arm and head. Though she had half-expected him to be there, she caught her breath, his sudden watching presence taking her by surprise. He did not look at her but silently began to unwind the leather straps from his arms.

Maya turned to fill the coffee pot with water from the bucket—and her breath caught in her throat. The bucket! Water! She had used that as her excuse to leave so early—mumbled to Yankel that she would go to fill the bucket from the communal tap, but in her hurry, in her flurry to leave, she had forgotten the bucket behind. Not to mention that such an outing should take no longer than twenty minutes and she had been gone the better part of an hour. Shame and panic rose in her all at once.

"Perhaps what you find is not what you were looking for?" Yankel said suddenly.

She did not say anything. Her breathing was quick and frenzied now. He would surely be furious. She turned to face him, to discover the furrows of his expression so she could prepare herself for blame or anger. But his face was lowered and his beard covered his expression, which bore the traces of sadness.

"I was looking for coffee for your morning cup, Yankel, my husband, and yet I discover we are out of sugar. Indeed, Yankel, what I find is not what I was looking for. I shall rush out and borrow some from the Tanchels."

"Don't," he said. "A man cannot always expect that things will be sweet. Let us thank *Hashem* for the coffee."

She lit the flint, ignited the kindling. Yankel moved silently around her, folding away his *tefillen*, winding and winding those long leather straps while she knelt and blew the flames for his coffee.

The twirl inside her, the gloriousness of her dance on the dawn frost had vanished. She was his bitter coffee.

The newly pruned rosebushes at the far end of the garden, April 1972

The pruning was done. A decent job, even if she said so herself. Her rosebushes stood proud and regimented in the sun. Two Boy was cleaning up the garden debris and she was ready for a cup of tea. Wasn't it that time of day? After that, she intended to check up on Mia—it wasn't that she had forgotten. She would attend to it.

It had only been an hour ago that Mia had bolted into the garden, hysterical, something about burning her hands. There was no point in panicking. She was accustomed to these bizarre outbursts. Detached containment was the sensible approach. Mia could not have literally burned herself—there was nothing cooking on the stove, it wasn't Sarafina's ironing day—and god, how she hated to be interrupted while pruning. Still, she had pulled off one of her muddied gloves, glanced briefly at Mia's hands, unscorched, and felt Mia's forehead. It was burning. "Sarafinaaaa," she had called, "Come and help Mia get into her pyjamas. She's not well."

Sarafina had emerged from the house wiping her hands on her apron.

"Meeaa, sick?" she had asked.

Mia had shaken her head. "My hands are burning, look!"

Sarafina had taken Mia's hands in hers and looked.

"Come, come," Sarafina had said, ushering her into the house. "We make Mia betta now. *Amanzi, amanzi** for hands,

* 'water,' in Zulu.

water puts fire out."

Fran had returned to her roses. The adrenaline in her veins slowly subsided as she snipped and shaped.

"Two Boy, those ones are *not* weeds, okay?" Two Boy had nodded, "*Yebo**, Missie Fren."

Perhaps the time had come to see someone about this. It was not that she felt responsible for Mia's nightmares, hallucinations and outbursts. But she was beginning really to despise the interference with her own life. Godonlyknows what other people said behind her back. The indignity welled up in her like venom. She stood up and surveyed the rosebushes. They were sturdy and ready for new blooms. Fran sighed, turned and walked towards the main house.

The lounge floor was strewn with crayons and papers. Fran bent down to gather the papers—she hated mess—but froze in mid-kneel. Involuntarily, her eyes fell upon Mia's words. All this had *nothing* to do with her. But then why did the A4 page in her hand, ascrawl with Mia's writing, feel like such an accusation? Surely only the guilty feel blame? These were words twisted from a desolate nightmare.

"She's a very clever little thing," Mrs Sweetnam had said. "Very clever—the best in class at writing and reading. But, in my opinion, something is... well, disturbing her," she had said nervously. "I keep telling her that news is what happens at home. But still... I get this sort of thing." And she had pushed across Mia's 'news book' for Fran to look at.

Fran had leaned back in her chair as a thicket sprung up between them.

"She's just going through a difficult stage," Fran had smiled tersely. "We're aware of it and are handling it. Thanks for your

* 'yes,' in Zulu.

concern." She pulled the strap of her handbag over her shoulder. "Will that be all?"

Now, bent over on the lounge floor, Fran cleared her throat. She massaged her face with both her hands, squeezed her temples. She slowly pursed her lips and ran her fingers through her hair. She stood up and headed towards the stairwell.

As she reached the top of the staircase, she paused. Whatever softness she had in her had given way to anger. It wasn't right. Somehow, she had to take charge. Once and for all.

Mia's eyes were closed in sleep. Fran sat down on the side of her bed and put her hand on Mia's forehead. The fever had gone. Fran gently shook Mia awake.

"Mia, where did this come from?" she said slapping the back of her hand against the page. "Did you copy it from somewhere?"

Mia shook her head.

"Where did it come from?"

"It's just a story in my head."

"Where do you get such stories from?"

Mia shrugged.

"I don't like such horrible stories, do you understand me?"

"I'm sorry Mom," Mia said softly.

"Sorry isn't good enough! You should be writing about fairies and happy things. You are seven years old, for god's sake. Enough of these stories. Do you hear me? Enough! I want *happy* stories!"

Mia looked at her mother with sorrowful eyes. The world was scary when moms were afraid. It was only Sarafina who didn't mind where stories came from and who told her scary stories of the *tokolosh** who eats little children, and when she cried, said, "Cry, Mia, the *tokolosh* will eat you."

---

* a small African bogeyman with evil intent, a possessor of souls believed to steal your spirit while you are asleep.

Mia turned her face into her pillow. How would she stop her fingers from telling stories?

"It's serious, Issey. We can't ignore it any more," said Fran, not looking up from her knitting.

"I'm sure it is, Fran," Issey said, bending down to kiss her hello, "but whatever it is, it can wait a few minutes." She did not tilt her head to meet his lips so that he could see the way her neck fanned into her jawline—that curve that had so enchanted him when he still smoked Gauloises cigarettes, wore his Tevya hat and drank that watery coffee from the university canteen. That was more than a decade ago and it was that line of her neck becoming jaw that had remained constantly beautiful, reminding him of the choices he had made.

"I'm tired of drawing it to your attention and having you downplay it all the time."

"Oh, I know what this is about," Issey sighed.

She had, all the Fine Arts students agreed, a compelling face. Composed, but fiery, and she could sit still for hours, only the blink of her hazelnut eyes, disturbing the stillness of her countenance. He'd studied her for close to an hour before he began. In a matter of minutes he had completed his assignment.

At the end of the class she had unfrozen, stretched, and walked from easel to easel, eager to see the images her still life had provoked. At his easel she had stopped dead. Her own large eyes stared back at her in unforgiving charcoal. Was it only she or could everyone see the tearlessness of those eyes that stopped crying when Uncle Max made her promise that it was just *their little secret*? She had felt her nakedness not in her body, but there, in that canvas. But when she had turned to him, coy, a paintbrush lodged behind his ear, and so badly dressed, with anger flaming from the aloed depths of her irises, all he had said, was, "You like it? It's yours."

She had carried it home on the bus, rolled up under her arm, and in the back garden with a box of Lion matches, she had watched it crinkle into ash. The next time she saw him on campus she had gone up to him with the boldness of a deep familiarity and asked him if he wanted to go see Sean Connery, a rising new talent, in *Dr No*. It was showing at the Civic. In town. Just a friendly outing to the bioscope. How could he say no?

For a while their lives had passed for happy. They were naive, certainly, but making the most of youth and whatever hopes came with it. Morning lovemaking, he, furtive and urgent, she, quiet and resigned, and late-night coffee in Hillbrow after the bioscope. She liked that he did not push to know too much. He was content with her faraway presence. Her beauty was enough for him and he was grateful for the space she took up in his life: an elegant statue of femininity— cold, distant, unreachable, as women were.

That curve in her neck remained enchanting even after her body dropped their baby like a dead weight onto the birthing table. Blame? He blamed himself for too much wanting. The doctors had wrapped the baby to cover the crushed skull. But Fran only saw what was lost, beyond love. And as much as Issey wished, he couldn't unpaint that.

From then on she relinquished hope, gently set it free. Perhaps it would come back to her. At night she closed her eyes against the darkness and reached for her Dormicum, in the drawer in her bedside table, swallowed the tablets in pairs without water, and waited for their soporific caress.

In the waiting room of her slumber images of her cousin Desiree and their thirteen-year-old bodies running through the sprinkler on the lawn would slither into her thoughts, and then her Uncle Max and his boisterous laugh, his eyes clasping her like the wet underside of a starfish on a rock. She must have said 'please don't', but maybe she had just thought that, maybe the words had stuck in her beautiful throat. How could someone who bought you a roll of Imperial Mints and Liquorice Allsorts for which you said 'thank you so much' hurt you? Maybe she had just thought the hurt. But she had not just thought the bleeding. But maybe that was the 'time of the month', that Desiree had told her about. And why did her mother and father make her go on holiday with Desiree and Uncle Max and Aunty Lily, and when Desiree said 'what's the matter with you?' why didn't she say 'something terrible has happened'?

At least she knew why good things always slipped away from her. There was comfort in that. And then the hum of bees would calm her as sleep nudged her into dreamless oblivion.

Issey thrummed his fingers on the doorpost, watching hers purling, crossing and uncrossing the miniature spears she had chosen as her weapons. He had never stopped finding her beautiful, but more often found that he liked to look at her from a distance rather than close up.

"You'll never guess who I'm tendering to paint," he said.

Fran said nothing.

"John Vorster's wife."

"I want to talk about Mia."

"I know you do. Just let me share this with you. This will be the biggest break I've ever had."

Fran sighed. "As long as you don't think there's a moral issue here," she muttered.

His fingers stopped tapping. "What's the moral issue with five thousand rand? That's if I get it. I'm up against some serious talent. Foreign talent too."

Fran knitted silently for a few moments. "They're Nats. We've just voted for the Progressives."

"And so?"

Fran said nothing and Issey turned to leave the room, stopped in the frame of the doorway and came back to finish.

"Don't confuse art and politics. I'm an artist. I draw faces. Evil faces make just as great art as holy faces. This has fuck-all to do with apartheid. I've got to feed you lot and whether I have to beg, borrow or steal, I frankly don't give much of a damn."

Issey stomped out of the lounge and headed for the bathroom. He took his time in there, scrubbing the paint ingrained in the margins of his fingernails. She always insisted he touch her with clean hands. As if those hands were somehow tainted in the spilling of blood, like he was a butcher. His grandfather, Zaide Yankel's father, had been apprenticed as a *shochet** for a week, so his father told him, but he had a weak stomach and would look away every time he was supposed to find the exact spot on the neck to slice neatly. Issey had inherited that weak stomach for bloody things. Even long before he had held his firstborn son, searching his little features for his own.

He looked into the mirror above the basin and pulled a face at himself. It was true, the Nats were racists, but Vorster wasn't as bad as his predecessors. He'd allowed mixed sports, blacks and whites playing together. That was a step in the right direction. He would spend the evening examining the photographs of Mrs Vorster and maybe do a sketch or two just to get a feel for her face. A face is a face. Coming out of the bathroom he called down the passage to the kitchen, "Mia, guess who's home?"

Back in the lounge, he avoided Fran's gaze, which was fixed on the pattern she was knitting. "Purl six, drop two, purl ten," she whispered, memorizing. Next to her lay Mia's story. Issey picked it up and sat down far into the crease of his Eaziboy.

"She's more prolific than Barbara Cartland," he mumbled.

"And as unstable as Sylvia Plath," Fran said, "Thanks to all the *meshugenah*† genes she inherited from your side of the family."

* Jewish ritual slaughterer.
† 'mad,' in Yiddish.

"Well, at least she inherited some artistic talent too—unfortunately no sense of humour, but that she didn't get from me."

Fran laid her knitting down and turned squarely to face her husband.

"We have a child who writes about houses burning, babies dying, dogs with one eye, goats that bleed, hearts tearing, limbs in dustbins. No, I don't have a sense of humour about it. I think she's in trouble, but don't let that interfere with your art, please, whatever you do." Her voice crackled.

"Okay," Issey said. He raked his fingers through his hair. "Sarafina..."

"Yes *Baas*,"* came the voice from the kitchen.

"Make me a gin and tonic, will you?"

He waited for her answer. "Did you hear me, Sarafina?"

Sarafina put her head around the door. "*Baas*?"

"A gin and tonic—in a big glass."

"Ja, I hear the first time," she said, as she turned to leave.

"Well, all you needed to do was answer. I'm not a mind reader."

Issey looked at the page again. "*Ag*, it's not as creepy as the others," he said. "Maybe she's getting better."

Fran purled and plained, purled and plained, furiously.

"Okay, what if we speak to Rabbi Goldenbaum?"

Fran stopped knitting and looked up at him.

"It can't hurt. It could be we've got an *eyin horah*.† Maybe we just need a *brochah*.** Shmooley tells me the Hurwitz's got rid of the buzzing in their roof last week. They tried Pest Control, Bug Busters, Anti-Ants Anonymous and nobody could find a thing wrong. Eventually they got the Rabbi to go through the house, taking down all the *mezzuzahs*. They found

* 'boss,' in Afrikaans.
† 'evil eye,' in Hebrew.
** 'blessing,' in Hebrew.

Joanne Fedler

that the one for the family room had two spelling mistakes. Since then, the buzzing's gone. Just like that." He looked up at Fran, who held her knitting in mid-stitch.

"You think that the problem with our child is that we've got an unkosher *mezzuzah* on the door?"

"Could be. You never know. Keep an open mind."

Fran shrugged. "And the problem with our marriage is that there's a spelling mistake in our *ketubah*.* Fix a letter on a piece of parchment and your child's problems will disappear. Is that your solution?"

"Well, I haven't heard any better suggestions."

Fran tugged at the wool.

"It's worth a shot," Issey said after a time. "Maybe it will make Mia feel better."

Sarafina appeared with a gin and tonic wiping her hands on her apron.

"What a girl! Thanks," he said, taking the glass from her just as Mia came skipping into the lounge.

"Look at my flying angel," she said, holding up a plasticine figure with paper wings.

"Where's it flying to?" Issey asked.

"Back home."

"It's beautiful," Issey said.

Mia plunged into his lap and buried her head in his neck. He hugged her close, kissing the top of her head with its white lock of hair. Over the top of her head he looked at Fran and raised his eyes, as if to say, "See, she's okay." Fran looked away and counted stitches.

Turning to the page, Issey pinched Mia's bottom and gave out a snort of a laugh. "You'd better put it with your others," he said. "You remember Rabbi Goldenbaum?"

---

* Jewish marriage certificate.

Mrs Sweetnam's class, King Solomon Primary School, May, 1972

Shongolulus* lie curled in a defensive helpless coil. You can lift them just like that and they stay wound up, hugging their millions of little feet into themselves, flat and twisted, pretending to be dead and hoping you will just let them live and not scrunch them to hear the crackle of their bursting bodies. Grace's unmarried Aunt Rinky had eaten a shongolulu once, just to hear Grace scream in disgust. Ever since Mia had been told that, she nagged Grace to meet Aunt Rinky who was sure to have long black hair plaited with bats' tails and a humped nose with a big hairy mole.

From the very first day that Mia had walked into Grade One B at King Solomon Primary School, Mrs Sweetnam's class, she had marched her way through the noisy clusters of children like Moses through the Red Sea and made a direct line for Grace because she was the only one who didn't ask her about her white hair. While the others in the class crowded around Mia and pulled and tugged at the white strands that had come loose from her braid, saying, 'Wot's this?', 'Is it real?', 'How did you make it?', the only question Grace asked her, was, "Do you want some silkworms? I've got too many." Mia had nodded yes, though she did not know what silkworms were or what you did with them. When Grace brought them for her the next day in a shoebox with punched holes in its lid, she could barely conceal her disappointment at the little grey

* Zulu for 'millipede.'

moving bits on mulberry leaves. Only things with wings made her happy.

Grace said that if you watch really closely, with your nose up against the side of the cardboard box, and you breathe softly so as not to disturb them, so that they lift their heads up and turn to look first to the one side, then to the other, you can see a silkworm's teeth. They are inside the little black nose part that sniffs the mulberry leaves to make sure they are fresh. Grace told her that silkworms like the dark and sleep on their food and even make poos on it. When they are big and fat you can lift them up with your fingers and feel how cold and clammy their bellies are and how their feet stick to your fingers. They tickle the hairs on your arm as they crawl, but it doesn't feel nasty.

"But the best part," Grace had told her, holding the box, not yet parting with her offering, "is that when they get big enough, they spin cocoons and wait inside until one day they become moffs."

"With wings?"

"Uh-hu."

"And then what?"

"U-um, then they die."

Grace's two older brothers, Graham and Andrew, played in the rugby teams. They were loud and pushed in line at the tuck-shop and scratched between their legs and laughed too hard. In the beginning, Mia liked to sleep over at Grace. Boys mesmerized her. They made noise and dirt and loud music, things Not Allowed in Mia's house of manners, tidiness and early bedtimes. They seemed possessed with the same madness as bees, and sometimes—when you had built a house of chairs and blankets and you were crouching inside with a plate of Zoo biscuits and a tin of condensed milk, ready to tell stories—they would barge in, big and clumsy like two Alsatians, and break the house, and everything you had made gently would be broken.

Mia and Grace walked side by side. The final bell had rung

and Mia was getting a ride home with Grace. As Mia walked beside her friend, she listened to her sing.

'*Somewhere over the rainbow, bluebirds fly… Birds fly over the rainbow, why then oh why can't I?*' Grace's voice had lots of littler voices inside it that could wind around a sore place, until it didn't hurt so much.

On nights when she slept over at Grace, head to toe, Mia sometimes cried out from the dream of the needle and the blood on her hands. Grace would sit up on her elbow, come to lie head to head and sing of morning stars and yellow jellyfish who fell in love. Little loops of verses gently bobbing on the cadence and slopes of her voice, which drained the nightmare like a plug pulled.

In the morning Grace would never mention the midnight dream, and the holding of tight little hands in the dark together. But Mia remembered.

"Rinky," Grace yelped in delight when she saw the blue Volkswagen Beetle outside the gates. But as soon as Mia saw her, the hope of meeting Aunty Rinky, the shongolulu eater, shattered. Rinky was as ordinary as a brown envelope. No terrifying scars. No jangling silver necklace with crystal pieces. She did not laugh in a ghastly manner, but she had hundreds and thousands of freckles, all down her neck and arms.

Mia had wanted to ask Aunt Rinky why she did it and what it tasted like and would she do it again so she could see?

Grace asked, "Where's Mom?"

"At the gynie," said Rinky.

"What's that?" asked Mia.

"A doctor who fiddles with your girl parts to see they work okay," Aunt Rinky said playfully.

Mia said '*sies*'* and turned to get Grace to laugh with her, but

* Afrikaans for 'yuck.'

Part 2 121

Grace had a funny look on her face like when Mrs Sweetnam put a red line through her jotter page so hard it tore the page and said, 'Are your ears on your head today or did you leave them at home?' and some of the others in the class started to laugh.

In the backseat of the car Mia strained to catch a glimpse of Rinky in the rear view mirror. Perhaps the whole shongolulu-eating story was a lie. Maybe Grace was just a big fat liar. As they approached Grace's house Mia felt time slipping away.

Rinky indicated right and turned into the driveway. "Cheers girls," she said, without switching the engine off. Grace scrambled out the car and it was all too late and Mia hadn't asked anything.

Mia sat fixed to the backseat of the car.

"Are you coming or not?" Grace said, putting her head back into the car.

Mia didn't move. Rinky turned around in her seat and asked, "Are you alright?"

Mia didn't answer. Rinky had a space between her two front teeth. Maybe the shongolulu squished out of the space like a piece of spaghetti.

"What's the matter, sweetie?" Rinky asked.

"Will you do it again?" Mia asked.

Rinky smiled so that the gap in her teeth showed. She leaned over to stroke Mia's black hair and the white strands that had pried themselves free. "Of course I will. I often come to pick Grace up," she smiled.

Grace pulled at Mia's uniform. "Come on, Mia."

"Go," nudged Rinky and Mia pulled herself towards the door. Her bum had gotten stuck to the plastic seat and it stung like a plaster when it's time to come off and your skin gets ripped.

After lunch Mia said, "I don't want to play with the silkworms anymore. Let's go down to the dam and watch the dragonflies."

All they had to do was cross the road—as long as Fancy, Grace's nanny, watched them—and jump over the green fence and they'd be at the water's edge of Emmarentia Dam, where the bulrushes grew and the dragonflies hummed. They had to wear their shoes across the road, but once they were on the grass they could go barefoot and even dangle their toes in the water. In summer, boys in Speedos sailed on the dam, wearing rubber suits and holding tight to big sailing kites that zig-zagged across the water. Girls in bikinis lay on the banks, slippery with baby oil, waving to the boys with the kites. But today, apart from two nannies sitting on the other side of the dam, it was theirs.

Grace was trailing a stick in the water, singing softly, *"A froggy went a walking on a summer's day, a-hum, a-hum; a froggy went a walking on a summer's day; he met Miss Mousie on his way, a-hum, a-hum, a-hum; he said, 'Miss Mousie will you marry me…'"*

"She didn't *really* eat a shongolulu, did she?" Mia interrupted.

"She did, I saw her. *'We'll live together in the apple tree, a-hum, a-hum, a-hum.'"*

"Maybe she just pretended."

"I heard the scrunch and she stuck out her tongue with the chewed bits to show me and then she swallowed it," Grace said.

Mia watched an ant crawl over the arch of her foot and disappear in between her toes. She had seen seven dragonflies already, but only red ones. The blue ones seemed to be somewhere else today.

"Why would she do that? Eat a shongolulu?" she asked again.

"I don't know, she just did. Mia, will you sleep over at my house on Saturday night?"

"Are you telling the truth, Grace?" Mia asked.

"Yes, I am."

"Why would she do that?"

"She's crazy. Dad says she's mad. He says she's a *kaffir-boetie.*[*] Will you? Will you sleep here?"

"What's a *kaffir-boetie*?"

"Someone who kisses blacks. You know, like Fancy. Sometimes there's a black man and a white lady and they've got children—I've seen them."

Mia wondered about this a while. She threw a stone into the water and it ker-plunked. "Do you think it's maybe because of the shongolulu?"

"What?"

"That she's not married."

Grace paused and then said, "Naah. Mia, please sleep at me on the weekend."

"Would you kiss someone who ate a shongolulu?" Mia asked.

"Yuck, gross. I saw a shongolulu in the road—I one it," Grace said.

"No, Grace, no..."

"Come on, I one it—you have to."

"I two it," Mia said, covering her face with her hands.

"I three it," Grace yelled.

"You're so unfair," Mia said, although she knew there was no way out. If one of them started, the other had no choice but to do the count. "I don't like it when you ask like that."

"I three it," Grace repeated.

"I four it," Mia murmured reluctantly.

"Why? I want you to sleep over. I five it."

"I six it. Because 'y' is a crooked letter and you can't make it straight."

"I seven it," Grace pouted, but knew Mia's no. They both started a smile at what they both dreaded was to come.

---

[*] racist term for people who befriended blacks, literally a 'black-brother.'

Joanne Fedler

"I ate it," Mia said, and they both jumped around going, "Yuck, yuck, yuck," the way they always did when one of them ate the despised object.

"Why not? Why won't you, Mia?"

"I can't—the Rabbi's coming."

It was a sunny Highveld Sunday morning. The air was windless and nothing swayed. The washing hung like parchment on the line. Sarafina was polishing the brass on the steps of the laundry. She sat on the back steps where the sun was and hummed. Mia came down the steps behind her and Sarafina shifted her weight to the left to let her pass. Mia came and stood right in front of her. Sarafina was sitting wide-legged with the brass jug from the mantelpiece weighing in her lap. With her right hand she was rub-rub-rubbing the curve of the jug till all the black came off. The orange *lappie** in her hand was stained with grey marks where she had rubbed the jug clean. Mia loved the smell of Brasso on her hands.

"You coming to help me?" she asked.

"To watch you," Mia answered.

"Ha!" Sarafina said. "Come help—the pot doesn't get clean from watching."

"But I've just washed my hands and they'll get dirty again," Mia said. "And I'm all clean for the Rabbi."

Sarafina didn't answer for a while. She just carried on rubbing. Her knees were whitened with cracks and looked hard as leather. A fly came to sit on her knee just below the hemline of her blue uniform. Sarafina didn't swat it away, but carried on rubbing, twisting the jug around in her lap. Mia

* Afrikaans for 'rag.'

smacked Sarafina's knee and the fly flew away.

"How many times do I wash my hands?" Sarafina asked.

"I don't know," Mia said, pulling at the Elephant's Ear that grew next to the tap.

"How many times?" Sarafina repeated.

"Ten times," Mia said, tearing the leaf.

"Don't do that," Sarafina said, stopping her rubbing. "Why you do that?" She looked at Mia and clicked her tongue, "Eish". The jug on her lap caught the sun and blinded Mia as it twisted and turned under the fingers that rubbed it.

"A hundred times," Mia said.

"Ja, a hundred times," Sarafina repeated.

"One two three four five six seven eight nine ten 'leven twelve thirteen..."

"*Kunye, isibili, kuthatu, okune...*" Sarafina started.

Mia stopped.

"*Kunye, isibili, kuthatu, okune...* count in Zulu."

"I can't," laughed Mia. "Say it again, Fina."

"*Kunye*—say it also, *kunye. Kunye* is one."

"*Kunye,*" said Mia.

"*Isi-bili.*"

"*Isi-bili,*" Mia repeated.

"*Ku-tha-thu.*"

"*Ku-tha-thu.*"

"See, *kunye, isibili, kuthathu*. One two three," and Sarafina held up three fingers on her left hand, blackened with brass stains.

"*Ahe Mma,*" came a voice from behind Mia. Mia turned and saw a black man coming out of Sarafina's room. He wore no shirt and had a big fat belly. He was holding his trousers up with both his hands, with the fly undone. The man disappeared into the little room, which was the toilet.

Mia turned to Sarafina. "Is he your husband?"

"My husband? Ha!" she laughed.

"Is he?"

Sarafina clicked her tongue and shook her head.

"Who is he then?" Mia started to tear the piece of Elephant's Ear she had in her hand into little pieces, which she let drop onto the ground.

"My brother," Sarafina said.

"Oh, is he?" Mia asked. "I didn't know you had a brother."

"Six."

"Six brothers!" Mia exclaimed. "Where are they?"

Sarafina shrugged her shoulders. She wiped her forehead with the back of her hand. "The baby died last of last year. That is Amos. The oldest is Sam. He works in Middelburg. The middle is Citizen. He is a witchdoctor."

Mia counted. Amos, Sam, Citizen. "That's only three. What about the others?"

Sarafina shrugged her shoulders again. The brass jug was shiny new. In it's curved abdomen Sarafina's doeked face was distorted and long. Sarafina put it down next to her on the step and picked up the brass platter. The orange rag was almost completely black. She found a small inch of orange, poured some Brasso onto it and began to rub the platter.

"Where is your husband?" Mia asked.

"I don't have," she said.

"But what about Zolisa? Where is her daddy?"

"Men are too much trouble," Sarafina said.

"Why, Fina?"

"'Y' is a crooked letter and you can't make it straight," she said.

"No man, Fina—why?"

"*Ag* they want this this this and that that that," she said, chopping her hand in the air.

Mia had no idea what this or that was, but she nodded. Just then they heard the sound of a toilet flushing and Mia turned to look. The black man came out of the toilet, his pants done up this time. He nodded at her as she gazed at him and walked to the door of Sarafina's room.

Turning back to Sarafina, Mia asked, "Is your brother also too much trouble?"

"Too much," she said.

Mia thought about the kind of trouble men were. Grace's brothers were always teasing. They made her cry. And Zaide Yankel was truly horrible. Men were definitely trouble.

"But some are good," Sarafina added.

"Some are, hey?" Mia agreed. "Dad is good."

Sarafina looked at her. "Ja, but he makes a mess."

Mia nodded. "If he didn't make a mess. Uncle Shmooley's good, isn't he?"

Sarafina didn't answer. She rubbed the inner circle of the plate and held it up like a mirror. "Put the jug back for me on the mantelpiece," she said.

"What about Uncle Shmooley? He's good, hey Fina?"

"*Ag*, you. Take this to the mantelpiece."

"What will you give me if I do?" Mia asked.

"I give you the wooden spoon if you don't," Sarafina said. "And pick up the mess you made." She gestured to the bits of Elephant Ear on the ground. "I'm not tidy your mess."

Mia picked up the bits of torn leaf on the ground and collected them in her hand. With her right hand she picked up the jug by its handle and marched up the steps past Sarafina.

"I'll tell Mom if you hit me with the wooden spoon," she said spitefully.

Sarafina did not turn around to look at her. "Tell," she said. "Tell her."

"I won't have," Rabbi Goldenbaum gestured with both hands as if in surrender.

Fran poured black tea and there was plum jam which Sarafina made every summer from the tree in the backyard to mix into it. When the tree in the back became heavy with plums sometime in mid-summer, Sarafina would call Mia to help her. Mia couldn't reach, but she would hold the bucket while Sarafina picked and plopped them in. Then hours later the whole house would fill with the purple smell of sweet and sour, and Sarafina would let her fish out the plum skins that floated to the top of the boiling red paste and suck on them so that her lips curled into themselves and her eyes watered. But the Rabbi didn't want any jam—or tea for that matter.

They were assembled on the *stoep* that looked out into the garden. From where she sat on the swing, Mia could see Mrs Kruger—who was a drunkard and a violin teacher across the road in number forty-one and the only Afrikaner in the neighbourhood—talking to her flowers. Mia knew she was talking to them and not just looking at them up close because once, when Sarafina had taken her for a walk to the café and they had crossed the road so they were up close, Mia had heard her say aloud, *'Moenie bang wees, om uit te kom'ie. Daar's genoeg son vir almal,'** and Sarafina had shaken her head and said, 'The white people, *eish,* they talk to the animal, they talk to the plant,' and then she had clicked her tongue.

Mia had been told that the Rabbi was coming at ten thirty sharp and that she should put on a clean dress and tidy her room.

The Rabbi had been taken on a tour of the house. He stopped at the door of every room and unscrewed all the *mezzuzahs,* which had little tubes of folded paper inside them that Mia had not known about. At the door of her room, he had paused a long time, holding the little piece of paper up to the light and examining all the letters. Eventually, he put the paper in his pocket and took out another little scroll in a plastic cover, which he inserted into the rectangular box before screwing it back onto the doorframe.

* 'Don't be afraid to come out. There's enough sun for everyone,' in Afrikaans.

"Did you find anything?" Issey asked.

"One step at a time," he said. "Nothing is ever so simple. Answers are sometimes difficult to find. Moses didn't part the Red Sea first shot."

Fran offered him some biscuits. There were Maries and finger biscuits and two Eet-sum-mors." Mia hoped the Rabbi wouldn't take the Eet-sum-mors. They were her favourite.

"I won't have," the Rabbi repeated, gesturing with both his hands as if to ward off the biscuits.

"But the *mezzuzah* on her door is not kosher?" Issey asked.

"Not completely kosher. A smudged letter, which is often the cause of unhappiness in a household."

"We're a happy family, Rabbi Goldenbaum, I assure you," Fran said.

Mia took one of the Eet-sum-mors.

"A child with an emotional problem spells unhappiness in my books, but if you'd prefer it, I won't call it by that name. Let's just call it—a difficulty. As I said, smudging is sometimes connected to the… difficulty, but there could be other causes."

"Other causes?" Issey repeated.

"Like what?" Fran asked.

"Well, I don't want to rush to any conclusions. I have a hunch about it. I could be wrong—Rabbi's are not always right. But my feeling is that it is connected with something broader, a kind of collective unconscious—have you ever read Jung?"

Fran raised her eyebrows and said, "Rabbi, I majored in psychology in my BA."

Issey said, "I know bits and pieces."

"I have a theory about South African Jews. I call it 'Destabilized and Detribalized'—it's my own name for what in layman's terms could be called confused identity. Or multiple identities. Don't forget that our ancestors left Eastern Europe, escaping pogroms and anti-Semitism, scattered into the diaspora, and settled wherever they were allowed to stay. South

Africa allowed them in. Not all countries were so generous. And here, we hoped to find acceptance. But what happened when we got here? We found that we had little in common with the *schwartzes** who hate us because we're white and have a work ethic and contribute to the economy. And on the other hand we had little in common culturally with the Afrikaners who hate us because they think we're all communists. Joe Slovo is a Jew, did you know that?"

Fran and Issey both nodded their heads.

"Scapegoats, in the diaspora, lost from the fold, unable to find our way back again. That's the fate of Jews in South Africa. It *tsetumlts*† the spirit, and that's why a name is so important," the Rabbi said.

Issey crossed his legs. Uncrossed them again. They had spent long nights in bed balancing popcorn on Fran's belly deciding on names like the queen in *Rumpelstiltskin*, finally choosing one, as if decreeing it to be lived in. But that name was now chiselled in stone on a grave the size of a mother's cradling arms.

"She has a name," Fran said.

"She may have a name, but what kind of name?" asked the Rabbi.

"She's named after my late mother, Maya." Issey shuffled in his seat.

"It's an honour to bear the name of an ancestor," said the Rabbi thoughtfully, stroking his beard. "But what, if I may ask without offending, was she like as a Jewess?"

Issey blinked. "As good as any other," he said, shifting his weight from the left buttock to the right and crossing his legs.

"Was she a *tzadeket?*** A true daughter of Israel?"

"She was my mother," Issey said. "She was a gifted and

* 'blacks,' in Yiddish, generally derogatory.
† 'confuses' or 'bewilders' in Yiddish.
** 'a righteous Jewish woman' in Hebrew.

wonderful woman. Tragically, she died when I was very small."

"May her soul rest in peace," said the Rabbi. "When a child bears the name of an ancestor, there is a link, a very important bond that is created between the two souls. I simply inquire about your late mother's spirit as perhaps a way of understanding what is happening with…"

"Mia," Mia spoke.

"Yes, thank you, Mia," said the Rabbi without looking at her.

"A name is a very powerful force. It is the root of who you are. It is the sound that summons the individual, the cluster of letters that signifies who you are. Think of all of *Hashem's* names in the Torah. Even His full name, we cannot speak. Abraham was Abram until he had a *bris*,* and then a '*hay*' was added to his name, to show he had an encounter with the Almighty. A name houses the soul of the object or person it represents."

Fran chewed her lip. Issey nodded.

"A name has a resonance, spiritually, both in this world and in *olam habah*.† When my father had smallpox as a young boy, his father went to *shul*** and prayed for his son to live and he renamed his child 'Chaim'—life. *Nu*††, my father lived," said the Rabbi.

"Can I go now?" Mia said, getting up.

"No, you sit down. We're not finished," Fran said.

"What, may I ask, did your late mother die from?"

"I think it was a heart attack."

"She was very young to have a heart attack," said the Rabbi.

"Nonetheless, that is what she died from," said Issey, his body rigid. "In those days, who knew what was what? She had a weak heart."

* Jewish ritual circumcision.
† 'The world to come,' in Hebrew.
** synagogue.
†† 'well?' or 'come on' in Yiddish.

"Yes, modern medicine has answered many questions," said Rabbi Goldenbaum.

"What are you getting at?" asked Issey.

"I'm trying to establish if there is any, shall we say, 'spiritual residue' that has been passed on, through the name, to…"

"Mia," said Mia.

"Yes, to Mia."

Issey looked at Fran, who rolled her eyes.

"In any event, we perhaps can, for the sake of this instance, assume that some residue has been passed on that is perhaps causing some disturbance. We need some shock therapy Jewish input—a jolt or two, just to get things straight."

"And how do we do that?" asked Fran.

"A Hebrew name, for starters. And some private lessons with me, just to instil some *Yiddishkeit** into her—no charge."

The Rabbi took out a little pad of paper from his top pocket and a fountain pen which he gently unscrewed, and began to write with its silver nib which had a split in it like a girlspot, and black ink flowed out of its tip like honey. "Here is a nice Jewish name, the name of one of the four mothers of Israel. Rachel. That's how you spell it, in English and in Hebrew. Keep it. Learn it. It is your true identity—the part of you that has been missing."

"Thank you, Rabbi Goldenbaum," Fran prompted Mia, as he handed her the paper. Mia just lowered her head and said nothing.

"Mia, say thank you to the Rabbi for his time."

Mia clutched her chest and her whole body began to shake.

"If you could come to synagogue next *Shabbat*, I will call you up to the *bimah*,† and we can formalize it then. A small donation to the shul on your part and that is that," he smiled.

"What's the matter?" Issey asked, bending down to Mia, but

* 'Jewishness,' in Yiddish.
† the podium in the synagogue from which the Torah is read.

Mia could not talk for the tears.

"Just excuse her," Fran said, ushering the Rabbi out.

"I can see this is going to be a challenge," said Rabbi Goldenbaum thoughtfully.

"We are very grateful to you," said Fran.

"I don't do this for gratitude. If I had to wait for gratitude, I'd be waiting for the Messiah. All rewards will be delivered in the world to come. What is a Rabbi here for? To bring home all the strays," he said, screwing the lid back onto his pen and putting it back in his pocket. "Jewish survival. That's what it's about."

fray tsu zine:

to be free:
move about at will;
not be in the power of anyone;
safe from, untroubled by

Perhaps it was Hirshke the pyromaniac who caused the fire that burned down the seamstress's home. Perhaps it was the will of God. It caused Maya anguish to see her bent, like an old woman, her face sooty from smoke and ash, her young son strapped stony-eyed to her back, with a lead pipe in her hand, poking through the debris for any remains of her heap of small possessions.

Maya fell to her knees for she knew what needed to be saved from that fire, and she reached her hands into the crinkled crumbled deadness of wood. Her hand burned as it touched a kettle still scorched with the heat. And Maya and her seamstress, on bended knees clutched at one another's hands, her for Maya's simmering flesh and Maya for her dreams.

"*Hashem* gives and He takes away," she said.

"*Hashem* has given you to me, but He will not take you away," Maya replied.

The synagogue housed her and her young boy for the two days it took Maya to plead with her husband to bring the widow to live with them. To share the little they had. "She can stitch the old blanket, your overcoat…" Maya implored.

The widow arrived *Erev Shabbos**, with empty hands. They lit candles together. They recited the *brocha* in the same breath.

---

* the evening before the Sabbath, Friday night.

When Yankel returned from the Friday night service, they ate a modest meal. And perhaps it was then that Maya's life truly began. The widow taught her to sew. Maya watched her nimble fingers and made a shawl. Maya read her poetry. The seamstress could not write.

"Let me teach you," Maya offered.

"Such a gift is yours, not mine," she smiled softly.

They cooked meals together, cabbage, beetroots and sometimes meat on a week when Yankel brought home pennies and not just his bag of carpenter's tools. She shared Maya's clothes—hers had been destroyed, and by the second month, her and Maya became unclean on the same day, drank hot tea to relieve the pressure in the hips, and laughed in relief when they ended on the same day. She even accompanied Maya to the *mikvah,** so that Maya could make herself clean for her husband, though she, husbandless, need not have.

Yankel resigned himself to the presence behind the tablecloth, but soon felt that the stranger in his house was not the figure of the seamstress but himself. He was a good husband, as far as husbands go. But Maya married for survival and not for love. For who can know love who has never known pleasure? Suffering they knew. Hardship they knew. Yankel was sturdy. His father had been a pillar of the community. Maya was lucky, neighbours whispered. Yankel was a good man. She should have been grateful. But the mongrel that finds a morsel of food does not pause for gratitude. It takes what it finds.

And so she wrote. To make a place for gratitude, loneliness, longing, and all the stuff not solid enough to eat, nor useful for warmth or physical comfort. In her writing, pain was more than the rat gnawing in the cavern of her

* Jewish ritual cleansing baths for women after they have finished menstruating before they can resume sexual relations with their husbands.

empty belly, harsher than the biting agony of split skin, axed by the blade of the cold. Her pain had knocked at her heart for long years and finally she broke down those doors to let it out. What did her husband know? He was a simple carpenter. A God-fearing man with a very good memory for detail. Especially of the afflictions of neighbours. But not the stuff of which poetry is made.

The widow, on the other hand, was tormented and Maya's heart trembled for her. The widow wove herself into a place of happiness. A square was all she needed. Maya was impassioned by the humility of her task, the courage of her insistence. Maya collected scraps for her. Buttons, bits of straw, old coins, feathers, threads (she even snipped one off Yankel's *talit**), and all the bits and lost edges she could find. And so the widow made a new dream cloth, sadder than the rest, for now it spoke of hope, and joy and love—things she had never sewn before— and she put it under Maya's pillow, for she had ceased to hold onto anything anymore.

And when Yankel informed Maya of his uncle's offer to pay for his passage to South Africa, Maya bent her head, covered her eyes, lest he suspect that her tears were not of despair. She helped him pack his small suitcase, full of new clothes the widow sewed for him, each stitch sending him away so they might love without eyes watching. And when he left for South Africa, finally they had their own paradise.

The tablecloth found its rightful home on the table, the boy occupied a corner which they kept separate with Maya's shawl. And the widow lay in Maya's bed beside her, and let Maya— with a longing that had waited beyond what was bearable— touch her hair and her eyelashes that swept her lids to show her sadness and her neck, so soft, that who would not want to kiss it? And they murmured stories and words of songs and they

* Jewish prayer shawl.

made promises. And there, they knew pleasure such that they had not dared to think could be allowed. God had made the world in seven small days, such a small world, could it hold such happiness? Rochel's nimble fingers did not find a spot to squeeze or dent, but moved in whispery circles over Maya's flesh that she had lived in without knowing it could feel in so many places.

"What is that?" Maya asked.

"A spot where hairs grow faint and fine like a newborn rabbit," and her fingers, and oh, sometimes her lips would wake them to a shivering.

They knew one another not by smell alone, but by the harmony of smells their bodies made. A woman alone in a bed smells of the days she has worked and not washed, she reeks of the weeks between the washing of sheets. A pair of bodies in a bed smells of women. The sharp warmth of the body's crevices, places that breathe in darkness and only come up for light with the touch of a lover's hand or tongue.

The sheets, where torn, Rochel sewed, immaculately fixing the unfixable, the rent, the jagged edge with her seamstress fingers which knew how to darn and ravel the shreds of bedclothes into new wholeness, so that what was once exposed, was now covered, no longer open to the bite of the chill.

Rochel's body would cover Maya's like a *talit*. Maya had always thought—why so, she could not recall—that a man's body better fitted that of a woman. They learned together that parts can be made to fit the way a roll of cloth is cut according to the body it will clothe.

Some nights they would dance, hands to hands, gleeful and beyond any joy they imagined swept through the universe. The boy coughed from behind the shawl, but he was easily forgotten. Sometimes they caught his dark eyes peeping at them, but those little eyes did not know from smiling. They knew their love was not made of the stuff of Kovno, and so

Joanne Fedler

each night, each meal for three years was a celebration they knew would someday end. For what flames can burn in secret?

His letters came often. Maya put them in a wooden box, some of them unopened. She did not believe it would come. But it did. On a morning in the month of *Tevet*,* when the days were warming, Bilke, his sister, arrived at her door. Maya first saw the silver *kiddush* cup that belonged to Yankel's father in her left hand. And some smelling salts in a small pouch. "For seasickness," Bilke said.

But still Maya did not believe it had come.

Bilke handed Maya the *kiddush* cup and held out her right hand. Another letter? And still Maya smiled. But perhaps that was the last one. "I very much await your safe arrival," was written in his hand in the inside flap of the envelope. Inside was a one-way ticket to South Africa. Leaving in a matter of weeks.

The *kiddush* cup made a clattering sound on the stone threshold of the doorway.

* one of the months of the Jewish calendar.

Part 3

Now the Lord said unto Abram
Get thee out of thy country and from they kindred
And from thy father's house unto a land that I will show thee
And I will make of thee a great nation
And I will bless thee and make thy name great...
And I will bless them that bless thee
and curse him that curseth thee...

Genesis, Chapter 12

***

Love is so short, forgetting is so long.

Pablo Neruda

***

Everything ends in weeping.

Yiddish proverb

Henri's flat, 16 Katoomba Heights,
Fortesque Road, Yeoville,
21 March 1994

Before she opened her eyes, the headache warned her to do it slowly. As her lids lifted, a filter of light from between her lashes caused her to wince. Daylight hurt. She pressed them tight again. The sounds of Henri tinkering in the bathroom whipped her with the memory of last night like a hard slap to the face. Mia rolled over onto her stomach, pulling the cushion over her ears with both hands.

The night's pieces filtered back to her. The Black Sun, Rockey Street. Double scotches on ice. Handsome black men smoking. *Not the Midnight Mass*. Hilarous as ever. Henri's snorting laughter. 'Bye, bye December African rain...' playing. Reminiscing, telling stories. More whiskey. Blokes' smooth face. Is that you? It's me. Happiness. Sadness. Arms and bodies in a hug. When did you get back? Ancient longing. And then, 'This is Lebo. Mother of my child.' Smiles. Hands shaken. Pulling away. Nausea. Must leave. See you around. Warm evening air. Henri's arms on shoulders. 'What did you expect? Seven years is a long time.' Walking back. At some point sleep. Now the craving for biltong.

The swirl of awakening, the disbelief in the dream or 'did it really happen' stirred her back to Henri's bed. There was comfort in being back where things she had loved remained. She touched her lips that had longed to be kissed last night. She wished she had not been drunk when he had come up from behind her and laid his fingers on her shoulder to whisper, 'Hello my settler woman'. She had not expected the lurch in her chest when she heard his voice, so near to her face. She wished she had smelled of her gypsy self and not Bells when he brushed her cheek with his lips, which had not lost their invitation to hers. Lost to Lebo.

She moved her fingers to her crotch, let them snuggle down below her pubic hair, to where the softness began. She took her fingers out and sniffed them deeply. The loamy smell, which she had discovered after she bled for the first time, was rich like earth, like a place that had been watered and was soggy with soil and roots. Her own secret garden. At first, she would touch the little hairs tentatively, not wanting to part them or disturb how they coiled at the heart of her desire. Then she would sniff her fingers for the softness of bulrushes.

But soon others discovered it and called it names. Boys snickered and made the smell ugly. Scaly. Slimy. A rank bit of flesh needing plenty of washing. She had not stopped sniffing her fingers, but when she did, she would pull her nose away in disgust. And dig deep into the humus and sniff again. The bulrushes were clogged with rottenness. The smell was to retch for. The sound of boys' laughter. "Blind man walks past a fish factory and says 'Hello ladies'." Ha ha ha. Scratch and sniff. Scratch and laugh.

She hated the laughter that was hungry for her smell, disgusting as it was. When Grace's Aunt Rinky was raped, she had wondered if perhaps God had given girls a bad smell so that men wouldn't rape them. In its filthy shamefulness, it became sacred—a cross to ward off vampires.

But she soon discovered how to break the laughter of boys by lowering her lips to the source of their greed. While boys agitated to snap her bra open, to cup her 34Bs and to sneak a finger into the rim of her panties for a brush with what was spoken of by older boys with callous entitlement, she would whisper, "Oh no, you don't," her hand already clasping the unfurling eagerness in their jeans.

Out of fright for what might be discovered by another

before she got there herself, she always deflected the hands and tongues of gruff trespassers from what she suspected was treasurable beneath her own panty-triangle that showed when she didn't cross her legs enough.

Dropping her head into their laps, she would feel their fingers becoming limp and lost as she turned laughter into desperate whispers.

She vowed never to permit mockers into her Paradise, which grew wetter and softer and more inviting to her own fingers, as if sadness were its destiny. Touch and weep. Touch and sigh.

Boys laugh. Girls cry.

Unless you left them first.

The sound of Henri's voice broke her reverie. "Hey girl. I'm going to Westpark—wanna come with?" muffled its way through the cushion.

Mia rolled on to her side and opened her eyes to look at Henri, giving out a small, "Owwww," and pressing her fingers to her temples. "What you going to the cemetery for?" she asked.

Henri left the bedroom and returned holding a glass of misty fluid. "To visit my *boet*.*" She propped Mia up against the headboard and made her sip.

"Disprin extra strength—shouldn't be drunk on an empty stomach—gives you ulcers, but an emergency is an emergency."

The cool sweet salty fizz made a beeline for her groin and suddenly the urge to urinate became unbearable.

"Gotta wee..." Mia mumbled, scrambling to the side of the bed and racing to the bathroom.

* 'brother,' in Afrikaans.

She collapsed onto the toilet seat and pulled down her panties, resting her head in her hands.

A pain shot through her groin, releasing a night of too much whiskey—a clipsh clapsh of relief.

When she opened her eyes, her bladder was empty. Some of the headache had retracted. She had lost him. It was a pain as suffocating as indigestion. It hung heavy beneath her ribs.

"Stay," he had implored her. *Could that really have been seven years ago?*

"I can't," she had said.

"Don't make me make promises."

"I won't," she had said, feigning lightness.

He had pulled away, making distance. "I won't wait for you to come back."

"You will," she had said.

He had taught her everything she knew about race politics despite his first accusation that her 'good intentions were not enough'. 'You've got to put your body where your mouth is,' he'd said. With freedom comes the responsibility to fight for the freedom of others. What you gonna do with your white privilege? Make it matter.

She had been dancing with Henri at Andries Joubert's flat in Yeoville. She hadn't noticed him at first, standing in a corner, drinking Fanta—'alcohol just makes you weak'—watching her. Once she felt his eyes on her, she lost her rhythm. He had taken a packet of Winstons and a Bic lighter from his pocket, smacked the underside of the carton, caught the single cigarette that jumped at his touch, put it in his mouth and looked at her before he rolled the grinding wheel, lit and inhaled to capacity. As he exhaled he had walked over to her.

The silver cross that hung around his neck was the length of her baby finger. Her heart thrummed with the craving of all she had been warned against. Don't go too near the edge. Stay close to the herd. Danger lies beyond the walls. A mystery lay beneath the seam of his jeans. She had only ever been face-to-face with the naked stretched penises of Jewish boys. New land beckoned, a call a gypsy cannot refuse.

"Touched by an angel." He motioned to her hair, but made no attempt to touch it. The elegance of his restraint was unfamiliar. Jewish boys had always fingered the goods, laid hands on what was not theirs. Her heartbeat quickened. She wanted to cross the distance between them, to the cleanliness of a place that held no remembrances.

She reached up to touch her birthmark. "More like a devil," she said.

He had started to move to the sounds of Sipho 'Hotstix' Mabuze. She felt awkward, rhythmless, but her body didn't care. Her hips made circles.

They danced without talking, moved without brushing bodies.

When they finally left at 3am, the silent chorus of her body's nerve endings was begging him to touch her. As they stood on the pavement, he turned to her and said, "I didn't get your name."

"Mia."

"Blokes," he said.

They shook hands. And then hands touched arms, which became shoulders, and entwined around necks. When he finally lay down on her, on the mattress on the floor of his digs, his cross poked at her breasts as the initiating taste of his lips pressed into hers. His flesh was salty and soft, like moist biltong. He spoke little. Murmurs between them sufficed, and he had held her with such gentle insistence, that she had feared then that if she did not leave him, she would need him.

He had been circumcised. "It's an African thing," he had told her. Funny, she had been so sure it was just a Jewish thing.

In Henri's bathroom, Mia flushed the toilet and examined her face in the mirror, mouthing, 'Mirror, mirror on the wall, nobody asked your opinion this morning'. She washed her hands in the sink and brushed her teeth. Henri walked in just as Mia was spitting out the toothpaste. Her hair was spiked back with gel. A small dab of lipstick brown-sugared her lips.

"You're all dressed up for him," Mia smiled, wiping her mouth with the back of her hand.

"He would have been thirty-four today. Just want to go say 'howzit, many happy returns', you know," she murmured, as she rolled her upper lip over her lower lip, smudging the lipstick.

Mia leaned over and, wiping the smudged lipstick with her finger, said, "If you're gonna act like a girl today, you've got to keep the lipstick *on* your lips."

haltn:

hold:
keeping in hand; grasping;
confinement, custody, imprisonment;
keep from falling;
a place of refuge or shelter

Maya saved her. Thrust her hands into the steaming rubble and branded her own flesh, leaving a half-moon of her palm on the handle of a kettle. Took the widow and her boy into her home, sheltered them, nudged them to the spot closest to the *pripetshok* so that they could thaw their bones. Her and her kind husband halved their plates of food so that they too could eat, so that Rochel did not have to become like Tamara the *meshugenah** who sold her annual offspring to childless couples outside the *shtetl* to keep the roof over her head.

Rochel never anticipated happiness. She had looked into the eyes of her mother, ringed with darkness from a young age, and there it was written—happiness was something behind your eyes, imaginary, mythical, like the stories of Jonah in the belly of the whale and of the courage of David who felled the giant, Goliath. Only in sleep could she be far from the cold, the frostbite, the dizzying hunger. In dreams she danced, sang and laughed until pain melted away and a kind of glory opened up. She would spend her days waiting for her nights, where she lived the life that she knew was more real than the stark emptinesses of her waking hours. Like most girls, she was not sent to the *cheder* to learn to read and write—she stayed

* 'mad person' in Yiddish.

where girls were needed, at home, in the kitchen, near the stove. Her older brother, Yossi, would come home from *cheder* full of stories of golden calves, seas that swallow nations, the hand of god that smites firstborns. But the plague of tuberculosis took him coughing and frothing at the mouth, three months after his barmitzvah, together with the twins, not yet walking.

She did not expect a marriage. Her older sister Rivkah had not found a suitor and Rochel was getting no younger. But Zalman, the organ grinder, made it his business to find her, offer her a roof, and though he was skinny and had lost most of his toes in the unforgettable winter of 1916, he was generous to her. Always sipped his soup to half and then handed her his bowl, making as if he were full and she should drink. "Drink, drink," he would say softly. "Fill yourself." He gave her a boy, so that when he died, she was not left alone, mistakenly bequeathing her a burden rather than a bulwark against her loneliness.

Rochel's fingers spoke to her, but not in the way of her father, who could recite blessings to ward off evil eyes with his hands. Her hands knew a different kind of dance. By candlelight, a patter of needle pricks this way and that, twisting and furling and bringing to life the scraps she kept in a box, kept her from disintegrating, shredding in half from a frail seam, like so many of the clothes people wore until they could not be worn. She kept them hidden, her dream cloths, little prayers and fantasies, under the mattress, so that sometimes at night, she could curve her arm under the bed, and through the springs, feel their pulsing texture. She found it easier to survive having a secret. It kept her alive, just holding it from being known.

It was a late afternoon in the bathhouse a few moons after the festival of *Shavuot*,* when she felt the soft touch of eyes

---

* the Festival of Weeks, the Pentecost, which marks the giving of the Torah at Mount Sinai.

on her. Turning to face the looker, she met those eyes, dark and changeable as velvet, held up to the light. She had a nose like a horse—big and strong. But Rochel averted her gaze, for eyes have a sadness that clings, refusing to be shaken out. One had to be certain one would not drown in other's sorrows, so numerous were one's own. So she allowed her eyes to fall upon the mouth. Those lips were not chapped and brittle like those of a man, but plump and perhaps soft like a ripe fruit to the touch. Those lips pulled her cheeks into a whisper of a smile, and Rochel had to look down lest her blushing be naked.

And then this stranger spoke a handful of words that caused a great upset in her belly, as if she had been spun around on a maypole.

"Your heart and my heart are very old friends."

Rochel was not a great companion of language. Words cluttered her world and drowned out the soft music she could hear in silence, but these words hooked a rumbling deep in her belly and caused her to lift her eyes to this woman's. Rochel swallowed a stone of unspoken things, and nodded her head. The onion in its paper jacket does not suggest that it can cause great tears. All human company felt to Rochel like unpeeled onions jostling about in a sack. So much weeping held inside that paper covering, never shared though one could be right up close. But in this instant, her own paper jacket had been rent and the tears began to spill from her eyes. Whatever had come before this encounter, even the hardships, suddenly cleared a pathway to this moment, like the Red Sea at Moses' touch, even though she had often closed her eyes in sleep and mentioned to God that He need not wake her.

Maya—that was her name—and what more need the world offer? She only asked if at the next bath time she might be blessed with Rochel's company. Company. Rochel felt the sensation of an insect scampering down her spine. She nodded and turned to leave.

She left the bathhouse gulping air as if she had discovered its taste for the first time. Her head cleared, her eyes washed. My heart and your heart are very old friends. The words circled around inside her veins and to every part of her body they travelled, causing a trilling and a tra-la-la-ing.

She closed her eyes in sleep for more than a handful of days before it was time, yes, time to return to the bathhouse. And there she stood waiting, patient for her company, her eyes expectant and welcoming when welcomes were few and far between.

The following week she need not have waited a full seven sunrises, for the day before she was due at the bathhouse, she was thick in examination of the potatoes at Mendel's stall at the market, when the hand of the stranger closed over her own as it held a potato, larger than a chicken's liver, but smaller than a chicken's thigh. And together, a potato between their clasped hands, they held one another.

They wandered the market that day. Maya asked her questions. A manna of words, so many things she wanted Rochel to relate. Rochel spoke little. She did not lust after friendship. Too many in her family had left the world of the living the winter before. She was weary of graveyards. But Maya did not want to speak of the poor daylight or the gossip of the village—that the Rabbi's wife had lost her third pregnancy in a row, that the flour was overrun with weevils and what would they bake for the breaking of the fast of *Shiva Asar b'Tamuz?** Maya had a feeling for deeper things. She said, "I am a poet", and Rochel was given something new to look upon—a creature she had never before seen. What did a poet do, Rochel wondered. But her wondering turned to a longing to share the cloths she sewed in secret as she wept.

---

* the fast of the 17th of Tamuz to commemorate the day the Romans breached the wall of Jerusalem.

The next day at the bathhouse, Maya spoke of dreams she hinged to words, and how that swirl of darkness in the belly needing a voice, a sound, a mark on paper, would haunt her, drive her near to madness, and how she fished for words, bringing them up out of nowhere and fed herself to plumpness with the delicacy of her catch. When Rochel told her she could not read nor write, Maya reminded her of her ears by gently lifting Rochel's hair, and cupping them with the warmth of her hands.

They met at the water pump where Maya took her aside and read her poems. Later in the week, they collected coal, and in the sooty surrounds, Maya read her another. To Rochel, afraid of words and their strange indecipherable markings on paper, and the way they took up space in the air and between people, these times left her feeling fragile, as if words perhaps could break her.

And so their times at the bathhouse became the beginning and end of the week, something to count towards, something to live for, to long for, in those days when expectations were a luxury. And Rochel wondered why she had been chosen, from all the hooded faces pressed together in those lines. Once chosen, one is never ordinary again. For when Maya looked at her, she saw something beautiful—enough to remark upon it with her eyes, as if it were not so very common a thing to find. Rochel was caught between the thrill of the joy Maya's poor sight gave her and the fear that someday Maya's eyes would focus and leave her grieved at the sharpness of her repaired vision. The widow with the swollen ankles, the aching hip, the wife of a toe-less organ grinder, dead within the year— such a *rachmonas,** that people would think to send her a few coins or a handful of flour *Erev Shabbos*, in pursuit of the *mitzvah* of

* 'Pitiful one,' in Yiddish.

tzedokah,[*] seemed hidden from Maya. So Rochel kept more secrets from her, as if the mysticism and shrouded corners of herself were what she was seeking. Rochel, not one to close her eyes to God, began to pray for the endlessness of Maya's delusion. To be found beautiful left Rochel with a feeling as if her dream world and her life intersected at precisely these moments of being looked upon.

But there came a time when all that had been thought was moved by a thumbnail into the language of touch, and two women found themselves saying things about sharing. Rochel spoke to her of her cloths, stitched full of dreams, of the lands she could visit in their beauty. Maya did not laugh or toss her head or wind her finger to her ear as so many did when they spoke of Tamara the *meshugenah*, but she bent closer to her, and tied Rochel's headcloth with fingers that dusted her eyebrows, so that Rochel could feel her impatience for her dreams.

It was easy to show her. Rochel felt more naked when she folded it out in her hand than when they had stood under the cold water together, scrubbing off stains from their feet and hands. Maya began to cry and her tears gave Rochel an end to the loneliness into which she had been born. Perhaps her cloths had served their earthly purpose in that moment, for why else would they have been drowned in the flames of that fire Hirshke the pyromaniac was always blamed for starting? Rochel could not hate him, for she knew that what drove a man to set fire to a building was the delirious yearning for colour.

Rochel's boy was safe, though sickly with a cough that rattled his chest like a lone thimble in a box. The air was no good for him to breathe, the fumes made him wheeze. She did not believe that her hidden cloths under the mattress would survive the orange banquet of heat and sizzle that danced until

[*] the good deed of giving charity.

Joanne Fedler

it died, leaving grey powder and black odds and ends twisted into new shapes, did she?

To start from nothing seemed more than she could do alone. Even God saved the animals when he destroyed the world. The smallest, most useless of creatures, cockroaches and flies. Yet her world hissed and smoked before her, an abyss of destruction. And then, she felt a presence at her back, and Maya sank to her knees, and before Rochel could warn her that the softness of ash can scald beyond fixing, Maya scrimmaged for her, for the pieces of the old world.

Rochel cried, holding Maya's blackened hand smelling of scorched meat, weeping with pink and red. And like Ruth said to Naomi, Maya told her, "Where you go, I shall go, where you need rest, my home is your home."

In her home Rochel found the taste of potatoes. There were so many things to say where before there were no words. So many things to see, where before looking hurt. When Maya's husband left them, they stopped lighting *Shabbos* candles, and saved them for during the week—sometimes when there was a new moon, or an unexpected teaspoon of something sweet to eat. Rochel was muddled by the riddle of those warm nights, all strange and close. They seemed undeserved, like a second helping of something delicious which should be left for another more needy—her sickly child or one of the other homeless wandering the streets at night. The twirly tickle from her bellybutton to her throat that made her shiver was laced with madness and was about something less sure than being saved. But only a breath away from it. In Maya's arms, Rochel knew the velvety surrender of being part of a largeness slowly sinking. And it was a fearless sinking. Such a seldom thing, this love thing, Rochel thought.

Maya gave her many more years than she was given at birth. At fifteen, Rochel had determined that it was not worth living into her twenties. What was destroyed in the fire, Maya made new, and doubled. When it came time for her to leave, Rochel urged, "Go, go", to save from the pogroms, the shattered windows, the hardness of life, the one who had saved her. Her boy would survive, there was always pity for children.

They whispered late into the nights, about the separation. Rochel knew it must come and that Maya had to go. But there is a grasping even in leaving. How could they hold this happiness between them? Rochel berated, more than once, the cruelty of her fingers that could not write letters, the uselessness of her eyes that could not read. On the final night of their togetherness, they sat at the window, without any words between them, just hand holding hand. Loneliness circled them, waiting to pounce. The pale night outside beckoned them to lift their sadness to the full moon. A silver ball of beauty, like a sequin on a dream cloth. And Maya said, "The moon is our only witness. It shall hold us together. The moon I see from Afrika is the same as you see from Kovno." Rochel nodded, knowing even then that the moon, though it could pull the waters, would not be strong enough to clench them. But it was poetry, and beautiful. Maya promised she would never be touched again by another, for her body was imprinted with only one kind of love.

She left Rochel with her poems, which Rochel could not read, but knew by heart from Maya's reciting them.

As she watched Maya ascend the few steps onto the train that would take her to her ship, Rochel reached for the hand of her boy, feeling the world tipped to its side, and all the happiness siphoned off, like the fat from the chicken in the preparation of the Friday night meal. She tilted her head to her shoulder, and sure enough, she could feel the great emptiness that had come in like an unstemmable tide. Everything was finishing. As she raised her hand to wave at Maya, clutching the railings, she knew with the certainty of winter's approach that her hand was waving goodbye for the last time. Her and the boy stood a long time at the empty train station. The boy was soiled and wet by the time Rochel dragged him back to their front door.

She did not curse *Hashem* for taking Maya away, but thanked Him for sparing her from this wretched place. It was shameful and she was thankful that she was never asked to speak such a terrible truth: had she been asked to choose between saving Maya and saving her son, poetry would have won over flesh. But she was not condemned to choose. Only to suffer.

It began in her fingertips. She passed through another five snows alone, with her boy confined to the indoors all winter on account of his being without shoes. But by the time the spring of her fifth year suggested itself in the tender light at her window, she knew it had come. Sensation was leaving her. She no longer felt the pricks to her fingers while stitching, nor the scorch while cooking or tending to the fire. Slowly the numbness moved to her wrists, then up her arms, into her elbows, her shoulders, so that by the third week of spring, her arms hung limply from the sleeves of her dress and neighbours, behind their palms, remarked on her skinny limbs. It was only a matter of time.

Maya sent letters. Rochel took these precious missives to the shack on the outskirts of Kovno where Shlomi the disgraced *Chazan** still sang, but only to himself. Shomi had been found with his hands in his trousers by his wife during her unclean days, and she had run screeching to the Rabbi. It was a *shande.*† It was God's commandment not to spill seed. Shlomi had been banished from the synagogue, for not a Kovnite wanted to listen to the voice of a nightingale who could not keep his hands on the outside of his own trousers. But Rochel could forgive such things, for Shlomi was a learned man, who welcomed visitors with a herring tail and a hot cup of soup. And he read her letters aloud without curiosity, only commenting on the beauty of Maya's prose.

* singer in the synagogue.
† 'a scandal' in Yiddish.

When his words reached her ears: that Maya had birthed children, Rochel had choked at the vision of that rough carpenter's hands on her body, in the knowledge that what had been taken from her, was taken by force. Shlomi offered her the corner of the tablecloth to stem her tears. Rochel excused herself, thanked him with a small handkerchief she had sewn, and wept for the bruises she imagined, developed some dark blue patches on her own thighs in sympathy, marvelled at their colour, and wept for their infliction. But from that day she no longer covered herself in her shawl and tiptoed to the door lest she wake the sleeping boy, to steal into the shadows of the night to look for the moon's face.

Winter didn't change the dam, except that the grass was dry and yellow and stuck to their clothes when they rolled in it and that it was too cold to go barefoot or put their feet in the water. The baby ducks had grown so you couldn't tell the difference between the mommies and the babies anymore. Mia and Grace sat at the edge of the dam with a plastic packet full of dry bread and crusts Fancy had cut off for them. They took turns in breaking off pieces and throwing them into the water. They sat and waited for the ducks to come and gobble the bits before they got too soggy and sank beneath the surface. Mia stood at the rim of the dam where the water lapped sometimes, though today it was still, and broke bread. Grace did not join her, but sat on the grass and pushed all the dry grass flakes into a little pile, scraping her hands together.

"Come help," Mia said, turning to see what she was doing.

She was scratching her girlspot.

"What you doing?" Mia asked

"Itchy," Grace said.

"Come feed the ducks."

"I don't feel like it."

Mia clicked her tongue, the way Sarafina did when she was cross. Grace didn't feel like doing anything fun these days. It was as if a splinter of silence had broken off and wedged itself between them. She didn't like to sleep over at Grace anymore, for when she did, and woke to her nightmare, instead of singing to her, Grace sobbed with her. And the world would seem doubly terrible.

"Last night I had a dream about a magic stone," Mia started. Grace, who loved her stories and dreams, would ordinarily beg, "Tell me a story, Mia. Tell, tell." Mia turned to see whether Grace's interest might be tempted.

"And if you looked deep inside, you could see your home.
There was yellow and green and lots of blue
As if a rainbow was passing through."

Mia threw her broken bread bits further and further into the dam. There was no sign of the ducks.

"Some of the colours had no name," she continued,
But you could feel them and hold them all the same,
I dreamed I found one at the dam with you
And if you made a wish on it, it would come true."

Grace hurrumphed. "Wish pish," she mumbled.

Mia threw the last of the bread into the water and wiped her hands on her school skirt. Then she squatted and began ferreting amongst the bulrushes. She dipped her hand into the water and lifted a brown stone. She held it up to the light, but it was solid and the winter sun did not shine through. She chucked it back into the water and it plopped. Some ducks further along the bank turned at the sound, but did not come nearer. Mia turned to see if Grace was interested in looking for magic stones yet, but she was scratching herself again.

"Stoppit," Mia said, "it's rude." Her own hands had been spanked many times when her mother found them between her own legs, and Mia knew that touching your girlspot was something you did in private, like writing your stories or making a poo.

Grace stopped.

"You can only find a magic stone
If two people look—not on your own," Mia added.

Grace stood up and came to stand next to Mia by the water's edge. She bent down and put her hand into the water, and when she lifted it out, she had a handful of mud that dripped down her forearm and dirtied her jersey.

"Ja, they may be in the mud," Mia said encouragingly.

Grace dipped her hand back in the water and swooshed it around to get rid of the mud. When she pulled it out the water, she held two brown pebbles and a Chappie paper. She turned the Chappie paper over and read, "Did you know that the ant can lift fifty times its own weight, can pull thirty times its own weight and always falls over on its right side when in—tox—ayted. Intox…"

Mia came up and took the paper from her. "Intoxicated," she said.

"Who cares anyway?" Grace said, throwing the Chappie paper back into the water. She turned to leave.

"Not everything you dream is true, Mia," she said nastily. "And all the bread is gone, and the ducks didn't even come."

When they got back to the house, their skin chilly and prickled, Graham and Andrew were kicking a ball out in the front garden. Not wanting to cross the lawn in case they got hit, they edged around the boys.

"Hey Dis-Grace," Graham, the older of the two shouted, walloping the ball across the garden, "How's your friend with the crazy hairstyle?" Andrew laughed and kicked back.

"Jus shaddup," Grace said.

From behind, Mia pressed her elbow, a small touch to the inside of her funny-bone, in their system of tiny gestures that only they understood. Grace crossed her fingers behind her back to indicate, okay.

"Hey Mia, is that white bit *chaaf-chaaf** or real?" Andrew called out.

Mia didn't answer. It wasn't far to get to the front *stoep*.

"Wanna play soccer?" Graham said.

---

* South African slang for 'pretend.'

"We don't wanna play anything with you," Grace said.

Graham stopped the ball with his foot as it hurtled to his feet, and bent to pick it up. In two large strides he had blocked their path to the front door, standing tall and sweaty and grinning in front of them. And in a voice thick and ugly, he said each word like a little pellet, "Not even doctor-doctor? Or Grace goes to the gynie? I'm sure Mia would just looooove to play gynie-gynie."

From afar, Mia heard Andrew laugh again.

And then Mia saw Grace do something she'd never seen before. Thrusting her head forward like a snake, she spat at Graham. Her spit landed on his knuckles. Mia's heart became noisy and everything turned, like in her bad dream and she didn't know what would happen next. Graham laughed, and lifted his hand, examining the small gob of saliva all beaded with little bubbles on his hand, and with eyes that didn't move from Grace's face, he licked the spit off his hand, going, "Mmmm, delicious", like he was licking an icecream.

Grace pushed past him with a gasp caught in her throat and ran into the house, not waiting for Mia to follow.

In the late afternoon when it was nearly time for dads to come home from work, the shrieking of the *mielie** vendors began. Balancing hessian bags on their heads, the barefooted black women wound in cloths and scarves ragged with wearing, roamed the suburban streets, crying "*E-mielies, e-mielies*".

If you had never heard a mielie lady call, and had never shouted 'Mielies here' out the window, and run out to meet her, where she waited to see the money in your hands before lowering her load to the ground, you might be afraid. If you had never seen her eat a raw mielie, biting into the chalky flesh

* Afrikaans for 'corn.'

Joanne Fedler

and spitting out the white unchewable bits, leaving her half-eaten mielie on the ground while a baby on her back looked at you with big eyes, gummed at the corners with dirt and eye crust, you might feel nervous.

Though she had been sent many times to buy mielies, and she knew there was nothing to fear, Mia froze at the sound of the mielie lady's voice on that afternoon when the ducks did not come. It sounded like a shriek torn from nowhere, making her scared of things that had never scared her before.

When Fran came to fetch Mia, the girls couldn't be found, even when Graham and Andrew helped search for them. Eventually Fancy found them in the closet under the stairs, huddling close, hurt as lambs.

The chair on the other side of the Rabbi's desk. The Rabbi's house, January 1975

Sweat travels. She could smell him from where she was sitting across the expanse of the big oak desk strewn with heavy Hebraic texts covered in burgundy leather. His smell was sharp, like a pinprick to the palette on every inbreath, and made her think of stickiness. He rolled his beard between his thumb and forefinger. Trevor, her cousin, had whispered a rude thing at the *Shabbat* table last week—that Rabbis touch their beards and twirl their sideburns because they're not allowed to wank. Did she know what wank was? Trevor had asked. Of course, she had said. But she'd had to ask Grace on Monday, and now knowing made her sit on the edge of her chair wishing it was already time to leave. The rolling made her feel like he was doing something she shouldn't be watching.

He was making her read from the Book of Ruth. Did she know that Ruth and Esther are the only two women after whom a book in the Bible is named. No she did not. Women also had an impact on Jewish history and that was important to keep in mind, so she shouldn't forget that. She wouldn't forget, she would always remind herself, like all the other things she needed to remember. She was a Good Jewish Girl, the Rabbi had told her.

Good is like God with an extra hole, except Don't Ever Write God with the 'o'. It's G-d. He rewarded her with gifts of books and candlesticks when she memorized passages from the Ethics of the Fathers and knew the names of all twelve tribes of Israel, in English and in Hebrew without his even having to tell her to learn them. He would smile at her sometimes from under his beard and she knew he would tell her father what a wonderful girl she was, full of promise and potential. There would be *nachas* for everyone involved, and no-one would feel that those Sunday mornings for which the Rabbi was not getting paid, were a waste of time.

In those few weeks, Mia had learned many important things: Believe in G-d, pray to Him for health and happiness. He gave Us the Torah on Mount Sinai. Once We were slaves in Egypt, now We are free. Do a *mitzvah** a day—give charity, but not for thanks; honour your mother and father all the days of your life; no cheese burgers because thou shalt not seethe a kid in its mother's milk; don't speak about other people, even in praise—it leads to speaking evil.

"So *nu*, you've read the Book of Ruth during the week, have you?" the Rabbi said, clearing his throat.

"Yes, Rabbi Goldenbaum."

"And what do you find most remarkable about it?"

Usually he intimated the answer he was looking for so that she could not get it wrong. This time he was giving her nothing, his head bowed deep into the text as he reread what he must surely have known by heart by now. Mia had read it. It was a story about a girl whose mother-in-law tells her how to win the heart of the hero— by rubbing his feet.

Mia tried not to picture Rabbi Goldenbaum having his feet rubbed. She bet his feet had hair on them, and were chapped around the heels. The Rabbi was still rolling his beard. She wondered about other bits of his body that might be hairy and chapped.

"Not very much," she finally said.

"Not very much?" he repeated in disbelief. Her answer stopped the twirling in mid-twirl. "Think again," and the rolling began again.

* 'a good deed' in Hebrew.

Joanne Fedler

She looked down at the text on the page so that she didn't have to look at him and remember his disappointment held still between his thumb and forefinger. The black letters on the page teemed with activity and maybe it was the tears in her eyes that made them shimmer. They slid around like amoebas under a microscope, nothing would stay in one place. She started to count the number of times 'and' appears in the Book of Ruth. Such a humble little word, but it joins things, brings them together.

"Well..." he said.

She shook her head. Sixteen, seventeen....

"It's obvious isn't it? Ruth was a *shiksa.*"*

His look was earnest.

"Really?" she said, shaking her head from side to side. Perhaps that didn't sound shocked enough. So she repeated "Really?" with more intonation this time and looked at him for his response.

"Yes, a *shiksa* who ends up being the great grandmother of King David—one of the greatest heroes in Jewish history. Isn't that remarkable?"

"Remarkable," she repeated. Truly remarkable.

"The greatest taboo in the Jewish religion—intermarriage, and here we have Boaz doing just that. What does that tell you?"

There was a merciful knock at the door and his bloated pale wife apologetically shuffled in, wearing her dressing gown and carrying the tray with enough kosher breakfast on it to feed all twelve tribes of Israel. As she moved into view, Mia counted the number of slices of toast piled in a little stack on the side dish. Nine. Last week there were twelve. Maybe the Rabbi was on diet.

"Where would you like it?" murmured the Rabbi's wife.

* a 'non-Jewish woman,' in Hebrew.

"There," said the good Rabbi, not looking at her.

"Where?" asked the slippered Mashi, softly.

"There," he bellowed, pointing to the space on the desk where the wooden surface peeked out from under the books. It was that irritation Mia always feared when she answered him, as if some questions were too stupid to be answered nicely and some things a person should just know. She sneaked a look sideways at Mashi, who had a grey scarf around her head on such a hot day, but as she turned to leave, the light from the open bay window caught it and showed sparkles of glitter like Tinkerbell dust trapped inside the cloth. Beneath the paisley gown swelled the belly of something growing. Her face, peppered with red freckles, turned a pinkish colour that was creeping down her neck.

Just as she got to the door, Mia turned to face her, and asked, "Are shongolulus kosher?"

Mashi stopped but did not answer, not used to having questions directed at her.

"Is that a question?" frowned the Rabbi. "We are talking about Ruth."

"I know someone who ate one—a Jewish person."

"Is there a reason for this question? Can you tell me what this question has to do with Ruth?"

"Well, Ruth wasn't kosher..."

The Rabbi laughed and said to Mashi, who suddenly wondered about shongolulus too, "You can go now." Remembering herself and her seven children, she left and closed the door to the Rabbi's study behind her.

"We don't ordinarily talk about people as kosher or *traif*.* We only refer to that in the eating context," the Rabbi offered her an answer.

"People get eaten," she persisted.

* 'non-kosher,' in Hebrew.

"Not by humans they don't—maybe wild animals, but there's no commandment on animals to eat kosher."

"People do get eaten by other people."

"Cannibals? Are you talking about cannibals? Clearly that's not a Jewish practice."

"No, not cannibals. Grace's brother has a book that says boys eat girls."

The Rabbi stopped and looked at her. Locking her gaze for a moment, there was a flicker followed by a forbidding, utterly stern 'thou shalt not say another word'. Finally he said, "If you knew as much about the book of Ruth as you do about the books of Grace's brother, I would be visiting the sick instead of trying to make a person out of you. Can we get back to Ruth?"

Mia looked down at the Book of Ruth, the taste of a sweet smile gathered inside her mouth.

The Rabbi's ears had turned the same colour as Mashi's neck when he had shouted.

T he flower vendor on the grass outside Westpark motioned to them with a flurry of beckoning, like one conspiring to secrets, seeking allies.

"Special price for you today, ladies... Twelve rand a bunch."

He stood surrounded by old Plascon paint tins filled with water, and clasped bunches of red, white and pink carnations. He held a cigarette almost smoked down to the filter in the cupped claw of his hand. The smoke trickled in wisps from between his knuckles.

"No thanks," Henri said, "We know all about what goes on here, and God will get you for it."

Mia looked at her with surprise. "God?" she asked, chewing on a stick of biltong they had bought at the café in Rockey Street on the way. Henri hadn't seen the inside of a church since the Sunday morning the sergeant had appeared at their doorstep, with an envelope in his hand, and a sweaty upper lip informing them that Johan had 'not made it' in Angola—it was a loss to the country, eighteen was very young, yes, it was most unfortunate.

"You know what I mean."

"Special price," the vendor repeated.

"No thanks," Mia said, smiling at him. Turning to Henri, she pinched her under the elbow.

"Oww," Henri complained, rubbing the spot. "And finish that dry wildebeest before we get inside please—it's *mos* fuckin' rude to eat in a graveyard."

"Sorry..." She swallowed. "There, all gone."

The cemetery was dotted with the bereaved and the dutiful, walking the rows of plaques and stone slabs, searching in the ordered mass for names marking the spot beneath which their dead lay deep in the earth.

"Why didn't you get some flowers?" Mia asked.

"They sell them to you and then pay some streetkid fifty cents to run around after you've left to fetch them and then they resell them. I don't want flowers for Johan that have already been laid this morning."

Mia laughed. "Where are we going?"

"Way up to the top—to the wall where the plaques are."

"What, no grave?" Mia asked.

"*Ag* shame, no."

Five words and some dates and that was all. '*Johan Marius Stephanus van Staden, 4 March 1960 – 19 September 1978*', chiselled into the sandstone plaque in the wall. They had spent nearly five minutes looking for it. When she finally found it, Henri laid both her hands on the plaque, closed her eyes, and said, "Happy birthday, *boetie*, happy birthday."

Henri turned to face Mia. "Let's go," she said.

"Is that it?" Mia asked.

"Ja, what else can I do? He was cremated and his ashes were scattered. Scattered—imagine that being your fate—not having one small tiny patch of this earth to know as your own." She shook her head.

Mia linked her arm into Henri's. "Jews aren't allowed to be cremated. You have to be buried."

"That's better than going up in smoke," Henri said.

"No way," Mia said.

"Ja—it's just shit for those you leave behind. Like for Johan, I've got nowhere. I can't stand where he lies and feel the earth where he once was—it's all just fresh air up here."

"So if he was scattered, why can't you just remember him wherever you are? Why do you have to come to this plaque on the wall?" Mia asked.

"Because you need a place to stand. It's a holding thing—you can't be held if there's nothing holding you down. You know, it's gravity. You gotta be in your spot. It's like coming home."

Where were gypsies buried, Mia wondered? Where they died? Maybe if she could feel where she would want to be buried, she could find the place that made her feel like she wanted to stay.

"Let's leave a stone here for him," she said.

"A stone?" Henri asked.

"Ja, Jews leave stones—they last longer than flowers."

Henri wiped her eyes with the back of her hand. "That'll be *lekka*,* he'll like that."

Mia fumbled in her pocket and removed the tourmaline. "Here, just lay it somewhere."

Henri balanced the stone on the ledge where the little holder for flowers stood empty. The stone let the sunlight in and glowed.

"Where's your old man buried? Let's go to the Jewish section—you can leave him a stone too."

Mia paused. "Uh… Okay, ja."

Israel Theodor Kaslow. The name had been chiselled out in marble and looked strange and unfamiliar, not the name of one with whom you shared DNA. He had been named Israel by his father, who was a great Zionist. Theodor after Theodor Hertzl, the great Israeli statesman.

A few stones dotted the side of the grave and Mia wondered who had been there and what they were mourning.

She fell to her haunches and touched the grooves of the letters. The name was cold. Left too long without comfort.

* 'nice,' in Afrikaans.

"I'm back, Dad," she said quietly. "Can you believe it? It's me."

Mia looked up. Henri looked away. Turned her back.

"I've just got back, actually. And here's something maybe you'd like to see again."

She put her hand inside her bra, and brought out the dreamcloth. She opened it to its fullness and lay it down on the tombstone.

Henri stood by, silent and witnessing.

"And see, Dad, it's just an old rag, isn't it? Quite pretty, hey, but really, is this what the fuss was all about?"

She crouched low, her head in her hands. She still remembered how the child in her wailed, but the ghost in her howled, when her mother informed her, with a voice creamy with blame, that her father had taken 'an overdose'. Antidepressants hadn't done the trick. But two full bottles of *Dormicum* sure had. Mia's only consolation had been that he had died a true artist's death: misunderstood and self-inflicted. There was comfort in that. His madness had crept up on them over the years, a slow steam rising, clouding his face— smudging what she knew was her Issey, until there was just the ghostly shape of someone gone wrong, where his laugh, his magical moon-smile painting hands had once been.

She closed her eyes in that moment, and there she is standing alongside this grave with her mother on her left. Men are lowering a coffin into the gaping earth, yawning wide to swallow her father. Her mother's face is anguished and beautiful. Black so becomes her. At her father's graveside Fran has never looked more tragic and Mia remembers thinking how her father, in his old self, would have loved to have painted that face. The red earth is dirtying her black velvet shoes, but she dare not bend down to clean them, out of Respect. From inside her stockings, between her thighs she feels a wetness descending and is flooded with panic at the thought that her tampon is leaking. Though she is eighteen, which is the Jewish numeral for life, she is at death's flank, shamefully bleeding instead of crying. Rabbi Goldenbaum is looking solemn and nods at her. She feels her heart racing, wondering whether he, who has such a close relationship with the God of Abraham, Isaac and Jacob, intuitively knows that she is bleeding. At her father's graveside.

"Rabbi Goldenbaum is a good man," her mother had said as she blushed her cheeks and mascaraed her eyelashes in preparation for the funeral. Those who died of unnatural causes were not buried in the ordinary cemetery along with all the other souls that had bided their time waiting for God to decide. But the Rabbi, through some obscure interpretation of *Halacha** and the exercise of influence on the committee of the *Chevra Kedisha*, had managed to secure permission for Issey to be buried alongside his ancestors.

Shame had flooded her as she felt her panties getting wet. Blood feels just like the wetness of sex if you can't see the colour. The thud of the earth on the coffin had smacked her, like the slap of water—a rough shake of all that has been hurt and sacrificed. In that moment, she had felt, as she had done many times, the hand of the father falling, and there is no God to stop it, for God is bloodthirsty—isn't that what Asher had said? And Issey had lifted his hand. Like Abraham did to Isaac, and God did not stop his hand from falling to her face. And there, just as a leg is amputated, his connection to her, skin to skin, bone to bone, blood to blood, was severed. She had not been able to comfort him, like a mother after he had wept. She had stood her ground as his child, while her ghost buckled inside her. *Forgive me, forgive me.* But she could not. She had stopped talking to him. Renounced their shared world. How could words force their way back in between the raising and falling of the father's hand? Only a miracle could make it all

---

* the letter of the law as interpretted by the Rabbis.

into some horrible mistake—could call out, 'Don't sacrifice the child—find a ram instead.' Nothing could make it safe to be a daddy's girl again.

Now, ten years later at his graveside, she lifted her hand to her face to feel the burning of a father's hand fallen to the face that he loves more dearly than his own and she hears the knocking of the earth on the face of his coffin. Earth knocks, just like water against the belly of a ship.

On the warm marble of the tombstone, the dreamcloth caught the sun.

She felt Henri's arms around her shoulders. "Let's go," she whispered.

"Okay," Mia said.

She lifted the cloth off the tombstone, folded it up and put it back inside her bra. She pulled out an amethyst from deep in her pocket and put it on the grave. She stood up and turned towards Henri who was waiting for her.

Arm in arm, they turned and walked down the hill. "Tell me about your dad," she said.

Her special chair, Issey's studio,
March, 1975

If she sat back as far into the chair as she could, her feet did not touch the floor and swung freely under the seat. Against the ridges of her spine the cold of the pink plastic chair cooled her flesh, but warmed the longer she sat. With the studio door shut, the room became cosy, just her and her dad, the canvases, the oils, the smell of turpentine and the brushes. The room held them close, her on the pink chair, him on the one that swivelled round and round, which he sometimes let her spin on until her tummy screamed stop. She was allowed to lay out all his paintbrushes on the floor, those with the golden squirrel on them, others with 'Kolinsky' printed in black letters on their slender bodies.

"A brush is the artist's harp. It is the instrument of his music," Issey told her. "Each, a work of art in itself."

Mia held the brushes in her hands, letting the bristles caress her palm, her cheeks, under her neck. Some were rough and prickly, others were soft as a tickle. Issey took almost as much care of his brushes as he did of the cloth he let Mia hold while they sat together in his studio. Each brush had a wooden hand piece, some in striated mahogany, some jet-black—all varnished and shiny. They had names like *rounds, flats, filberts, mops, fans, liners.* Each formed a beautifully shaped tip and had its own way of speaking to the paint and whispering the stories in her father's hands onto the canvas. With a brush, Issey swirled colours and shapes and painted lines in faces, worlds in expressions.

The Kolinskys were made from the winter harvest of the kolinsky sable and only the hair of the males was used. Could she work out why? Issey watched her as she crinkled her nose and scrunched her eyes, trying to solve the riddle. Give up? It's because the males are hunters and spend most of the winter in the snow. Because of this, over the centuries they have developed thicker hair than the females. And thicker hair makes for a better brush.

"Where are the females?" Mia asked.

"Probably in the den protecting their young, the way Nature intended."

Perhaps Nature's intentions for humans were different. Mia curled her fingers inadvertently around the white hairs of her birthmark and considered the hunting of male kolinskys in the winter months so that artists could paint perfect profiles. Then a terrible thought—did the hunters kill the kolinskys or let them go once they had taken their hair? Issey shrugged. He didn't know. But it was important to know, wasn't it? she pressed. There was a big difference between a haircut and a massacre. Perhaps, from the kolinskys' point of view, Issey conceded. To produce great art, sacrifice was inevitable. But yes, it was unfair, as life is.

Mixing the oils with one of his favourite mops, he glanced at his daughter. A curious mixture of affinity and alienation gathered in his chest. She was a mystery unfurling, her questions unpredictable, often disquieting. An ancient soul— who could say? But—as he dabbed the canvas with aquamarine, not quite the right colour, maybe a dash of teal would do it—she suffered because of it, and that hurt him in a way that his own suffering did not. It could be that all artists were troubled as children, growing into the great Expressionists and Romantics of history. Perhaps, in the end, that is all art was: exhaled pain. In his studio, he filled the stretches of silence between them with stories of all the great artists—Kandinsky, Van Gogh, Gauguin, Monet, and his favourite, Chagall.

"You could even see the gobs of snot and tears in Van Gogh's paintings. He would sometimes use paint as thick as my thumb," Issey told Mia. "And before he died, Van Gogh went mad, and I'm sorry to tell you this, cut off his own ear." He looked up at her—maybe too much detail for a child...?

But Mia paused. "Why?"

"Nobody really knows why. A bit like the old lady who swallowed a fly."

"And what did he do with it?" she asked. "Did he throw it in the bin? Flush it down the toilet? Keep it in a matchbox? Press it between the pages of a book?"

"Actually he gave it to a pros... umm, a woman called Rachel, and asked her to keep it for him."

Mia nodded. "That was the right thing to do," she said.

Issey smiled. "Was it, really?"

In this way, afternoons would pass, as they sat and pondered the enigmas of life.

Issey sat back and squinted at his canvas. "What does it need?" he would ask.

Mia stared at the image on his easel for a long time without speaking.

"More sadness." Or sometimes, "To remember better."

He drew pleasure from the labyrinth of her mind, a world where fantasy and phenomena meshed into a glorious universe of quasi-things and thought bubbles, finding colours to match.

"You have a gift, Miala," he once told her.

The description of this fullness of words that bloated her, giving her cramps in her fingers and chest, as a "gift" was confusing to Mia. A gift was a delight, a happy surprise. But her "gift" of words pushed her thoughts into dark spaces, inside cupboards, under beds, behind doors, where she dreaded the finding, like dipping her hand into a nightmare.

"But it hurts sometimes, Dad," she said.

"Well, my love, art comes from suffering," he declared. "And the work of the artist is to share the suffering with others, which is why words come to you, whether you want them or not." He paused, searching for an analogy. He scratched under his arm. "Think of a tortoise crossing a road, and a car driving towards it." He made his right hand into a fist of tortoise-shell and his left into the hood of a car. "All the tortoise knows is plod, plod, plod, crush." He smacked his palm against his fist. "A tortoise's tragedy. But it's not art. All the driver knows is vroom, vroom, vroom (here he gestured holding the steering wheel of a car), crush. But for him, it's not art. When does it become art?"

Mia thought a long time about this. "When somebody sees it."

"Yes!" Issey exclaimed. "When someone who is neither the tortoise nor the driver, sees the whole thing happening. The artist sees the driver zooming towards the tortoise and the tortoise going about its business, plodding away. Who cries? Not the tortoise—it's dead. Not the driver—he's squeamish. The one who cries is the artist, because he is the one who hopes that it may be different, that the tortoise is going to make it across the road before the car wheels smash it. The artist reads past, present and future all in one moment. And that's like knowing too much. And knowing too much is painful. That's why it hurts, Mia."

By the time he had reached the end of his soliloquy, her eyes were wide and afraid and suddenly he felt unequipped, like he'd gone too far without a compass.

"Get me a Kolinsky long hair round 10.3," he said.

For a few moments, she did not move, as if struck still by oncoming headlights, but slowly the vapour condensed to fill her eyes, with their dark liquid centres. She shook her head, blinked a few times and returned to the world, her fingers sorting through the brushes to find the exact one he needed. She passed it to him, and he said, "Thank you, nurse. Now can I have a hug and a kiss?"

She flung her arms around his neck and planted a loud kiss on his cheek.

"What a cuddler!" he said, squeezing her. "Just like my

mamma. I don't remember much about her, but I do remember, she was a great hugger. And I remember her hands—they were rough from hard work, but they were gentle on my back. I don't remember her smile, or her smell, or the way she used to laugh. But your mother's cuddles lifting you out of the bath, that you never forget."

Mia was thoughtful. Did mother's cuddle?

"Why did she die, Dad?" she asked once.

"Zaide Yankel says she went crazy, until one day her heart exploded." He repeated the story he had been told many times.

Mia stopped sorting out the brushes.

"Zaide Yankel is a liar," she said.

"Mia, you are not allowed to talk about your Zaide like that—that is very rude," Issey scolded.

Mia put all the brushes together in a pile and then lifted them up and put them back in their glass jar.

"But he's lying."

"Just because you don't like him, for whatever silly reason, does not give you the right to call him a liar. You have to respect him. He is my father and your grandfather, and you are never to call him a liar again, do you get it?"

Mia looked at him with those eyes, feeling the sadness into which she had been born. She did not know whether the sadness was there before she had come or whether it was her coming that had brought the sadness.

"Miaaaa..." She heard Fran call her from upstairs.

Mia did not answer.

"Answer your mother," Issey said.

"Do I have to?"

"Yes, you do. One of the most important commandments is to answer your mother and father."

"It's *honour* your mother and father."

"Same thing.'"

"But she's only gonna want me to tidy my room or something."

"Well, maybe that's what she wants—or maybe she has a surprise for you. But you'll never know unless you answer her."

And Mia had to leave the studio and follow her mother's voice into her bedroom, or the lounge or the kitchen and put the knife she'd left out back in the drawer, or hang up her dress, or tidy her toys. Mia could never understand why, just as she was getting enough of something, her mother would find a way to finish it.

Mia had been summonsed to The Bedroom. Fran sat on the bed and looked at her.

"I've just received a call from Mrs Radcliffe." Mia looked away from her mother's pinching eyes. "Well, what do you have to say for yourself?" Fran asked.

"It wasn't me," she said.

"What wasn't you?"

"That wrote 'Mrs Radcliffe is a shit' on the board," she said.

"Mrs Radcliffe seems to think that you had something to do with it. Now why would she think that?" Fran looked straight at her.

Mia shook her head and shrugged her shoulders.

"If it wasn't you who wrote it, who did?" Fran asked. "Just out of interest."

"I don't know," Mia said.

"And why did whoever wrote this write such a nasty thing about Mrs Radcliffe?"

"Because she pulled Grace's ear," Mia said.

"Why did she do that?"

"Because she didn't do her homework."

"Well, maybe she shouldn't have pulled her ear, but Grace should have done her homework, shouldn't she?" Fran said impatiently.

Mia stood and looked at her toes. She wriggled them all in

a row, starting with her left baby toe and working her way to her right baby toe.

"Can I go now?" she asked.

"No, I'm not finished with you," Fran said. "It's bad enough that Mrs Radcliffe thinks there's something wrong with you, given what you write in class. But I will not have people think that I use that kind of language in my home. I won't have bad manners from you. I've brought you up properly. To be a lady."

Mia looked at her mother. Her face was blotchy with trying not to shout. A wetness, not quite tears, had gathered and was being held by the fine lashes of her lower eyecup.

Mia nodded and turned to leave. Mrs Radcliffe had stood facing the board for a long time before she turned around to face the class. Her eye was twitching. "This is most disappointing," she had said—twitch, twitch. "Not what one would expect from Jewish children." She had made them all write, "The Rolled cuff is short," on a piece of paper and send them to the front. Michelle Orelowitz was told to collect them and she glared at Mia as she went past her.

Standing with her back to the class, Mrs Radcliffe had flicked through the pieces of paper, pausing every so often to compare it with the big yellow letters on the board. Finally she had said, "I know who did it, and the person who did it knows, and that is enough of a punishment."

When Mia got to her bedroom, she closed the door, flopped on her belly onto her bed, hid her face in her pillow and remembered that she had not heard Grace sing 'Somewhere Over the Rainbow' since the blue dragonflies disappeared.

The only time Mia ever remembered seeing her mother happy, and not just smiling, but happy like in the song— enough to clap her hands and stamp her feet—was on a

Sunday in summertime when the whole family drove to the market in Newtown. They parked the car under the bridge and walked down the skinny aisles of the market stalls, touching the cloths and the jangly beady things that hung on little boards. And it was not bitter. Fran drifted curiously, giggling when she tried on silver necklaces with stones, or scarves with flowers, and Mia felt content to follow her, for there was no bitterness in the sound of her laughter, the radiance of her step.

Issey bought Mia a piece of dry *wors** and held onto her hand as she chewed and sucked the salt from the meat. And then he bought her a Banana Boy and even ate the rest of it when it dripped down her arm and she said she'd had enough.

Each time Fran tried on a dress or some earrings or a ring, Issey would say, "Take it, I want to buy it for you," but she'd put it back, and say, "I'll never wear it at home," and so what was bitter?

"People get over these things," she had heard Issey say, one full moon night, when her nightmare had woken her and she had tiptoed to their door, held back by their voices. "It wasn't your fault. Why won't you let it go?"

Mia had held her breath. There was only silence.

"You're bitter," he then said.

"I'm sorry you think so." Her mother's voice sounded like a little girl's.

And then she heard crying and didn't know where it came from. Sadness filled the world as mommies and daddies sobbed, cradling their unburied grief.

Issey bought Mia a book of Wally Serote's poetry and a belt with an Ndebele design on it for himself. They watched the Zulu dancing and Mia wasn't sure whether it was the

* 'sausage', in Afrikaans

stamping of feet, the banging of drums, the crush of the crowd or the heat of the afternoon, but she was sure she saw her mother and father hold hands for the first time without her having to make them.

avekgeyn:

to leave: to go away;
that which remains after death;
to stop holding;
to fail to take or bring

It is the curse in the Bible, that the Jew must wander—travel great distances and be a stranger in a strange land. But Maya would rather have welcomed a curse of barrenness, like Sarah, *Avraham Avinu's** wife. For it is easier to mourn what one has never had than to leave behind a love one has known.

She would have stayed. She should have stayed. But Rochel prodded her, "Go, go."

She had grabbed Rochel's arms with her hands, "But how shall I go from you?"

"There is no future here," she whispered. "You go. Bring me when you are settled."

But such distances, for someone who had only ever travelled miles by foot, and several miles by wagon, were impossible to imagine. It was said that the world was round, but one needed to believe in such things, for it is not possible to know these things with one's own eyes, and Maya had come only to trust the distances between her eyes and what they could behold in her short-sighted clarity.

She packed her suitcase, a small leather valise she had brought

---

* 'Abraham, our forefather' in Hebrew.

with her from her father's home into her marriage. It sat gaping on their bed, an open wound, a silent screaming mouth into which she placed a few precious garments Rochel had made for her. The shawl with seven triangles of red velvet she had sewn on. The dress with the five buttons, one of brass, three smaller ones mottled in colour and one she had treasured from a wedding gown (replacing it with a lace ribbon) last winter that looked like a pearl. Maya folded each garment in half, then again, and again. How small things can become, folded in upon themselves.

Rochel sat beside her on the bed, stitching a jacket, which had a rent in it from the winter of 1918, when the goat was underfed. Maya folded and tucked. Rochel threaded and pulled. Silent motions of the hands, which knew only happiness when clasped together. The room was filled with hands and their tasks, as if all the things that needed to be said had found their way into fingers, for the things to be spoken were immense and words could not hold them. Not even poetry.

When the stitching was done, she bit the thread off with her teeth, smoothed down the collar, pressed it with her rough fingers and lifted the jacket for Maya to try on. Maya slipped her hands into the sleeves and Rochel lifted it up around her shoulders. As Rochel's fingers touched Maya's body, even through the layers of fabric, Maya felt her slipping. Rochel grabbed onto Maya's shoulders with both hands and Maya grasped them with hers. Rochel laid her head to rest in the soft place between Maya's shoulder blades. Maya laid her hands over those of the seamstress and leaned back into the crown of her head, closing her eyes.

From this desolate place, a place deeper than memory, for Maya had no rememberances of her mother's voice, she began to sing an old Yiddish lullaby her mother must have sung to her.

"*Kinder yoren, zishe sheine blumen… zurik tzu mir vet ir*

Joanne Fedler

shein mer nisht kumen…"[*]

It is our mistake: we think the places we leave are rooms and walls and bricks. But we are misled, for the places we never see again are not etched in the soil or marked in the earth, for we can always return in memory to such places. No, what we leave behind are spaces in time. It is moments we lose when we leave what we love behind. For what is life, but the time we have spent; the sharing of the clock's hours, the partaking of mouthfuls in the same breath, the laughter that coincides at a joke well-told? Lines of longitude? Who could pine for imaginary hems along the earth? Only one inclined to abstractions. But for those of us with an eye for finer things, it is the lines of grief on her face with that goodbye look in her eyes that distance steals from us. Such lines, small folds of skin scrolling the stories of her smile, her frown, her whispery glee, touchable in the moment with nothing more insistent than the pillow of a fingertip, such lines dissolve, are taken from us in parting. For what is place but a confusion of geography with time? The places we leave are days not addresses. And since time changes everything, places can never be where we left them. And memory cannot guide us back to them.

"This room, this cold dark place—I shall return to it every time I close my eyes, for you made it warm and bright," Maya whispered. "You, with your copper hair and your nimble fingers. You, my Rochel-a. You."

It was not a garment she cast off on that day, but a skin she tore off with her own hands, to leave Rochel behind, with her own heart made sweet with hunger and thirst.

As she stood at the window of the train and looked out at her, an illness rose up from her heart, like the rise of stomach acid or the expulsion of a meal eaten several days too late for

[*] 'The years of childhood, sweet, beautiful flowers, you will never return to me….'

freshness, and she clutched the window ledge to stop herself from falling. It was a sense that froze to knowledge as she met Rochel's gaze, that joy had come and left. That day, her heart split open like the belly of an ox under a *shochet's* blade, as the full bodied image of her Rochel diminished to the body and then the dot of an 'i' on the horizon, before vanishing from her sight. When she finally boarded the ship, she retched into the waters each day of those thirty-nine days on the ocean.

Water does not lap. A lap is a place of comfort, the cup of a mother's body where the child nestles. The rough tongue of a grateful goat on the open palm after the hand has filled the goat's bucket, perhaps also laps. No, water does not lap. It knocks. A menacing visitor, a knock that is never answered, a slap against the boat's laden belly full of the sharp smells of weary bodies stifled and expectant. Knock knock sloosh knock knock, who is there? She is not. She is not there.

Maya counted knocks, but not as one drifting to sleep counts. Rather, she counted to clip herself, to pinch herself to stay awake, so she could know, as if each knock were a measurement of space, how many knocks away from Rochel this ship of immigrants was taking her. Fourteen thousand, seven hundred, eighty three, four, …sloosh sloosh, five…" She moved between her vigil and her dream in which she was caught in a ship's belly, searching amongst all these people for that face, those hands, the smell of potatoes.

People around her spoke of sunshine, of a land of dark-skinned natives, of a city built on gold. Their laughter, counting of money, and prayers three times a day became a tapestry of time passed. At the three appointed prayer times, instead of taking out her *siddur,** she, sheltered by the poor light, removed

---

* prayer book.

from her bosom a square of embroidered cloth and smelled it as if it were air itself. The good Mrs Tuvel of whom, it was said, could make from an old chicken bone and a cabbage that had seen better days, a feast, shuffled over to her on many of those days, and fed her with a broth of beetroot and vinegar that sustained her.

"Eat, eat," Mrs Tuvel encouraged. "Your Yankel will say the neighbours did not feed you, if you arrive in Sud Afrika wit no flesh on your bones, like a stray dog in Kovno," she bellowed. She spoke of a garden she would grow in a place where the sun shone. "Cebbeges, cerrots, celery, my own parsley. And fruit." She spoke in dreamy phrases about lemon trees and peach trees. Trees, the fruit of which they had never tasted. But Maya did not want a sun that did not warm the skin of Rochel. She would have lived in the biting winters of Kovno for a thousand lifetimes if those lifetimes could have been shared with her widow Stzupak.

Part 4

'But the stranger that dwelleth with you
shall be unto you as one born among you,
and thou shalt love him as thyself;
for ye were strangers in the land of Egypt.'

Leviticus 19:34

★★★

Beware of your friends, not your enemies.

Yiddish proverb

The front door, 48 Komatie Road,
April, 1975

Perhaps they were her cup of tea after all, Mia thought… It was something in the way Fran held her neck. Something she did with her chin and her shoulder. Mia watched her mother. Mrs Drewmore said in Biology that animals expose their necks when they surrender, signalling that the fight is over. Fran's eyes were smooth. The voice that came from her throat was soft with fur. Mia could not tell whether it was this new stranger with the rose that had brought the clamouring in her ears and the rattling in her chest, or if it was the stranger in her mother.

"They're not my cup of tea," Fran had declared at a full *Shabbat* table in front of Zaide Yankel, Shmooley and Selma, two Friday nights before. Issey, with his mouth full of the grey pulp of the *kneidel** had just shared the news about a letter, dated January 1975, posted in Jerusalem, he had received from a stranger called Asher Trubik—the son of one of his mother's old friends in Lithuania. The letter said that the stranger was intending to travel to South Africa and that he planned to be in Johannesburg in a matter of weeks. He hoped to meet with "the family of his late mother's dear friend", to whom, in the meanwhile, he sent "hot hellos", the literal translation from the Hebrew quaint and endearing. Issey passed the letter around the table for everyone to examine, Mia too. Mia had rubbed

* dumpling in chicken soup.

her fingers over the signature, slanted to the left, A-s-h-e-r-T-r-u-b-k—the 'i' had been swallowed up by the 'k'.

Now Mia moved her gaze to the sender of the letter, signed with a missing 'i' in his name. She felt herself tilting her own head, but quickly put her hand to her throat and looked him straight on. Though he was lovely to be near and Mia wanted to sit next to him at the table, she worried about his eyes. He was browner than most white people, from "living by the sun", he explained in his gravelly accent that was made up of so many bits and pieces of places that her ears quivered like the strings of a lute to listen.

"I've never met a decent Israeli," Fran had said, passing the letter to Zaide Yankel. "What do you want to get involved for?"

"He's had an interesting life," Issey had said, pushing through the brambles she was growing between them. "Lost both his parents when he was young, was adopted by a Jewish family that emigrated to America, and when he was twenty-four, he went to Israel. He's fought in a couple of wars there—the Sinai campaign, maybe even the Six-Day war."

"*Tah-ke?*"* Zaide Yankel had nodded, impressed

Mia had listened to this, her eyes wide with questions. That letter in her father's hand held so many new things: abandoned orphans and wars shorter than the time it took to make the world. Even his name shook something enormous and startling inside her: Asher.

"Well, if I wasn't Jewish, they'd be reason enough for me to become an Anti-Semite," Fran had said, as she dished up a second *kneidel* for Uncle Shmooley, who always had a second one, and claimed that no-one could make *kneidlach* like Fran, though it was Sarafina who made them.

"That's a bit harsh, Frannie," Uncle Shmooley had said.

* 'Really?' in Yiddish.

Joanne Fedler

"But, you shouldn't trust Israelis," he continued, shaking his head with authority. "They're the biggest crooks next to *coolies*."*

"I've got an Israeli friend," Aunt Selma said timidly. "She's a lovely pers…" but trailed off, ignored.

"They are all obsessed with money," Fran had said. "And this Asher is a soldier. You wouldn't know," she said, reminding Issey of the fact that he had never served in the South African army, "but it does strange things to people's heads."

Issey had just shrugged, folded his letter and put it back in his front pocket. He used to believe that opposites attract—the Yin-Yang thing. A relationship could only survive one difficult person and he had assumed that his artistic sensibility naturally entitled him to that role. Over time though, Fran's retreat from life had surreptitiously displaced the mantle of 'difficult' to her, a relationship transgression he struggled to forgive. It was artists who were supposed to be eccentric, not miserable housewives. Slowly, his interest in her interpretation of events and human motives waned, bristled, while he nurtured patience, and finally resignation to the fact that they were like Siamese twins joined at the back, never seeing the same world at the same time.

"He wants to know about Mom, Shmooley. I mean, I can't tell him a whole lot, I hardly knew her, but Pop, you can tell him."

Zaide Yankel looked up at Issey. "About your mother?"

"Ja, he's very interested in finding out more about her."

"His name again?" Zaide Yankel asked, bits of *kneidel* gathered at the corners of his mouth.

"Asher Trubik."

"It doesn't rink a bell."

For several moments, there were slurps from soup spoons.

"Odd," Fran said, shaking her head a little.

* derogatory slang for 'Indians.'

"What's odd about it?" Issey asked, in a voice strung out thinly, grasping for tolerance.

"Why now? What's taken him so long? What does he really want?"

"He's just looking for pieces of his past. Jewish families all over the world have been broken and scattered and people have spent years trying to piece them back together," Issey said.

The vacuum inside him that had been created by the early loss of his mother had left him with an unnamed pining evoked at unexpected moments. He knew what it was to want answers. To be near those who were near her, as if their touching her and his touching them kept her alive, like a sentient broken telephone.

Issey sighed. "Let's be hospitable, civil, at least. Let's treat him like a guest in this house."

"Don't let him in," Mia said softly, tugging at Issey's hand.

"Don't be silly, darling," Issey said. "He'll be like an old friend to the family."

That night, Mia had sat at her window, looking out. The night sky was clear with a half-moon, like a pale orange slice, with only a hint of the half dipped in shadow. She said the name 'Asher' over and over in her mouth, until it sounded like a made-up word that had no sense to it. "Ash. Er. A. Sher."

"Please let something good happen," she whispered. But when she looked up, the moon had slipped behind a hanging cloud that had come from nowhere.

That night she worried about the moon, feeling as if everything that she could hold was slipping from her. As if danger was biding its time. Looking for someplace soft to strike.

Now he was before her, younger than she had imagined him, but older than he looked. He smoked small cigarillos from some Arabic country, sweet-smelling tobacco wrapped in dried leaf and tied in the centre with a small piece of thread, which he allowed her to undo on one of them, even though it was a waste.

When he held out his hand to her and she gingerly extended hers, only to have him bend down to kiss it, Mia took a few deep gulps, felt her tongue swell under her palette with nothing to say.

"And this is my beautiful wife," Issey said, introducing Fran. Fran blushed.

"Beautiful indeed," Asher said, taking her left hand in his right, and placing a kiss on the knuckle of her middle finger. And then, from the inside pocket of his jacket he produced a single rose, with blended petals of whites and pinks, which he had cut with his Swiss Army knife on his walk through the Rose Gardens, in full view of the sign that said, 'Do Not Pick The Roses'. But he'd not had an opportunity to stop for something on his way, and arriving empty-handed seemed suspiciously desperate.

Fran did not care for visitors, ordinarily. Strangers in her house felt like open day to the private realm of her losses. Someone who did not know you was bound to ask, in the glib way strangers do, why they only had one child, and wasn't her daughter lonely? She could hold her world and its tragedies if she kept them close to her chest, not exposed for observation and opinion. She would tolerate Issey's fascination with his new guest with moderated civility. A homecooked welcome dinner, followed up in a month or two with a meal at a decent restaurant—their treat, of course, nice to have met you, all the best. Contempt followed on all too easily from the naïve delights of familiarity. Issey was too easily drawn into other people's agendas, never suspecting an ulterior motive, a skeleton in the closet or an undisclosed secret. She took it as a personal slight when people took advantage of him. Boundaries were her department.

For these reasons, she had not dressed especially glamorously for the occasion of his first visit. But she instantly regretted her plaid skirt and green blouse buttoned to her throat. His eyes came to rest on her, like a hand cupping her neck, under her chin, never straying below her collarbone. She longed for him to flick his lashes to take in the length and breadth of her body. But he resisted, as though confusing hunger with greed was a sign of weakness.

She could not help noticing that beneath the rough calico of his tan-brown shirt, the prominence of muscular lines boasted strength. The brown hairs on his chest that peeked from over his top button were tinged with the same silver of his short-cropped head of hair.

Issey helped him with his jacket. Fran wondered whether it would be obvious if she excused herself and changed into something more appropriate, and decided that it would be. She excused herself to check on the dinner, but sneaked into the bathroom, undid the top button of her blouse and pinched her cheeks to draw attention to the height of their bones, licked her index finger, and wiped beneath her eyes, in case any stray mascara had darkened the pads beneath them, which could make one look *so* much older. This she did without pausing to wonder at her behaviour. Adolescence infected her, holding the promise of a time before happiness had fallen from her.

Fran came from a line of beautiful women. The most beautiful of all, her great-great grandmother, had the face of an angel. Over time, in combination with other genes from generation to generation, the beauty had been fractionally eroded, so that Fran's great grandmother was said to have been as beautiful as a Modigliani painting, her grandmother as beautiful as a doll, her mother, Olive, as captivating as a filmstar. Fran herself had only inherited the residues of such lofty comparisons. Unlike the magnificent purity of the faces of her ancestors, she had a face craggy with transmuted beauty and diluted innocence.

As a young girl, she found in the attention of young boys and older men, which she never voluntarily sought, a terrifying conspicuousness. Male attention gravitated to her like 'bees around a honey pot', her mother had scolded, as if she were somehow to blame. It was shameful. Uncle Max had said that she drove boys to it. She held both her guilt and her bewildered ignorance as to how to prevent it hidden inside her like a diseased organ.

It didn't surprise her to learn that the degree of beauty of her matrilineal line was in direct proportion to the unhappiness of their marriages. It was said that her great-great grandmother, with the angel's face, had spent the entire twenty years of her married life cooped up in a small house, in a deep depression. Her great grandmother had died of an unknown disease six years into her married life, and family lore had it that the cause was her husband's affair with the bottle. Her grandmother had divorced her grandfather, even though it was known that, in those days, a divorce was a disgrace second only to conceiving out of wedlock. Her mother, well, her mother had been having affairs on the side for as many years as it took her father finally to die of a brain aneurysm at the age of forty-seven.

Fran determined at the age of thirteen, after her fall-out with her cousin Desiree, that she would marry someone who saw something other than beauty in her. She thus dismissed all suitors who ever mentioned her appearance. When she found Issey at the easel of her portrait, its ugliness misled her into believing he saw no beauty in her. In this she was mistaken, and luckily so, for even though mention of her beauty had driven her from the arms of many, she loved to be reminded of the very quality in herself that had ruined the lives of all her predecessors.

Asher's words were spoken slowly, in a drawl, like he was enjoying them in his mouth, and only reluctantly letting them go. He tugged gently at his thoughts, revealing them like a rope of scarves from a magician's sleeve. He had had a sad life, beset with losses and miseries. He spoke of fighting for what you believe in; defending your country; being prepared to die for what matters. He told of his adventures. Times of war and times of peace. He had never married. But women had always been his comfort and delight, keeping the world a place of exquisite wonder.

"It's just an ordinary supper," Fran apologized, carving the chicken and interrupting the stream of endless stories of glory and sorrows. "Nothing fancy."

Asher turned to her, and cocked his head. "Wonderful," he crooned. She blinked at him with smiling eyes, wanting to take all the pain of his motherless life from him, to comfort him. "There's seconds," she said, "if you're still hungry after that."

"Thank you, but I eat slowly. I like to taste what you make," he said. Fran sat down and swallowed quickly. She felt a silky peep between her thighs.

"Here's the parson's nose for you, Mia," Issey said, holding it out to her on a fork. Mia plucked it off with her fingers, and was about to pop it in her mouth, when Asher's hand closed over hers.

"Aah, a girl who loves the tail," he exclaimed, "Do you know what they say about the one 'oo eats, what do you call it, the person's nose?"

"The *parson's* nose," Mia giggled.

"'Oo dares to eat the tail of the beast is the one without fear. In South America, there is a tribe with a tradition, that if you touch the tail of the crocodile, no-one ever will 'arm you. This is you, Mia," he said wistfully.

Mia held the parson's nose in her fingers. "Does that mean that I'm safe?" she asked quietly.

"Of course you're safe, silly billy," Issey said, chewing half a potato. "You're safe my mate."

But Asher did not allow Issey's glib comforting to intervene. He pondered her question, the way adults seldom do and then he said, marking a spot on his chest, "Safe from the outside, but no-one can protect you from the evil inside."

"Mia, let Asher eat his dinner," Fran said.

Mia lowered her ear to her shoulder as if shyness was overtaking her. She knew then that she could ask Asher anything and he would know the answer that would put the asking to rest.

P erhaps the nightmares were gone for good. It had been the longest stretch of time without them. With Asher's arrival, like a parachute from the sky, the pieces she had always felt were lost or missing inside her were all gathered together. She wrote stories about lost things being found and unexpected treasures. She even carved a family of wingless angels, holding hands.

Asher said he wanted to rest a while in South Africa, because there was enough beauty here to keep him interested, at least until the 'travel insect' bit him. Issey took a day off work to help him find a flat to rent in Hillbrow, made several phonecalls to get him the best bargain on a second-hand Mazda, which, even though it had an oil-leak leaving little puddles if the car stood still for too long, was a real find. They lent him the bed from the spare-room, some linen and a blanket Fran had knitted two winters ago.

Fran collected things around the house to put in a box for his flat, crockery for one, a bar of lily-scented soap, and on the spur of the moment, a tin of smoked oysters. Finally, she gently lifted one of her new rose bushes from her garden and put it in a potholder for him with handwritten instructions on 'exposure to the sun' and 'watering.' Mia gave him one of her plasticine angels, but she broke its wings, 'so it can't fly away'.

"Someday, I might 'ave to ask you to give 'im 'is wings back…" he smiled, accepting her housewarming gift.

Asher would often arrive around dinnertime and protest that he was not coming to eat, but just happened to be in the neighbourhood. "Stay, stay," Fran and Issey always insisted, and stay he always did, for a drink, a chat, a plate of food. More and more, Mia found herself, around dinnertime, waiting in the garden for the sound of his oil-leaking Mazda. When she heard it, puttering up outside and the squeak of his handbrake, she'd rush to open the front door for him, clamouring to be the first to welcome him. But on evenings when the streets offered no sounds of his arrival, Sarafina would need to be sent out to bring her in because her dinner was getting cold.

In summer, they would *braai** on the lawn, and sometimes Issey grabbed his camera, taking pictures of Asher tickling Mia, or Fran putting a piece of *boerewors*† in his mouth. Sometimes, Issey would set up the camera so that he'd rush to join them, squashed on the swing. While the camera's little red light flashed 'hurry up, hurry up', Issey would say, "Everyone say *Vasbyt!*"** and all four of them, Fran included, would shout '*Vasbyt*' like a big happy family—though Asher's sounded more like 'frostbite', which made Mia laugh 'til she almost wee-ed. She loved him desperately for the joy he had brought, fixing everything that had been wrong.

"What do you do, Asher?" Fran once asked.

"Do?" he repeated.

"Yes, *do*—I mean, all day, what do you do?"

"Odd jobs—whatever I can find. I'm not fussy."

"And what are you doing now?"

"Making a living. Making money."

"To what end?"

"To be rich. I want someday to be so rich that if I cannot buy something it cannot be bought." He laughed at his own dreams.

"Isn't there more to life than money?" she smiled, ringing the bell. Sarafina came in from the kitchen carrying a tray. She

---

* 'barbeque,' in Afrikaans.
† 'a thick sausage,' in Afrikaans.
** 'Hang on,' in Afrikaans.

was wearing her pink Monday uniform, even though it was Wednesday. "Evening master," she murmured.

He looked into Fran's wondrous eyes inherited from her great-great grandmother, and said, "I do not say money is everything. But it can buy you everything."

" What about happiness?" Fran asked.

Asher nodded at Sarafina. "I inherited some money many years ago from the man 'oo adopt me. It was a lot of money for a young man. I spend it all in two months." He held up two fingers, allowing the dramatic effect of his words to sink in. "In that time, I was free for the first time in my life. I bought whatever I wanted. That was freedom and that is not something I am imagining. I speak out of experiences."

"But money can't buy you friendship," Fran said. "Or love."

Sarafina returned to the kitchen.

"Love? What is love?" he asked. "If you 'ave money, you can buy the most beautiful woman in the world."

"For an hour or so," Issey said.

Indignation choked Fran. "Please, not in front of the child…" she said.

"For the rest of your life. Take it from me—money can get you everything. Love. Fame. Freedom. You think this woman," he said gesturing to the kitchen, "would clean your plates if she 'ad money?"

"We pay her very well," Fran said hushingly.

"'ow much?" Asher asked.

"Enough. She also gets free board and lodging, and every Thursday off— most Sundays too."

"What does she do with 'er Thursday and Sunday off?" he persisted.

"She goes to the maintenance court on Thursday," Mia said. All three adults turned to look at her. "And church on Sunday—if she's not working."

"This is adult's conversation, Mia," Fran quipped.

"But Mom, that's where she goes on Thursd…"

"A child can 'ave a conversation with an adult, no?" Asher said.

Mia held her breath and looked at her mother. Fran narrowed her eyes at Asher. The gall of the man!

"This child never knows when to keep quiet—it's a question of manners."

Asher turned and winked at Mia, who turned her head so that her mother could not see her smile.

"If she 'ad money, she'd never 'ave to stand in court for money from anyone, and she would not 'ave to ask you 'please can I do this' or 'please can I do that'," he resumed.

"If it wasn't for this job, she'd be out on the streets. If you think she's doing me any favours by being here, you're wrong. I don't want a servant. I don't need the intrusion into my privacy, my broken dishes or the guilt of having more than she has because I'm white. She needs a job. And if there's one thing I hate more than having a servant, it's when foreigners come here, full of superior knowledge and judgemental moralism." She began to stack up dirty plates as she spoke.

Asher laughed. "I'm not judging you. I'm judging the black man. 'e is a barbarian. Primitive— 'e never learn that money is power. That's why 'e stay like a monkey in the bush. But if 'e 'ad money, 'e would be free. You make a big mistake if you think money cannot buy everything."

Fran rang the bell again. Sarafina came back for the rest of the plates. Fran said, "Anyone for more pie before she takes everything off?"

"Me," said Asher, offering his plate for more. "Thursday, Sunday and everything off," he whispered to Mia.

"My friend, there are some things money can't buy," Issey said.

"Like what?"

"I have something I inherited from my mother, for example, and that is priceless."

Asher's eyes shone. "Let me see it."

"Okay," Issey said.

"Can I get it, Dad?" Mia asked.

"Sure, love."

In minutes Mia was back at the table, holding the *talit* bag in her hand. She gently unzipped the bag and furrowed her fingers inside to remove a small piece of cloth. She opened it and held it in her hands.

Asher was silent, his eyes all over it. "'ow much you want for this cloth?" he asked.

"Are you joking? No amount in the world," Issey said. "It exists outside your world of currency."

"'ow much?" Asher repeated.

"It's not for sale," Issey said.

Asher took the cloth from Mia's hands and his rough hands touched its surfaces, greedily, madly.

"Just be gentle," Issey said. "It's very old."

"I want it," Asher said.

"I'm sorry, my friend. You cannot have it."

"I 'ave to 'ave it."

"Listen, my mother gave this to me on her deathbed. It's been with me all my life. It's all I have left of her. I would never part with it."

Issey put his hand out and gestured for Asher to return it. Asher did not give it back.

"You can't have it," Mia said. "It takes away my nightmares."

Asher looked at Mia. "Does it now?"

Mia nodded. Asher handed the cloth back to her and Mia gave it back to Issey.

"And where did your mother get such a priceless object of beauty?"

"A very close friend, is all I know."

Asher's face grew soft with shadows. His eyes flicked slowly. He drew in a long breath. "You are right," he said. "Some things even money can't buy."

"I love women," Asher once told Mia, when they were sitting alone on the swing in the garden. Since the first night when he had observed how she watched in fascination as he lit his cigarillos with a silver lighter that burst into a flame as long as an index finger, he had let her light them for him. You needed to click the head of the lighter open, roll your thumb backwards over the little round wheel, and press hard. It was difficult to get it right the first time, but three or four more attempts and the flame would shoot upwards, surprising her each time. Once he had dipped his cigarillo into the tip or belly of the flame, you needed to click the head back down and the flame would suffocate and be snuffed out. Somehow the way he said 'women', made her know she was included in that circle of lovely things.

He turned to look at her and drew on his cigarillo. In his watching, she felt no need to shrug her shoulders with the uneasiness of the examined. He said, "Your eyes, they are older than you are. They are 'iding a secret."

"What secret?"

He took a deep breath in of his cigarillo, held it for a while, and said, as the smoke trickled from his nostrils, "If I tell you, it won't be a secret."

The smoke curled around his face, a misty moustache, and disappeared. He was watching her closely. A fly landed on the knee of his crossed leg. They both looked at it and, in a fraction of a moment, his hand slapped his knee. When he turned his palm over, the fly was squashed in its centre. Asher flicked its flattened remains off his hand and turned back to look at Mia.

"How will I find out about my secret?" she asked him.

"Mia, the world is full of things—some so beautiful. But not only beautiful things. Also very sad things. And you will understand why there must be sadness in the world. When you see 'ow everything that 'as gone before and everything that will 'appen is connected. You are too young for your secret. But you will know it when you see it."

"When will I see it?" Mia asked in wonder.

"When you are old enough and have some titties," he said with a growl, as he exaggerated two enormous mounds in front of his own chest, "in place of your pimples."

The talk of the secret became their secret and drew her near to him, but then the secret with no answer left her disquieted and incomplete. Without knowing its whereabouts or even its shape, she feared her secret might slip out of her unless she knew how to hold it.

Sometimes they would know he was in the house from the sounds of the piano that came from the lounge.

"Asher, is that you?" Fran would call from the landing.

He would never answer in words, but would start a new melody.

"Don't you learn your manners from Asher, you hear me, Mia?" Fran warned, as she smoothed her blouse to emphasize the fullness of her bosom and checked her mascara. "And how the hell did he get in? It's like he's got his own key to the front door."

"Maybe Sarafina let him in through the back," Mia suggested.

Mia knew only that Asher was happiness and sadness all knotted into one person because she could never say whether he was going to laugh or shout or sometimes cry from the look on his face. He could be reclining on the swing in the garden with a drink in his hand, or sitting on the couch cursing some 'asshole' who 'ad 'fuck with him', when suddenly, he would jump up and make his way to the corner of the lounge where the old piano sat. Mia would follow him and sit on the arm of the easy chair as he let his brown fingers press onto the white slivers of the chords as they made music.

"This one is for you, my little girlfriend, soon to be a beautiful woman," and his fingers would begin to play a sad lullaby from a distant time and place.

He told Mia that his father was a musician and that, though he had died when Asher was just a young boy, he had inherited the talent of making music with his hands. There was not an instrument he could not pick up and caress into a weeping song.

"Time for bed, Mia," Fran would say, just as she felt she could bear his playing for the longest time. Asher would never argue and suggest she be allowed to stay down longer, but he would take her hand in his and hold his index finger out, yellowed with cigarillo smoke, to touch the tip of her little index finger. Then, taking her other hand, he would make her rub up and down so that she touched his finger and her finger all at once. "Touch the finger of a dead man," he would smile. She would shiver because it was a half-feeling, something not quite alive. Then he would kiss her on her forehead. By the end of the evening, he would smell heavily of cigarillos and alcohol, and she always wanted to leave before he stopped wanting to play with her. Before he began arguing with her father in his studio, watching him while he painted.

"Sleep tight and don't let the boys bite," he would say, giving her a hug.

"It's 'bugs', Asher. Don't let the bugs bite," she said crossly.

"More important for you to look out for the boys. *Leila tov, motek.*"*

Leaving him at the dining room table or in her father's studio, she would climb the stairs to her bedroom, each step, a heartache. By the time she reached the landing, the loss felt unendurable, and she would lie awake in bed, a cushion wedged between her thighs and listen for the sounds of his drunken laughter or melancholy, which both terrified and thrilled her.

---

* 'Goodnight, sweetie,' in Hebrew.

Joanne Fedler

He was full of riddles, which could all be solved if she asked the right questions. As for him, he could only answer yes or no.

'A dead man is found next to a walking stick. Next to that lies a small piece of the stick. What 'appened?'

She worked out that the dead man was blind, that's why the stick. She even worked out that he had killed himself, but that's where she got stuck. He helped her—"see 'e was a tiny circus clown".

"A what?"

"A small man, 'ow you say it? Like Snow White's seven little friends."

"A dwarf—do you mean a dwarf?"

"Yes, yes a dwarf... sometimes I make mistakes translating between 'ere and 'ere," he said gesturing to his brain and his mouth.

Someone had cut off a piece of the walking stick, but being blind, he could not see. He thought he had grown because his stick was shorter than usual. And because there would be no place in the circus for him, he had taken his life.

"See?"

"Who would do such a cruel thing?" and "why?" Mia wanted to know.

"It's not important to the riddle," Asher said. When she became upset, he threw his head back and began to laugh. Mia felt her heart grow sore. She had never thought about a dead circus dwarf before, dead on his caravan floor, dead only because someone had played a practical joke on him.

"I don't like your riddles," she scolded. "They give me a tummy ache."

Asher put his cigarillo to his lips, inhaled deeply, and smiled with his silvery eyes in which words sometimes got stuck in translation.

"You are my favourite girl," he would whisper to her when Fran left to check on the dinner or her rosebushes, and Issey was late from work. He would touch the white hairs of her birthmark, wind them around his finger and let them loose. Mia would close her eyes and let his fingers drop to touch her closed eyelids. Then he would run his fingertips along her eyelashes, so that it tickled, and move to her nose, softly squeezing it between his thumb and index finger. When he got to her mouth, she'd feel something warm but full of loss hovering close, and he'd bend his head forward and hold his mouth just centimetres away from hers, so she could feel his breathing on her lips.

"My favourite," he'd whisper again, moving his head away, and it would all be gone. And she'd open her eyes.

"I know," she said, squeezing his hand, although she said it quietly, so no-one else could hear. When he confessed to her in this way, something shameful surfaced in her, as if he'd told a secret she had to keep, or spoken out aloud his birthday wish. In the Bible, Joseph's brothers sold him into slavery because he was the favourite. Though it made you feel special, being the favourite was also dangerous: jealous eyes followed you everywhere.

Mia started to fear Asher. Because he said things she knew were supposed to be unheard.

The Passover table,
April 1977

"Why is tonight different from all other nights?" Zaide Yankel asked slowly, balancing the tip of the spine of the blue bound *Haggadah*[*] on the table ledge.

The table was decked in bridal white. Two brass candlesticks stood in the centre, with their long white limbs boasting flames that would consume them by the end of the *Seder.*[†] In the centre sat a huge bronze platter like a witch's salver with little indents to hold a chicken neck; a roasted egg (burnt and cracked on its side); a twisted piece of horseradish; and other little dishes of strange concoctions. Unleavened bread was everywhere. The smell of *kneidlach,*[**] with their ginger and onion hearts, bubbling in chicken broth had roused Mia before the arrival of the guests, and she had entered the dining room and stood still. Fran's voice had carried from the kitchen, "…the saltwater must be poured *over* the eggs…" and "don't forget to brown the *tsimmes*[††]" and "what is the chopped herring doing here? It needs to be in the fridge". She had heard Fina clattering plates, preparing for the Seder, different from all others because tonight both Asher and Grace were coming. Mia had put her palm on her chest at the spot where the madness rattled—couldthatbeherheart? All these objects

[*] book which tells the story of Passover.
[†] Passover dinner in which the story of the Jews leaving slavery in Egypt is told through songs and rituals.
[**] dumplings in chicken soup.
[††] a stew made with prunes, carrots, sweet potatoes and brisket.

and strange smells recalled a distant time when God had smote firstborn sons and rivers had turned to blood.

Now, the thumping in her chest had quietened. Under the table, her and Grace held hands.

Across from her sat Asher. He looked up at her and his smile made her quiver with uncertainty.

"Well, *kinderlach*?"* Zaide Yankel's voice broke their gaze across the table. "Why is this night different from all other nights?"

"We love riddles, don't we?" Asher whispered, leaning across to Mia.

"Grace and I know," Mia said. "Tell them, Grace."

Grace smiled. "Because God led us out of Egypt, from slavery to freedom."

"Very good," Zaide Yankel proclaimed. Mia looked at Issey, who winked back.

"And God sent ten plagues to the Egyptians—blood, frogs, lice, beasts, pestilence, boils, hail, locusts, darkness and then He killed all the boys, and then Pharoah said we could go," Mia continued.

"Not all the boys—the firstborn," Zaide Yankel corrected her.

"Yes, I meant the firstborn," Mia said.

"And what did the Jews do to stop God from smitink their first born?" Zaide Yankel asked.

"They had to put blood on their doorposts so God would pass over them," Grace said.

"So the Angel of Death would know Jews were there and wouldn't kill their firstborn," Mia continued.

Zaide Yankel nodded in agreement.

"God likes the taste of blood."

Everyone turned to look at Asher.

"What do you mean?" Fran asked.

* Yiddish for 'children.'

"God 'as a taste for blood, wouldn't you say? First plague—'e turns a river to blood, God asks for the blood of a sacrificed beast, and before that, Isaac on the altar, waiting for 'is own father to kill him—at God's command."

Mia's stomach lurched.

"But God stopped him in time," Issey said, a quaver of laughter in his voice.

"Do you think Isaac knew 'e would be saved? 'e was just an innocent boy, trusting of 'is father. Do you think Isaac ever trusted 'is father again?"

Uncle Shmooley cackled, "He's got a point." Selma laughed softly, and soon Issey was laughing too. Mia looked in confusion from one smile to the next.

"It's not funny," Mia said softly, squeezing Grace's hand.

Asher looked her full in the face. "You are right, Mia, my child. It is not funny. It takes a child to understand that."

"It was different in those days," Zaide Yankel said. "People believed in God. Isaac understood."

Asher turned slowly to face Zaide Yankel, "We can never know what Isaac knew or felt, can we?"

Zaide Yankel shrugged. "No-one can know anythink for sure."

"We can know only our own experiences, not so?" Asher pressed.

"Mostly."

Mia looked at her Zaide. Like Isaac, he did not know he was being led to the slaughter. She looked at Asher. His smiling eyes were telling tales.

It was time for hiding the *Afikoman*.* Issey broke the middle *matza* and excused himself from the table warning the children

* piece of *matza* (unleavened bread) that is traditionally hidden for children to find later on.

'not to look', while he went into the lounge to hide it. Mia gulped down her second glass of the sweet red wine.

"No more, hear?" said Fran. "You'll be sick."

After they had dipped their fingers in the wine and shouted out the ten plagues, and it was almost time for dinner, Asher turned to Zaide Yankel. "It is strange that you don't remember my mother," he said slowly. "It was such a small *shtetl*—everybody knew everybody."

"*Nu,*˙ it just show you—a person can never know everybody," Zaide Yankel said.

"Do you remember a boy?" Asher asked quietly, "a young friend of mine I played with—Moshe Stzupak. I always wonder what happened to 'im..." His voice trailed off.

A vein on the side of Zaide Yankel's neck began to jump. "Stzupak? Stzupak?" His voice unsteadied, teetering into high-pitch. "Ja, I remember—this boy came to live with us—with his mother. Their house was burned down in a fire." His knobbly hand came up to his face, adjusted his glasses. "I was like a father to him—poor boy lost his father very younk."

Asher did not move. His eyes were steady, watching. "What appened to 'im?"

Zaide Yankel coughed. "To be poifectly honest with you, I don't know. I assume his mother brought him up. We left for South Africa and lost touch with them."

"'is mother committed suicide." Asher's voice was as blunt as hammer.

Zaide Yankel did not look up. "Really? What a tragedy. Perhaps the neighbours took care of him. He was just a boy." Zaide Yankel began to cough. Issey patted him on the back. The coughing grew more agitated.

"Yes, just an innocent boy," Asher said.

Issey handed his father a glass of water and helped him to

˙Yiddish for 'so,' or 'go on,' or 'well.'

Joanne Fedler

swallow a few sips.

Asher leaned back, with his arms behind his head.

"Let's get back to the *seder*, shall we?" said Issey, "otherwise we'll never get to the food."

When Zaide Yankel had recovered from his coughing fit, Issey took over from him in leading. The old man had grown hunched in his chair. His eyes did not move from the page in his *Hagaddah*. Asher did not release him from his gaze and Zaide Yankel stayed stooped like a question mark.

"Mia, open the front door for Elijah the Prophet," Issey said.

Mia ran to open the front door. It was a warm evening outside and the moon was not overhead yet, but dangled halfway between earth and sky. She looked into it, but could not see the smears of shadow on its face as she sometimes could. On this night, it was white and bright, a moon for a Passover night. Back at the table everyone had already started to eat their eggs and Mia was cross that they hadn't waited for her—not even Grace. Trevor's egg was already finished.

After the chopped herring and soup with *kneidlach*, Mia and Grace both complained that they were full. But Fran warned that there was still meat *tsimmes* with carrots, potatoes and prunes, and brisket. Mia wished everyone would hurry up and finish eating so they could get back to the songs, so everyone could hear Grace sing, *she has the best voice in the school— they always make her sing* Hatikvah* *and* Die Stem† *at assembly.* Grace, through her smile, shushed her *don't embarrass me*. After fruit salad and sticky syrupy *teiglach*,** Issey announced that it was time for the children to go look for the *Afikoman*. Mia, Grace and Trevor jumped up and raced each other to the lounge. "A

* Israeli national anthem.
† old South African national anthem.
** sweet dessert in the shape of a donut made with syrup and ginger.

reward for the first one to find it," Issey reminded them.

"We're not children," Dale said, but Shmooley insisted, and her and Karen slouched out of their chairs after giving each other meaningful looks, and headed to the lounge.

Mia lifted the cushions on the couch, Trevor looked in the record player holder. "I've got a guts ache," Grace whispered to Mia, "I'm going to the loo."

"Okay, if I find it, I'll share the reward with you," Mia said.

Trevor had his head inside the cabinet with the glasses, and Dale and Karen were whispering on the couch, Dale picking her split ends, so it was only Mia who heard. A sound came from upstairs, something falling or things being brushed by Bo Jangles' tail. Mia stopped.

"Did you hear a noise upstairs?" she asked.

"Nope," said Trevor, ferreting among the pot plants. Dale and Karen were talking about 'Jason Lipschitz who invited Dezi Stein to the matric dance when Lisa Nathan was sure he would ask her'.

Curiosity pushed Mia to the bottom of the stairwell. From upstairs she heard a rustle. She climbed the stairs slowly, her ears pricked. At the top of the landing, she held her breath. The door to her parents' room was half closed. She peeked through the crack of the door where it was joined at the hinges, and peered in. There was a shuffling, a busyness coming from within. A streetchild, like those you always saw begging, was at her mother's dressing table—barefoot, emptying the contents of Fran's drawer into a plastic Checkers packet.

Just then, from downstairs, Mia heard, "I found it." Trevor's victory. She turned slowly and made her way down the stairs. When she got back to the dining room, Zaide Yankel was giving Trevor two rand for having found the *Afikoman*.

"It was behind the TV," Trevor said to Mia.

"Come here, Mia. You too will get somethink," her Zaide said, motioning towards her with a crooked hand. "And somethink for your friend too."

"There's someone upstairs," Mia said.

"What do you mean?" Fran asked.

"I saw someone upstairs."

"A black?" Fran asked.

"Ja. And he's taking your things, Mom," Mia said.

"Oh my God," Fran panicked, clasping her face.

"Ja," Mia said. "But he's small."

"Has he got a gun?" Issey asked.

"I don't think so." Mia shrugged her shoulders. Asher was reclining in his chair, rolling a cigarillo.

"I'll sort this out," Shmooley said. "Issey, have you got a gun or a golf club or something?"

"Cool, Dad, can I come watch?" Trevor asked.

"You stay right here, with your mother and sisters."

"I'm calling the police," Fran announced, leaving the table, dropping her serviette on the carpet.

"He must have come in through the front door," Selma mused aloud, to no-one in particular.

In a moment the whole table emptied, except for Zaide Yankel who continued to eat his fruit salad. Selma waited a moment, grabbed a *teigel* from the plate and pushed it quickly into her mouth, before joining the others. Issey and Shmooley were up the stairs, Shmooley first, holding a golf club in one hand and a bread knife in the other. Issey was behind him, with a tennis racket. There were a few moments of silence, and then from upstairs came a yelp, followed by shouting. "You bloody little thief," (Shmooley). "What the hell do you think you're doing?" (Issey). Fran stood at the phone with Selma on one side, and Dale and Karen on the other. Trevor was halfway up the stairs, unable to contain his curiosity.

"Mia, go close the front door immediately," Fran ordered, dialling. She held the phone tightly with both hands, as if it might wriggle from her grasp. "Typical—no answer when you need them," she muttered.

The men came down the stairs noisily, trundling a small

black child in front of them—a hand on each shoulder.

"Looks like we've got a little visitor," Issey said, holding the Checkers packet in his other hand.

The boy stood shrunken under their large hands. His bare feet were white with calluses and there was an open gash on one of his calves. It looked infected. He did not look up at the crowd of white eyes.

"Who taught you to be a thief?" Uncle Shmooley said, clipping the boy on the side of the face, so that he held up both his hands and whimpered, *"Jammer baasie, jammer."**

"Ja, you'll be good and sorry when the police get here," Uncle Shmooley said.

"Look Frannie, he was walking off with Mia's moneybox and half your jewellery," Issey said, shaking the packet at her. "I told you not to keep it in those drawers. You need to lock it away."

Fran, still hanging on for the police said, "I didn't tell you to leave the front door wide open so that any little *tsotsi*† could just waltz in and help himself to our things, did I?"

"Do you speak English?" Issey asked, nudging the child in the back.

The boy squirmed and shook his head.

"He's playing dumb—typical," said Uncle Shmooley. "Well, boy, you better find your tongue, or else you're in big trouble."

"He's in big trouble either way," Issey said.

"Try the Flying Squad," Selma suggested, trying to be helpful. Several *teigel* crumbs clung to the side of her mouth.

"This *is* the Flying Squad's number," Fran clipped back.

"Right," Selma mumbled.

The noise in the entrance hall caused Sarafina to come to the kitchen door and watch.

"Sarafina, look who we found trying to steal Fran's jewellery," Issey said.

* 'Sorry, master, sorry,' in Afrikaans.
† slang word for 'thief.'

Joanne Fedler

Sarafina leaned against the frame of the kitchen door, wearing Fran's old *takkies** with her shoelaces undone. She shook her head.

"Ask him what his name is," Uncle Shmooley said.

Sarafina's face darkened around the eyes.

"Go on, ask him," he repeated.

Sarafina said something in Zulu which sounded longer than just 'What's your name'. The boy mumbled something back.

"What did he say?" Issey asked.

"He said his name is Ben."

"Ben my arse!" Shmooley laughed. "What's his real name? His surname?"

Sarafina tried again. This time the boy just shrugged. He did not look up at her, nor at the others.

"He doesn't know," Sarafina said, turning to go to the diningroom to clear away some dishes.

"Hello. Yes, at last. Look, we've just had a burglary. Luckily we've caught the intruder. We're at 48 Komatie Road, Emmarentia..." Fran's voice trailed off. "Please don't be long, we're in the middle of a dinner party... Yes, fine, we're waiting…"

Mia watched the boy. He was so small next to her big father and uncle. His dirty little black fingers had been all over her moneybox. He was skinny, making his elbows and knees seem like swollen knots in the cricks of his arms and legs.

"Well, they'll be here in ten minutes," Fran said, clicking the receiver down. "In the meantime, he'll just have to wait in the kitchen."

Zaide Yankel roused himself from the table and stood in the doorway to the dining room with a napkin flowing from his neckline to which bits of chopped herring and red horseradish stuck.

* South African slang for 'trainers.'

"What will you do with this child?" he asked.

"We'll hand him over to the police when they get here," Fran said. "Sarafina," she called.

Sarafina came back holding dirty dishes. She had a set expression on her face, the kind she wore when Fran shouted at her.

"Keep him in the laundry with you, and just watch him. The police will be here soon," Fran said.

Uncle Shmooley poked the boy in the back, urging him towards the kitchen, wagging his finger at him, *"Wena—*" you don't try any funny business here, you hear me?"

"But he's just a child—a little boy," Zaide Yankel said. "What will the police do with him?"

"Pop, what are we supposed to do? Send him out the same front door he came into—let him back on the streets to go rob the next house?"

The old man shrugged and put his hand to his head.

"The police, they don't like blacks, that's for sure. They killed hundreds of children, little children, in the township last year. Didn't you see all this on the news? Children what wanted a better education. Like the Nazi's—they opened fire on innocent children." He shook with the emotion of his telling.

Suddenly silence descended on the troupe gathered in the entrance hall.

"He is just a child," Selma agreed quietly.

Uncle Shmooley's anger broke the reverie. "So what? Are you gonna send this kid back to his business? And when the Joffes phone us tomorrow and tell us they were robbed out of house and home, we can tell them to thank us for putting this little thief back on the streets. He'll never learn if we let him go!"

---

* 'you,' in Sotho.

"Just remember," Zaide Yankel said, "The police don't like blacks and they don't like Jews. This Verwoerd, before he was assassinated—and we can be very grateful for that—was the biggest anti-Semite, what didn't want to let the Jews from Germany into South Africa. If you send this boy to the police, you send him like a Jew back to Germany. That is all I have to say about this matter," he said.

"They can be brutal," Issey said. "I mean it wasn't really necessary to kill those kids. They could have dispersed them peacefully."

"Have you ever seen a hoard of hysterical blacks marching down the road?" Uncle Shmooley said. "A bunch of savages. The cops did what they had to. And what the hell has that got to do with this little *tsotsi*. He's not a kid—he's a gangster. He does this for a living. If you don't stop it in its tracks, he'll grow up into a thug, a rapist. He's got to learn now that wrong is wrong."

Issey glanced at his daughter. The country was changing. He needed to fortify his home and protect his woman and child against hurt.

"Pop, with all due respect, I can't argue with Shmooley. Your analogy with Jews isn't accurate. Jews don't steal. What happened in Soweto was politics. This is theft. The fact that he's black is neither here nor there. If the police are a bunch of thugs, then it's this kid's bad luck. The cops are here to protect the decent person. We don't have an option. Now let's just get back to the *Seder* and wait for the police to arrive," he said, gesturing to everyone to go back into the dining room.

Mia did not go back into the dining room, but slipped into the kitchen. The boy was on Sarafina's stool in the laundry, sitting on his hands, dry-eyed and tight-lipped. Sarafina was talking to him in her language and clicking her tongue at him.

"What you saying, Fina?" Mia asked.

Sarafina did not answer immediately, just shook her head at the skinny boy on the stool without shoes. "What, Fina?"

"I ask him where is his parents, but she say she have no parent."

No parents? Mia felt something soft and pitying wash over her.

"Where does he sleep, Fina?" Sarafina shrugged. "Doesn't he have a home? A place for his stories?"

"Ag, Mia, *wena*. He have no money," Sarafina said crossly, and turned away to wash the dishes at the sink.

Mia stood a little way from the boy, curling her finger in her hair. His hair was dirty and he smelt of wee. The gash on his leg oozed puss. It was disgusting. Mia turned and went to the fridge. In it she found an apple and she marched back to the boy, holding the apple out at him. He still did not look at her. Mia gestured again, pushing the apple closer. He peered up at Sarafina, who said something in Zulu to him. He shuffled on the stool to release one of his hands from under his bottom and reached out for the apple.

"You shouldn't have taken my piggy bank," Mia said.

The little hand snatched the apple from hers, stuffed it into the pocket of his shorts, and nudged its way back under his bottom.

"Miaaaaa, where are you?" Fran's voice called from the diningroom.

Mia turned to leave, but not before looking at her unlikely visitor and wondering whether he was a firstborn.

The police arrived forty-five minutes later, which was a lot quicker than the previous time. The last time it had taken them two hours to arrive, when one of Sarafina's boyfriends had got drunk and flayed her with a *sjambok*.* In the meantime, Issey, in his singular act of heroism, had taken an old golf club from the storeroom, stormed into the backroom and threatened the boyfriend, who had fled down the street in nothing but his underwear.

* whip made of wood, leather and rubber.

The two cops had asked to see Sarafina's pass book before they questioned her, as she sat crying in the kitchen. They had asked her questions in Afrikaans and she had shrugged her shoulders to show she did not understand, so they had translated into broken English. When they heard that the assailant was her boyfriend, they nodded smugly and left, telling Fran and Issey that they should tell Sarafina that if the boyfriend ever came back, they would fire her.

"That's the only way they'll ever learn," the cop had said.

This time Issey was relieved to see that one of the cops was black. Sergeant Mazibuko, and his partner, Lieutenant Kotze— young, Afrikaans, cold blue eyes.

"Amazing how many calls we get on a night like tonight," the white cop said.

Issey collected the boy from the kitchen and marched him out in front of him. The boy moved sluggishly, his eyes pinned to the ground. His bony limbs trembled.

"Listen," Fran said, "he's just a child. You will, I mean, you'll just take him in and do the regular procedures with him, won't you?"

"Of course, Lady," Lieutenant Kotze said. "What do you think we'll do with him?"

"Well, it's silly really, but we were afraid that maybe these kids get beaten up or something. We've read things in the newspapers."

"Not to worry," he said, "I got better things to do with my time than beat up a kid," he said, smiling. "Hey, *kaffirtjie*,"* he said, poking the boy in the shoulders. Sergeant Mazibuko said nothing.

"And what's in your pockets?" he said.

The boy remained motionless. The cop pointed at the bulging pocket of his shorts. "Empty them," he said, gesturing for the boy to give him what was in his pocket.

---

* 'little kaffir,' in Afrikaans.

Mia's heart stood still.

The boy dug his hand into his pocket and removed the apple.

"Stealing fruit, hey?" the cop said. He took the apple from the boy and handed it to Fran.

Mia swallowed hard. And for the first time, the boy's eyes peered at Mia from under the hoods of his eyelids. But God did not move her lips to stop the sacrifice. Mia's lips stayed sealed though the words in her wanted to speak out loud.

"Oh, he can keep the apple," Fran said. "If he's hungry."

"No, no, no," the cop said. "These kids don't need anything. They're parasites, they live off society. Don't give him anything."

"Listen younk man," Zaide Yankel said, clearing his throat. "Tonight the Jewish people celebrate freedom—liberation from slavery. This child has come into this house in a moment of freedom. The Egyptians, who enslaved the Jews, had many plagues fall upon them by the hand of God. Do not," he said, waving his finger at them, "do not lay your fingers on this child. He is a boy without freedom."

The two cops looked at each other and the white cop's lips curled in a smirk.

"We just doing our job, Sir," the white cop said. "You did the right thing by calling us."

They turned to leave through the door. They opened the back of the van and the boy climbed in tiredly with old limbs, scraping the gash on his calf as he pulled himself up, and wincing. The black cop locked the door behind him.

As the van pulled out of the driveway, the boy turned to face Mia and looked her full in the face with his hollow yellow eyes.

Back inside, Mia found Grace sitting alone at the table. "You've missed all the excitement," she said. "Where were you?"

"In...the toilet."

"A thief came in and tried to steal my piggy bank and my mom's jewellery."

Grace didn't look up at Mia, but nodded her head and picked at her nails. Her eyes were red and watery.

"Don't be upset," Mia consoled. "They promised they wouldn't hurt him."

Everyone came back in and sat around the Pesach table but the jubilance of the past few hours had slipped through the open door. No-one felt like singing the freedom songs. Not even *Chad Gad Ya,*[*] about the goat that was bought for two *zuzzim*. Mia sat paging the *Haggadah* in her fingers, irritated with Grace. Grace was silent. Sarafina took the dishes off sullenly, Zaide Yankel muttered that he was tired, Issey was bad-tempered, Shmooley self-satisfied, Fran busy, Selma fidgety, the children bored. Only Asher had a smile. Mia felt the weight of the apple inside her like a stone. As if something had come into the house and touched them all—an evil of a kind, in which each of them was boldly imprinted.

[*] one of the songs sung on Passover.

farloren, ongevoren:

lost;
perished or destroyed, especially morally or spiritually;
having gone astray;
to be forgotten by, unknown to the world

She could not wait to take her clothes off. Thirty-nine days at sea had not been kind to the garments Rochel had so lovingly sewed for her to keep her body from the corroding salt spray and a month without soap and water for washing. But more than the itch from the dirt, it was the heat that swelled her, so that she stripped down to her petticoat, there, at the dock, while Yankel tried to cover her with his jacket, berating, but lovingly, "Modesty, Maya, in public, we are."

Together, they boarded a train from Cape Town to Johannesburg. It was a gruelling eighteen hours during which Maya sat stone-faced while Yankel spoke without pausing for a breath about the new sights and adventures that awaited her in Africa. They passed through the oven of the Karoo, while Yankel wiped her brow, her arms, her upper lip, wet with moisture, and intermittently pointed out the barrenness of the land, almost like a desert. But there were people— Hottentots—who survived in this extreme heat, only wearing small loin cloths, like Adam and Eve wore in the Garden of Eden. He was taking English classes and had been attending night classes at the Jewish government school in Doornfontein. This he did after a long day's work. His English had come on. "How do you do?" he said to her in his best

English. "How *do* you do?' That is how they say it."

She nodded, without smiling. Even words, her beloved companions, sat in her mouth uncomfortably like bacon on the tongue of a Jew in a place where she could not understand the sounds people made from their mouths and those she spoke were foreign and clumsy.

Her strange demeanour he put down to exhaustion. And what did they call it? Culture Shock. It had taken him a few weeks himself to adjust to the new climate, strange accents and people of Africa. Perhaps she too might consider taking English classes. He would save up money so she could attend. She shrugged.

She asked him no questions. He opened his leather satchel and produced six kosher sausages wrapped in brown paper, a loaf of crusty bread and—the greatest surprise of all—a handful of summer fruit—a nectarine, a peach and a plum. He placed these in her lap.

"Taste, taste, Mayala. Such fruit you have never tasted."

She examined these with interest, inspecting each in turn, for the range of colours mottled into their skins. She took a bite of the peach and gasped at the sweetness. She looked at him with kindness.

"You shall not forget about the widow, shall you?" she said, more than asked.

"Of course not," Yankel patted her hand.

***

The old man sat on the bench next to the counter holding a folded hat in his hands. Yankel approached him with uncertain gratitude.

"Ah, I believe it is you who brought her here," he gestured to the police desk behind him.

"Yes *baas*,"* the old man said in a gravelly voice. In his hands, the hat was being twisted around and around.

"I tenk you with all my heart," he said. Maya's soft weeping could be heard from the corner where she sat on a wooden bench. Yankel felt a terror stalking inside him. He had given her such clear instructions. Get off the bus at Rissik Street, walk for three and a half blocks, turn left, and it was the second building, third floor. With exactly the right change for the bus in her hand. She was due back at four forty-five. When she had not come back from her English lesson by five, he had paced up and down. By five fifteen, he had his prayer book out and was reciting the *Shema Yisroel*, interspersed with his own, "Please let no harm come to her". By five thirty, he was sweating with panic. He was on a bus to town by five forty-five, and was standing outside the building, locked and dark, by six thirty. The sound of his heart beating was so loud inside his head, he could not hear the voices of the people passing by. By seven thirty he was back home pressing a piece of toilet paper against his cheek which had started to bleed from his picking at an ingrown hair. At five past eight the telephone rang and he urinated in his trousers at the sound of the shrill ring. It still took him time to understand the Afrikaans accent, for the pieces to fall into place. It was the Parkview Police Station— Constable Van Tonder. They had his wife. She had been brought in by a *kaffir*. Apparently she had gotten off at the wrong stop and was there, ready to be collected. He had bolted for the door, not changing his soiled trousers in the rush.

"The madam she be okay?" the old man nodded towards Maya.

"Ja, ja. Just confused," Yankel said, quietly.

The old man raised his eyes to meet those of Yankel. Something unfinished stretched out between them.

* 'boss' in Afrikaans.

"You can go now, John," Constable Van Tonder said from behind the counter.

The old man did not move. Yankel looked at him expectantly. "Tenk you," he said again, as if to seal his appreciation. Still the old man made no motion.

"You heard him, John. Go. *Voetsek,** get out of here."

Yankel turned towards the young policeman, with an imploring look.

"Just bugger off now, you're making a nuisance of yourself." And to Yankel he said, "He wants money, but just ignore it."

Slowly, the old man unfurled his fingers and, almost in slow motion, straightened out his hat. It had a frayed seam. He bent his head to meet his hands and pulled the hat down over his white peppercorn hair, first straightening it back to front and then left to right. Once again he looked at Yankel and bowed his head. Then he reached for a walking stick balancing against the wall, which had a knob of old newspapers tied together with rubber bands over the top to create a handle. He placed it in front of him and slowly lifted himself out of the seat.

He shuffled past Yankel and, as he passed by Maya, he stopped. She raised her eyes to meet his and put her hand on top of his gnarled fingers, clasping the walking stick.

"*Az dos harts iz laidik iz der moi'ech oich laidik.*"†

The old man stood there with Maya's hand on his.

"Tell him tenk you," Yankel said to Maya. "That is how they say it in English. English. We speak English now. Say 'tenk you'. If he had not found you, where should you be now? Wanderink around in the dark? Tell him tenk you."

Maya did not look at Yankel. "*A dank,*"*** she said softly.

Suddenly Yankel felt the sweat he had released in anxiety over the past few hours, could smell the urine from his trousers, and felt a bubbling rage that only a man humiliated in

* 'Get lost,' in Afrikaans.
† 'When the heart is empty, so is the brain', a Yiddish saying.
** 'thank you' in Yiddish.

the eyes of another man could feel. "Tenk you," he hissed to Maya. "Tell him tenk you."

Maya did not raise her eyes to look at her husband. English. What was English? A mirage of sounds, indecipherable with meanings she could not reach. Words with too many different meanings, all aswirl in her mind, making her giddy. She had not consented to this loss. Everything had been sacrificed. Every sensation, every taste, every sound, every moment that had ever coursed through her body, she had given up in the passage from there to here. But to lose even a world of meaning, where words, her most beloved treasures, could no longer offer comfort—that was more than a person could survive. She had not consented to this loss.

The old man shuffled past the angry young man smelling of a latrine and left the crazy young madam behind him.

"*Sala kahle,*"* he said, turning back and tipping his hat at her.

★★★

There were many mornings when she encountered on the bus a woman, her own age, sitting at the window in the second last row. She always clutched her handbag to her belly, though the strap was wound around her right shoulder. In the clam of her left hand she held a handkerchief, and her face was streaked with grey from the tears she let spill from her eyes. Tears in public—they do not invite a friendly inquiry, 'Are you alright?' Such tears carry with them a warning, 'Do not come close. My pain is so large that I do not care that I am crying and you are seeing. Stay where you are.' And so, on these many mornings when Maya encountered this woman on the bus at her same

---

* 'Remain well,' in Zulu, a farewell greeting.

spot each day, she held back from reaching out with a 'Good morning'. She certainly did not dare to put a hand on her shoulder, a gesture of knowing, of reaching, to comfort this woman in her nameless enduring pain, daily visible. People looked away, as public tears require, buried themselves in their newspapers, paperbacks, conversations or thoughts.

Sometimes she saw this same woman sitting in the third row in the women's section in the synagogue on a *Shabbat* morning. Maya would pick a seat several rows away and steal a glance at her every now and then, and then look away, never daring a smile or even a catching of the eye. She began to catch glimpses of this woman in the queue at the bank, at the checkout counter at Pick 'n' Pay, even on a bench at the Emmarentia Dam. There she would be, clutching her handbag, looking out to a place beyond. Weeping.

Maya was not moved by intrigue, godforbid curiosity. She had no use for gossip, no interest in stories. For a woman crying in public is no mystery. There is nothing strange, nothing that spurs the mind to wondering. It is all the life running through her veins going to waste. It is the unmet longing, the dreams she dreamed as a girl, that she took as promises, but that reveal themselves now as delusions. It is what spills from her spirit, squashed too tight in her life, like the ugly sister's feet in Cinderella's glass slipper. A woman crying in public cries for the loss of what was once possible, when the world charmed her with whispers of something she sensed in her dreams and felt in the chambers of her destiny.

And Maya came to recognize that it was not a private condition, not an exclusive birthright, but the situation of all womanly creatures, locked into places from which they could not fly away.

This stranger she passed, sometimes daily, gave her comfort that she was not alone.

And it took several years before she caught her breath, in a gasp of surprise, in recognizing that woman. *Why, it is I.*

The playground, King Solomon School,
August 1977

When the bell for break rang, Mia moved to Grace's side and stayed there like a guide dog. Grace's eyes were soft, like seeds soaked in water, and she had bitten her nails until they bled. She still clutched the note explaining her lateness in her hand, like a newborn baby who grabs hold of your finger and forgets to let go. Together they walked without speaking to their spot behind art class where the jasmine grew and where no-one ever went, and only when they sat down, did Mia ask.

"What happened?"

Grace tore at the shreds of her fingernails with her hands.

"Rinky," she said.

"What?"

Mia waited. Grace did not look up. Her head hung down and she tormented her fingers. Mia tried to feel the shape of the thing that needed to be said, but the sound of her heart gadoofing in her chest stole the silence. The last time Aunty Rinky had picked them up from school, she had driven them to the Zoo Lake where they had taken a little rowboat out into the middle of the lake. There, on a Thursday afternoon, with the lake deserted, except for some ducks and swans in a huddle on the far side and a couple of vagrants sleeping on the park benches, she had stood up in the middle of the boat, causing it to rock from side to side, and with a whoop of delight, had pulled up her blouse and bared her naked titties to the sun. Both Mia and Grace had yelled, "Stoppit! What are you doing? Some-one will see!" but Rinky had laughed until the tears streamed down her face.

Grace was really cross about it, though Mia had thought it was almost as good as seeing her eat a shongolulu. She had very nice titties.

"That felt so fucking good!" Rinky had said. "Sorry, shouldn't say 'fucking' in front of you. Your mom will kill me," she had said to Grace.

"We're not kids, you know," Grace had said. "I say 'fucking' all the time."

To make it up to them, Rinky had bought them each a Coke and a packet of Simba chips, and had made them 'swear on the sisterhood' that they'd never tell Grace's mom.

For a moment, as she sat there, Mia thought maybe Grace had told her mom about the titties incident on the Zoo Lake, but all the knowing inside her had knotted into a ball of fear. Whatever Grace was about to tell her was more serious than a shongolulu eaten or bared nipples.

"She's…in hospital." Grace stopped. Her thumb was bleeding, so she put it in her mouth. Mia waited. Grace still did not look up and Mia could not see her eyes. "They were in Hillbrow, at a club last night, and a man took her in his car, and hurt her. You know, raped her."

The feeling in her belly spread through her body and Mia felt a terror like in her twirly dream. "Raped her? What do you mean?"

"Raped her, Mia. Don't you know what rape is?" Mia kept still, a blinding ache in her chest. "It's when you say no, but a man fucks you anyway," Graces' voice was harsh and bitter.

"Why would someone do that to her?"

Grace shrugged. She lifted her head up and looked at Mia. "That's a dumb question."

Mia wanted to hold the sadness in her friend, but did not know how.

"My mom says maybe because she was holding hands with her girlfriend—you know she's a lesbian?"

Mia nodded. She had heard Grace use the word before,

244 Joanne Fedler

laughingly, about her Aunt Rinky.

They sat with the weight of Grace's news between them.

"Because they held hands? But we hold hands."

"But we're not lesbians, are we?" Grace said harshly. And then, "Maybe we shouldn't hold hands anymore."

A strange breathlessness caught in Mia's throat. It was a winded feeling—the kind you get when you hear about something evil out there, like the story of the flood or the sacrifice. Things that don't make sense, but are there to be endured nonetheless. Mia swallowed hard, she felt tears prick at the corners of her eyes. On the field some boys were playing basketball, shouting orders to one another. Girls sat in pairs alongside, watching.

"One day," Mia said, "we'll be so big and so strong that no boys will be able to hurt us."

Grace didn't answer for a while. And then she said, "I want to be like Anneline Kriel. Miss World. Then everyone thinks you're special and everyone wants to marry you. That's what I want. Then I won't wish I had never been born."

They sat quiet for a time.

"I'm glad you were born," Mia said. Grace did not smile or answer.

"Will Rinky be alright?" Mia asked.

"What do you mean?"

"Will all her parts still work okay?"

Grace looked at Mia. "Are you stupid or something, Mia?"

Mia sighed. "I'm sorry, what did I say wrong?"

"Everything!"

Mia looked down at her hands, a swelling ache inside her. "One day, we won't be scared anymore. And no-one will be able to hurt us."

Grace laughed bitterly.

The bell rang again. They got to their feet slowly, like two old people after a life of hardship. They walked back to class, Grace with her arms tightly around her waist and Mia with hers at her side, the distance between them now visible.

The front door, moving into the lounge,
October 1977

At first it looked like a smear of grease. When Mia opened the door to let him in, she noticed the ridge of dark brown above his right eye. But when she reached up to touch it with her hands, he pulled away from her. Too late. She had already felt its crustiness and knew it was a scab. And when she looked up into his face, she noticed a bruise on his forehead.

"What happened, Asher?" she asked.

"A little trouble on the weekend," he said, bending to kiss her. "Nothing very serious. Such curiosity, can a man come in?"

Mia blocked his entry into the house. For a moment she did not budge. Asher's eyes, which usually stayed in one place, were dancing like gypsies around a night fire. He ruffled her hair, but still she didn't move. She was his drawbridge into the house. She slowly gave way.

Fran appeared from the kitchen, breathless and smiling, then stopped. "Are you alright?" She moved up close to Asher, touched the bruise above his eye tenderly. "Can I get you something?"

"It's nothing to worry about. I got mugged in 'illbrow a few nights ago, that's all. They got off worse than me, I promise you." Asher laughed. He removed his denim jacket and hung it on the hook at the front door.

"Oh my God, you were mugged!" Fran exclaimed. "Jesus Christ—what is going on in this place? Sit down and let me make you a drink. Issey..." Fran called into the studio.

Issey did not emerge from his studio. His door remained shut. He was working very hard on a portrait of Elvis Presley. What a loss. That's what fame and fortune did—a drug overdose. What a waste of a life. He was sure to be able to sell it to someone. The portrait of Mrs Vorster stood facing the wall in the corner of his studio. Ah, it had just been bad luck. Shmooley said it was rank anti-Semitism. But he said that when someone cut him off in the traffic. Who could know? An uneasiness had begun to stir in Issey, which was somehow tied to Fran's happiness. The sunnier she became, the harder it was for him to paint. He sometimes even heard her humming to herself. It gnawed away at him. He found it hard to concentrate. He sat for hours in his closed studio, examining the little cloth, folding it this way and that. He couldn't remember when last Mia had sorted out his Kolinskys or told him one of her dreams. She was slipping from him. It was as if all the women in his household were slowing moving towards a lightness and jubilance for which he was not responsible. He was no longer the one who made things right. The pulse in his fingertips had become duller and duller, and a fear began to rattle in him that someday he would return to his studio and the magic in his fingers would have left him finally, utterly.

Fran's voice broke his reverie. It was shrill with alarm. He needed to pull himself together. He turned out the light in his studio, closed the door and joined the others in the lounge where he greeted Asher with a civil nod.

When Asher was comfortably seated, a Scotch in his hand, Mia at his side, he exhaled a long sigh. On Saturday night, he had been walking back to his flat with his groceries in his arms, when two blacks jumped out of an alley and held a knife to his throat. Asher held his forefinger at his neck. They demanded his money, his silver lighter. But before they had a chance, he grabbed a bottle from his parcel and smashed it over the head of the one. The other got such a fright that he ran away.

"So they took nothing of yours?" Fran asked eagerly.

"Nothing—what is mine, is mine. This lighter belongs to me. I must 'old on to what is mine."

"What happened to the guy you hit?" Issey asked.

Asher shrugged. "I don't know and I don't care. I leave 'im lying there. You can 'ave no mercy for people who will take what is yours."

"Well, do you know if you killed him?" Issey half-laughed.

"I don't know. I think 'e was okay." Turning to Mia, he said, "Always fight for what is yours. Your 'eart, your land, your freedom. Don't let anyone take this from you. I fight in three wars in Israel because the Arabs don't understand this is my land. The black man in this country also will fight for what is 'is. You cannot take what is somebody else's. This is what I believe."

"Did you report it to the police?" Fran asked.

"This is the most unbelievable thing of all. The other man who run away, 'e calls a policeman to tell him that *I* attacked '*im*. So the police come after me and arrest me. Last night, I spent in 'illbrow police station."

"That's outrageous!" Fran exclaimed.

Mia felt her heart constrict. As if the world was conspiring to take Asher from her.

"Do you need a lawyer?" Issey asked. "Shmooley's got contacts if you need someone."

"No!" Asher said emphatically. "I can sort this out by myself. I just tell you, not to worry you, but so that you know if I don't come every night, that I am sorting this business out."

"Are you sure you don't need a lawyer?" Fran asked.

He bent to take her hand in his, looking her deep in the eyes. "Please don't worry so much. Let us forget about this and just enjoy tonight."

Fran agreed and went to the kitchen to check on dinner, for which Asher would naturally stay.

For the first time, Mia asked to be excused from dinner. She had a terrible tummy ache.

tsu benken:

to long for:
have a yearning desire;
craving, lust for (see hunger)

Children survive their parents' atrocities. Beatings, a mother's hand that cannot take away the venom of hunger, a father's cries... Kovno was not a child's playground. A child can survive—even being an orphan. There are worse things. Like a mother's shame. Like the *loshen horah** of neighbours gossiping should they find out the truth of what made her life go on for five years after Maya left.

She knew her boy would be tended for. Jews do not leave their own to die. She knew the neighbours would take pity on him, that pity begets generosity. From her, what did he get? Since the day he was handed to her by the woodcutter's wife who doubled up as a midwife and she looked at his old man's face contorted in a cry, she knew with a certainty as sharp as despair that she could not take hunger from him, nor stop the icy morning air from biting his face, nor the smallpox from ravaging his body. No one had told her that to birth a child was to make a problem for oneself too big to solve. She was a simple seamstress. Her hands were made for fixing, making whole, creating beauty. She could not fix Kovno, nor make it beautiful for her child. His life was heavier for her to hold than her own.

And when their home got destroyed in the fire perhaps it

---

* Hebrew for 'gossip', or literally 'evil tongue.'

would have been easier had they burned with the few possessions they owned. But there was Maya. Her pull was stronger than the pull of dying. In the years they shared before she left Kovno, Rochel understood why people thought living was something good to do. She even loved the boy. She taught him to laugh. She thought maybe he would know a place of sunshine. And when Maya left, the boy was her burden. Rochel lived in hope for all those years, that Yankel would bring them to the new land of sunshine and gold. Can you guess how long that is in days? Meals? Pinpricks? Perhaps tears? She spoke to Maya every night, the moon her witness. She howled for her like, perhaps, a wolf. For she had never heard a wolf wail.

Time passed, of that she could be sure, for her boy stood at her hipbone, where once he was only at her knee. Letters arrived and she made the journey to the outskirts of the village, where Shlomi the Disgraced *Chazan* always welcomed her and read to her from the crinkled folds of the pages. Sometimes there were money orders, which she could cash to buy a little pot of sugar or some chicken necks for a soup.

Waiting is only bearable while the heart goes on. But soon there was talk in the market square that laws had been passed. For Sud Afrika, it was not so easy to get a visa. Like everywhere else in the world, Africa was closing her doors to Jews. And all around, panic was brewing as Germany's new leader and his terrifying propaganda was gaining strength. In such times, it was not possible to believe that the Promised Land lay just beyond the horizon. God led Moses to the threshold of the land of Canaan, but it was not Moses who led the Jewish people into the land of milk and honey. He only got to glimpse it from afar.

Taking life is easy. It is giving life that is hard. From the time her boy raged to be set free from her womb, bit her nipples until they bled red into white, coughed until his eyes watered, and held onto her hand with a need she could never promise to fulfil, it was only pain. She waited to hear him speak, saw the sickness in him dwindle and prayed for the kindness of neighbours who might find in him a pair of hands to work, and thus feed his mouth. As for her, what pain could there be in ending pain?

Finally, Rochel felt herself get to the end of her life. It was just like coming to the end of a thread or a ribbon. Suddenly, there it was. No matter that one still needed an inch or two, or even a foot to finish. The ribbon can only be as long as it is. And sometimes one had to make the garment fit the ribbon, not the other way around. That is how it came to her that morning. There was no more of her life that she could live.

And so that moment is not such a production or a clattering of the heavens. It is a small quiet seamstress standing to look out the window, patting down her skirts before she rummages through her sewing box to find a sufficiently long piece of sturdy cloth. It is her not finding a piece long enough, and her carefully sewing two, three, four pieces together, double-stitching, overstitching and re-stitching, making certain of their firmness. It is her winding the cloths around her neck in the manner of a scarf and opening the door, taking unhurried footsteps through the snow to the shed, because she, not mad nor deranged, does not want her boy to find her in a room in which perhaps he might still have to sleep some nights and she still cares that he may sleep. It is the loosening of her hair from its head cloth, so that the brown tresses, stiff and unwashed for many a week, fall to cover her eyes that do not need much more of their seeing. It is the creak of the shed door and the search for a chair, a ladder, a bucket. It is the rancid comforting smell of a goat and the finding of an enamel bucket used for milking, and it is being glad for the finding, as one might be for finding something lost. And then it is the unwinding of the scarf, the patting (for the last time) of the goat on its rough head. It is the foot placing itself on the bucket, losing its balance, for perhaps one has never noticed that the bottom of an enamel bucket is curved, not flat. And it is the trying again and the balancing of both feet as the arms stretch to the beam above, where the scarf is wound. It is the arms hanging onto the scarf to test that it will hold the body and it is the tying of a knot around the neck. It is the closing of the eyes, and then it is the feet, tiptoeing on the bucket, nudging the bucket to fall, so that the body can do what it does all by itself when left to hang.

Joanne Fedler

The playground, King Solomon School,
November 1977

"So, you wanna get fixed up?" Andrew asked. Mia knew that there could only be two reasons why Grace's brother wanted to get fixed up with her: either because she was one of the five standard six girls who wore a bra, or because he still thought that Mia was Grace's best friend. Grace, who was found kneeling in cubicle G with Stanley Lipschitz's penis in her mouth, had been giving blowjobs for 50 cents in the boys' toilets at break. Since then, a teacher was put on duty every break in the boy's toilets, putting an end to the smoking and the magazines that were being passed around there. Everyone blamed Grace. Stanley Lipschitz became something of a hero and the ramp girls (who were always chosen to be in the school fashion show), Melissa, Belinda and Michelle, all wanted to get fixed up with him. 'Silly slut, ha ha ha,' people laughed. Grace deserved all she got—that none of the girls wanted to be friendly with her anymore and whispered in huddles near the tuckshop and laughed when she walked past. That her parents were called in by Mr Seligman and that she had to go three times a week to the social worker at the school. Mia could feel the anger roping inside her. The laughter was shrill and ugly, but Mia just lowered her head. Grace was a liar after all.

"No thanks, Andrew," Mia said.

"What, you only like black boys now?" he snickered.

"Bugger off," she said, as he turned his hands in his pockets, a formal gesture of nonchalance. Andrew walked off in the direction of the rugby field and, from the corner of her eye,

Mia caught a glimpse of Grace walking across the field. Mia turned the other away.

Zachariah did not talk much in class. He never volunteered and only spoke when the teacher asked him specifically. He was very well behaved. His eyes did not tell stories and never danced to the corners, or down, or away, somewhere. They stayed fixed, firm, not like the moon that moved in the sky.

It was at the time when Issey had bought a television and Michael De Morgan read the news every night, and Mia had a crush on Eckhard Rabie in *The Villagers*, that Sipho Zikalala applied to King Solomon School to have his son, Zachariah, enrolled there. Sipho was a relation of the King of Swaziland, who recently moved to Soweto where he built a mansion. He wanted the best education for his son and was prepared to accept the terms of enrolment at King Solomon—that his child should learn Hebrew, the language of the Bible.

The issue plunged the Board of Deputies of the school into uncharted waters and a special meeting of all parents was held to discuss the problem. After many months of protracted debates, it was finally agreed, and all parents were informed in a memorandum sent home, that as long as parents could pay the high fees of the private school, and each child learned Hebrew, and that the school remained predominantly Jewish, there could, in principle, be no objection to the enrolment of Zachariah Zikalala.

There was much excitement the day Zachariah was brought to school in a chauffeur-driven BMW, and many of the children came to greet and welcome him. He stood, impeccably dressed in the King Solomon uniform, a small *yarmulka** on his head, but without clips, for his short hair

---

* Jewish head–covering.

could not hold the clips. And for some reason, he was much taller and bigger than all the standard four boys—almost as tall as Mia.

"Now, don't everyone stand around examining him like he's an animal in the zoo," Mrs Berkowitz said.

Mia smiled at him, but Zachariah, who had a name like a song, lowered his eyes and bent down to rub some dust off his shiny shoes.

Mia had wondered, looking down at his school shorts one day, whether he had to be specially circumcised to come to King Solomon, but she knew this was not a question she could ask. She wanted to be near him for his quiet ways, his interesting lunches of cold *pap* and gravy, which he ate with his fingers and his unroaming eyes.

"Do you mind being the only black at the school?" she asked one day.

He smiled remotely, and said, "I like it. It makes me different."

"Don't you wish there were more black kids?"

"It would be good, but this is only a school. In the rest of the country there are ten black children for every white one."

Mia looked at him with narrowed eyes.

"And in Swaziland," he continued, "you would be the only white child in a school of black kids."

The bell rang. He clicked the lid of his lunch tin down tight.

"It's like your hair—there's only a little white, the rest is black," he smiled.

Mia reached up and twirled her fingers in her hair.

"Why don't you sing *Die Stem* at assembly?" Mia asked.

He looked at her for a moment, as if considering whether he would tell her. "Afrikaans is the language of our oppressors. It is not my national anthem. I keep quiet as a form of protest."

"I won't tell anyone," she said.

He smiled. "It's no secret."

Mia felt a small tuft of deflation.

"Are you going to have a *barmitzvah*?" she asked.

"I'm not Jewish," he said. "Just because I sit next to you in class doesn't make me a Jew."

"Ja, but you're learning Hebrew."

"I'm here to get a good education. That's all. I also want to go to university, become a businessman and make lots of money."

Asher had been wrong about the black man. He wasn't going to stay like a monkey in the bush. "What will you study there?"

"History and political science," he said, standing up. "I'm sorry, I've got to go to Biology now." And he turned and left her standing there, coiling her fingers around the white hairs of her birthmark. But before he rounded the corner, he turned and said, "And so do you."

Mia ran after him. "I'll keep a place for you… if you like…."

Time Square Café, Rockey Street,
Yeoville,
28 March 1994

"Thanks for coming," he said. "Of course," she smiled. Time Square Café always seemed full, no matter what time of the day. Yeoville, once the place to hang out if one were living in disregard of the *Immorality Act,*[*] was now full of accents—Eastern European mostly, but also French and snatches of German.

"Do you want something to drink? To eat?" Blokes said, beckoning a waiter.

"An espresso would be great."

"They make a wicked thing here with mince and cheese, all toasted."

"No thanks," Mia laughed. "But I wouldn't say no to some biltong."

Blokes grinned. "I remember those days. Fondly. You sending me out at the crack of dawn to look for bloody biltong. Man, the times I thought you were pregnant with my baby…"

They smiled in shared memory of a lovemaking always superseded by a rush for a café, a butchery so that Mia could fill the emptinesses. When Blokes returned with a brown paper

[*] of 1949, followed by a ban on sexual relations between blacks and whites.

bag scrunched up tight at the edges, which he would hold behind his back, teasing, he would lift the sheets to find her nakedness so he that could press his cool lips to her belly, nudge her legs apart and enter her, warm and wet from their earlier love-making. The bag of biltong in his hand, released finally as his orgasm slackened his grip. She would grab it, without waiting for him to roll off her, and stuff her mouth with a handful of wet salty flesh, as he lay heavy on her body.

Even as a man Blokes looked like a boy of sixteen. His skin was smooth and he still had hardly any facial hair. Mia resisted the desire to lean over the table and touch his face with her hands.

"Did you ever see that Leon Schuster—the one with the butcher?" Mia asked.

Blokes shook his head.

"It was one of those Candid Camera things where they put a sign outside a butchery saying 'Fresh meat'. People come in and wait to be served. And you hear 'mooo, mooo, mooo' coming from the back. Then Schuster comes out, dressed like a butcher, holding a chain saw in one hand, dripping with what looks like blood, and plonks half a cow's carcass on the counter."

"I never saw it," Blokes said.

"It was hilarious. One of the old men said, '*Ag sies, daar's kinders en vroumense hierso.*'"*

Blokes laughed. "The bloodier, the better. Is that still how you like it?"

Mia laughed. "I must have been a cannibal in a previous life."

"So tell me, my gypsy woman, where have you been?"

"Everywhere," Mia said, looking into his eyes only briefly, and flicking her gaze.

* 'Shame on you, there's children and women here,' in Afrikaans.

Joanne Fedler

A woman with broken toes and bare feet, reeking of alcohol and carrying a small baby strapped to her back, hobbled by on crutches. She touched Mia's arm to get her attention and held out her hand for money. Mia looked at her, reached into her bag, fumbled for her wallet, but before she could find it, Blokes had reached into his pocket and deposited a two rand coin in the old woman's hand. "*Hamba kahle ma,*"* he said gently, and she brought her two knobbled hands, wrapped in rags like a boxer, together in a gesture of thanks. She shuffled on to the next table, but was swatted away like a fly by the occupants, two swarthy Eastern European men smoking some heavily tobaccoed European cigarettes and wearing shoes one wears to business meetings even though this was a Tuesday morning and if they had business meetings, they should have been in them.

"You've been writing?" he asked.

Mia nodded, but was cut short by the arrival of a waitress.

"What will it be?" the waitress asked, leaning into her hip the way girls do who are flirting or waiting for a pick up. Her fishnet stockings under her shorts had a ladder on the heel of her left foot and her shoes were scuffed and old. But her legs were long and willowy, so men wouldn't notice the shoes for the stockings.

"An espresso for me, please," Mia said.

"Brandy and Coke for me," Blokes said, winking at Mia.

"Since when do you drink?" Mia asked, wide-eyed.

"A lot's changed since those days…" Blokes said. "And a toasted cheese and mince," to the waitress. "Sure you don't want something to eat?"

"I'm fine, seriously. Just the coffee."

The waitress nodded, left in her scuffed shoes.

"Ja, been writing. I've seen some pretty fucked up people and places in the last seven years. The worst by far was Bosnia.

* 'Go well, mother,' in Zulu.

Christ, it is a holocaust what's going on there. The women are being destroyed there."

Blokes shook his head sadly. "We don't deserve this planet, hey."

"I've seen more sadness than I can describe. Words, you know, my tools for telling, have failed me."

He uttered no platitudes, made no inquiries. Unlike the newspapers she fed with her articles, Blokes did not push for lascivious detail.

A man plonked a wooden swinging pelican and a note on their table and, without pausing, moved to the other tables where he did the same. Mia picked up the note. *I have been deaf since birth. These are my handmade crafts. Thank you for supporting me. Samson.*

"I already have two," Blokes said.

"And I don't have a home to put it in," Mia said.

"Don't you?"

"I'm staying with Henri."

"Why don't you find your own place?"

"I don't know how long I'm here for."

Blokes let out a bitter laugh. "That's you, Mia—forever on the run. Running everywhere to everyone else's problems except your own."

"What does that mean, Blokes?" Mia said, adding, "Sorry, not today," to the Samson, deaf since birth, and handing him back the pelican.

"I'm buying it for you," Blokes said, reaching back for the pelican. "For your home. One day."

Mia sat back in her chair, watched Blokes pay for the pelican. Samson made exuberant gestures of appreciation and wrapped it in a Pick 'n' Pay packet he removed from his jacket pocket. Blokes nodded and smiled. He handed the wrapped up pelican to Mia. She took it reluctantly.

"What did you mean, running to everyone else's problems?" she asked.

"Well, it's not like history has passed us by. Lots has happened here in the past seven years. There were lots of stories to write about. We needed journalists here, people with a conscience."

"I had to leave."

"That's the chorus of your song."

"I'm restless."

"A good excuse."

"Well, I'm here now, aren't I?"

"Just until after the election, after a few good articles in the *Mail & Guardian*, and then you'll be off again to find another mess on the planet, more hearts to break."

"Sounds like you've missed me."

She reached over for his hand. He grabbed hers. His hands were warm. They interlaced fingers.

"Don't you ever get tired of moving?"

She smiled, shrugged. "I don't know how to stop."

The espresso and brandy arrived. Blokes and Mia broke their grasp to allow the waitress to put the drinks on the table. The espresso was more biting than she remembered. It stained her mouth and burned her throat—a yellowy-dark drink of bitter sweetness. She tinged the spoon on the side of the miniature cup.

"One day you'll stop running…" he said. "And I hope I'm there to see it…"

She downed the rest of her coffee.

"Blokes, how do we know when we've finished in a place? When our business is done, when we've what we came for or were sent for? We get no letters of resignation or termination. So how do we know?"

He considered her question. He looked past her and then back at her. "We wait for postcards, phonecalls. And when enough time has passed and there's nothing, we move on. To other pastures," he said wryly.

Mia smiled. "You did say you wouldn't wait."

"Yes… and you said you would write…"

"It doesn't mean I forgot…"

"It doesn't matter now," he smiled.

"No, I guess it doesn't. How old is your child?" Mia asked.

"He's four. My son, Xolile."

"That big?"

"I had to move on."

"I know."

The toasted cheese and mince arrived. It did look tempting. Blokes picked up his knife and fork. "Sure you don't want a bite?"

"I gotta go find some biltong," Mia said, standing to leave. She took a five rand note out of her bag and put it on the table. She squeezed Blokes on the shoulder, before striding down the steps of Time Square Café and disappearing into the throng of people on Rockey Street, leaving him to eat alone, and the wooden pelican on the table, forgotten.

Joanne Fedler

Part 5

And it came to pass when they were in the field
that Cain rose up against Abel his brother, and slew him.
And the Lord said unto Cain, 'Where is Abel, thy brother?'
And he said, 'I know not. Am I my brother's keeper?'
And he said 'What hast thou done?
The voice of thy brother's blood crieth unto me from the ground.'

Genesis, Chapter 4

★★★

How many shall pass away
And how many shall be brought into existence?
Who shall live and who shall die?
Who shall come to a timely end and who to an untimely end?
Who shall perish by fire and who by water?
Who by sword and who by beast?
Who by hunger and who by thirst?
Who by earthquake and who by plague?
Who by strangling and who by stoning?
Who shall be at ease and who shall wander about?
Who shall be at peace and who shall be molested?

Yom Kippur Service,
Mahzor

The patch at the end of the garden,
December 1977

Mia had nightmares about the ear. She worried that it might turn up somewhere unexpected, like in the breakfast cereal or between the pages of one of her stories. She was sitting at her patch at the end of the garden. The grass was long and the weeds had taken over, even in some of the flowerbeds. Maybe she had grown too big for her life. Or perhaps someone had cut off a piece of it when she wasn't looking. But, like a blind circus dwarf, she could not tell whether it was she who had grown or her life that had shrunk. Her world was slowly emptying, but the source of the leak remained a mystery.

She held the words in a small space in her head. Nervous. Breakdown. They had come easily off her mother's tongue. Rolling the words round and round in her mouth like a sourball, Mia repeated, 'Nervous Breakdown. Ner. Vous. Break. Down. Nerv. Ous. Br. Ache. Down.' Nervous was butterflies in your tummy before you had to go up on stage. Or how Grace's lie made you feel.

Or finding the broken Kolinskys in the bin.

Her hand had shaken as she pulled out the broken splinters of brushes and laid them out on the floor, dismembered wooden corpses, a portent of something horribly unfixable. With forensic dedication, she had found each brush's broken half, and stuck them together with sticky tape, the way she used to force her mother and father to hold hands. She asked Sarafina for an old jar, and stacked the brushes in them. She put it on the window sill in her bedroom alongside her flying figures—a vase of crippled flowers. Only the one he had used to paint her portrait 'Moonsmile', did she put it in her 'Just in Case': the small leather valise Issey had given her, belonging to his mother. There she also harvested all the signs she had taken down from around the house just after Fran drove him to hospital. A pale face behind a closed car window.

'*Beware the Jabberwock, my son,*' she had taken down from the fridge door, the black capital letters in his neat artist's hand strangely terrifying. '*How the winds are laughing, they laugh with all their might,*' she had removed from the door of his studio. She hated how weird it made her feel.

'Thou shalt honour thy mother and thy father,' the sign he had hung around his neck, with two pieces of string and worn for a week, had disappeared. She couldn't find it anywhere, even after rummaging through all the dustbins, her hands trembling in anticipation of finding a severed ear.

It had been eleven whole days since Asher's last supper. Only she wished she had known that it would be his last—that way she would have had a chance to say goodbye. But like with dying, you only knew too late all the things you should have done.

Now, sitting cross-legged at the end of the garden, she wrote:

Asher's last supper

Roast chicken and potatoes. Asher let her have the parson's nose.

Issey had asked lots of questions while Asher ate, not answering any as if Issey was not speaking at all. Questions about Soweto. Prime Minister BJ Vorster. Terrorism. Interrogations.

What happened to Steve B Co?

Asher had put his knife and fork down straight on his plate like you do when you have had enough, even though his plate was still full and said, "Why all these questions? 'ow would I know?" The red veins in Issey's eyes had pulsed with anger. He said things like 'spy' and 'Israeli intelligence', which had made Asher laugh until Mia had seen all the way into the back of his throat. And Asher had wiped his mouth slowly with a napkin and said he thought he should go, though Fran had reached out for his hand and said, 'No, don't'. And that's when Issey had punched the table. Asher had excused himself to go to the toilet. No-one around the table had spoken while he was gone. When he returned, Issey had said, "You are not welcome in my house anymore." Asher had shrugged. Fran had sobbed into her napkin. At the front door, Asher handed Issey a brown envelope from the folds of his jacket.

"This is for your father," he said. "Make sure 'e gets it."

Before anyone could speak or cry or remake what had just been broken, he had left.

In the silence that followed the starting up of the Mazda, and the swallowing of the sound of its engine in the Johannesburg night, Issey tore open the brown envelope. It was filled with a small wad of opened letters. Issey had removed one from its envelope, opened it, turned it one way and then another. They were all in Yiddish.

Stupid fucking asshole

Endangering this family

Just leave with him if that's what you want

That night the shouting had started. By the next morning, the drawers in Issey's studio had all been overturned. And the horrible terrible unbearable thing had happened: the dreamcloth was gone.

Dreamcloth gone

Asher was gone too. His flat was empty, the Mazda stood parked outside with no trace of a memory that he once was there, though its side-window was smashed and the radio had been stolen.

Asher gone

Later Uncle Shmooley had come by. His voice carried from the lounge up the staircase to the top stair where Mia sat, holding the stones in her hand. "Man, Solly Iserow told me. He's a police reservist, sits behind me in *shul*. He's working with the government, you know. I bet you he was working with the Secret Police here. Training them or something. And now he's probably gone underground."

Mia felt a cold flicking somewhere under her shoulder blades, the same she got when they told her White Lies. Like when Bruce Lee, their tabby cat had been run over by the blue Toyota, and they said he 'had to go for an operation'. One two three four five six seven days at the vet passed when she prayed he would get well. But at the end of the week, they said, 'sorry he didn't make it'. But then she found out he had been dead all that time. They said it was a White Lie, because they had wanted to 'prepare her for the bad news'. As if death had ever scared her. As if bad things in the world were ever hidden from her.

Maybe Asher had died, like Steve B.Co. Maybe he was hiding in a cave underground. But he was gone. And the valleys of loneliness stretched before her, her secret unreachable now.

Days later Fran had stood hesitantly at the entrance to Mia's room after softly knocking on the door. "Are you alright?" she had asked.

Mia had sat up on her elbow. Her mother's voice had changed. It was washed with something wet, its brittleness had melted, full of the sounds of a river or an ocean. Somewhere near water. A voice that has wept and lost.

Fran came to sit on the edge of the bed and Mia thought perhaps she might feel her mother's hands on her face, or in her hair. But Fran just clutched her fingers tightly together. The two of them held on, with only the silence that stretched the moment. When Fran spoke, her voice was clipped, as if the water had been chased back and the hard rocks had been found.

"Your father—is having—a nervous breakdown. I'm sorry to have to tell you."

Mia had hung her head down. "They're just signs around the house, that's all... He just wants us to understand..."

"No, Mia. He isn't well. He will need to go to hospital for a few days. It's all been a bit much for him. This business."

Mia had gone down the stairs into the kitchen to find Sarafina who always knew where things were that had been lost or stolen and who never told white lies. Sarafina was standing, frying fish because it was Wednesday.

"Fina, where's Asher gone?"

"I don't know," she said, lifting a sizzling brown fish piece from the oil and laying it on brown paper. She sniffed, and with the back of the hand that held the egg-lifter, wiped her nose. A drop of oil fell onto her uniform.

"But you *must* know, Fina," Mia shouted.

Sarafina turned to face her, and waving the egg-lifter at her, said, "Don't shout at me. How will I know where Mistah Troobeek is gone?"

Mia sighed and sat down on the plastic chair at the kitchen table, with her head in her hands. "Sorry, Fina," she murmured.

Bo Jangles had slunk her way into the kitchen, pressing up against cupboards. She paused, blinked at Mia, as if maybe she might snuggle in her lap, then turned and walked passed her to the bowl of water under the sink.

Sarafina sniffed and stretched her back. "It's better, Meeeyaa, better. Cry now. But it's better. Men are too much trouble."

Now as she sat at the end of the garden, with her 'Just In Case' in her lap, she flicked its clasps and they snapped at her hands. She sorted out its contents: the signs she had collected from around the house, the three stones, a broken taped-together Kolinsky and the matchbox. She curled her fingers around the cardboard corners of the matchbox. She picked it up and squeezed it tightly before pushing at the one end so that it opened like a coffin. From the corner of the box she removed the cigarillo stub and held it between her fingers. Then she lifted it to her mouth. It smelt old and dirty, not like the smoke that would come from his lips. She squeezed the box closed in her hand, and though she knew for sure it was empty, she shook it, holding it close to her ear. Even the last match makes a rattle—a little one, but a rattle nonetheless. It is the last lone match that is the difference between a little sound and none at all. 'No last matches in me,' Mia thought. 'Shake me up as hard as you like, no loose bits in there to make even the smallest sound.'

Then Mia laid out the three stones Asher had given her. She felt their solid weight all hardened into rough corners with her fingers, and pressed them together.

"These stones are for you," he had told her.

"What are they for?"

"What are they for? They are for 'olding."

"What must I do with them?"

"Keep them until it is time to let them go. They will 'old you to life so you do not float away like a balloon."

"And when must I let them go?"

"When it is time."

"You mean die?"

"Yes, but not before you have lived and solved the mysteries of your life. But you must listen closely, to solve the riddles." He had held the stones up to his ear, cocked his head to the side, and smiled, even with his eyes.

Now she held the three stones he had given her in her hand and remembered his story of how he couldn't speak for many years after his mother died. But then a kind family took him in and fed him and gave him a place to sleep, and the sister Malke, who was fifteen, held him in her arms and rocked him to sleep at night, singing to him, whispering for him to speak again. In all the years his mouth would not allow language to escape, he collected stones, the earth's rubble, and always kept some in his pocket. Little nuggets of gravity to keep his heart from flying away.

She examined them now as she had done hundreds of times.

The biggest stone was purple laced with white and lavender. A rainbow of purples, not just one kind, threaded into the nugget of semi-precious earthcrust. It looked like grape rock candy.

"Amethyst," Asher had told her as he placed it in her hand. "A gypsy with three eyes gave it to me for safe journeys. She put it in my 'and, and said, 'This amethyst comes from one big mountain that looks just like this stone.' Can such a thing be, Mia? A 'ole mountain?"

"No-one's got three eyes," she had said, but all the while nodded, imagining a valley of ribboned purples, maybe with yellow daisies pushing through the crevices.

"Tourmaline," he had said, placing the smaller stone in her palm. "In South West Africa you can pick up full 'ands of tourmaline on the beach. I give the natives beer, they give me a fist of stones. I lost them all, except this one, it is the last."

Finally he had placed an ordinary white stone in her hand, the size and shape of a bird's egg, which he had picked up off the beaches of Eilat. "Under water, it looks like the pearl's mother. A mermaid gives me this one."

"There's no such thing as real mermaids," she'd said, taking the stone.

"You don't believe? Because you are not 'ungry enough to see."

Now she rubbed the stones together and closed her fingers over them, holding them tight. If she held them like that long enough, they slowly warmed, as if her holding could squeeze their coldness out of them. You could do that with stones. When she opened her hand, her palm was whitened where the stones' edges had pressed into her flesh.

"They also 'ave life," he had told her. "'old them up to the sun and you see."

Now she held the amethyst up to the light, but it was too chunky for light to pass through it. It was only at the edges that the stone glowed. The tourmaline worked better, and she held it up as close to her eyeball as she could without it touching. She flapped her eyelashes over it. It was blurry, but a paler blue was at its centre. It was almost one of the colours of the magic stone in her dream and she thought she must show Grace, but then she remembered that she and Grace were no longer friends. She swapped it for the white egg stone, which she knew would never let light pass through it. It was only up close that you could tell what things are. What can you really tell from afar?

Mia put all the clues back into her 'Just in Case' and clicked the buckles closed. She touched her cheek, the site of the sacrifice, and shook her head, trying to let the pieces settle into their places. Her cheek still stung. She stuck her index finger into the soil of one of the overgrown flowerbeds and pulled it along, marking a line.

Some lines in the sand could not be crossed. Some places we will never reach again, for they are like moments in time, taken from us. Like the threshhold into his studio which she had not crossed in… months… maybe, no, could it be? A year? The closed door no longer felt inviting, like Aladdin's Cave to which one had to remember a secret code to be granted entry. It had happened so quietly she had hardly noticed. He had stopped coming out of his studio for dinner, often leaving her and Fran and Asher to eat, a happy family of strangers. Issey's plate would be put in the warming oven for later, and his place at the head of the table had stood open like the empty chair for Elijah the Prophet at the *Pesach seder.* He said he was busy. It was work. Deadlines. But now from where she sat she could see from afar how he had folded himself up smaller and smaller, becoming almost invisible. She had not heard him enter her room the day after Asher had gone.

And then his voice, a peculiar faraway sound: "Did he, did he ever hurt you? Did he ever touch you?"

Mia had felt the memory of Asher's fingers in her hair, on her face, on her lips, but the voice that came from her mouth said, "No, Dad, he never did."

And then from the softness of a father, whose voice never thundered or lightninged, or made the world cower from fear, came a voice from someplace else, "It's no use protecting that bastard. He's done enough to burn in hell, so you'd better tell me!"

"He didn't, Dad. I promise."

But a sea separated them now. A sea of closed studio doors, a tide of space absent of their togetherness, in which Asher and his cigarillos and all that had shifted in the years he had been part of their family swept through like an undercurrent. And something horrible changed in his eyes.

"Don't lie to me! I'm still your father!" he'd shouted.

And she'd shouted back, "I don't care! It's all *your* fault he's gone. I hate you! I loved him and I hate you!"

And then the hand, the one that painted faces with eyes full of stories, the one with the little brown freckle over the fourth knuckle, swung out to the side, and before she could turn and follow that hand, it came slamming down across her cheek and smashed the side of her nose, so that she felt as if she had fallen head first into the sand.

The hand stopped in meeting flesh, striking the heart still like the pendulum of a clock. And before she could shake her head to nudge the pendulum in motion again, so that feeling could return, he dropped to his knees, crying with those changed eyes, and she didn't know whether to call Sarafina or to scream to drown out his cries of, "Maaaaammmmmaaaa, Maaaammmaaaaa."

Mia closed her 'Just in Case' now. She stood up, clutching it like a firstborn child, brushed the grass off her stockings and walked back to the house.

"Is Meeya okay now?" Sarafina asked as she came in to Mia's room to dust.

"I don't want to live here anymore, Fina."

Sarafina laughed. "Why you want to not live here?"

"'Cos I hate Dad."

"He sick."

"He's having a nervous breakdown. Mom says."

Sarafina opened the curtains of the room wide. "Ja?"

"Ja," Mia said. "Do you know what that is, Fina?"

"He's upset."

"He's gone mad. Crazy in the head."

Fina clicked her tongue, "*Eish*, shame."

"He said Asher stole his special cloth. He's really lost his mind."

"Ja, Meesta Troobeek is a thief."

Mia looked at her. "No, he's not."

Sarafina shrugged.

"He is not. Don't be schewpit, Fina. Anyway, what do you know?"

Sarafina's *doek** was lopsided on her head, over her left eye. She was wearing her pink uniform she called her 'Jewniform', and her legs looked fatter.

"And you're getting fat," Mia said.

"Ja."

"Fina fina ballerina, went to bed with a vacuum cleaner," Mia said, laughing.

"Ja," Sarafina smiled. "I'm be getting old now."

* headcovering.

tsu benken:

remember; keep in memory;
call back into the mind with feeling or intention;
take care not to forget

What would we poor mortals be if remembering were taken from us? What would become of our history, our traditions, our stories, if the archives of memory went up in smoke, or were washed away in a flood? Perhaps we would be happy. Only those cursed with memory suffer. So Maya remembered. She undertook the task of holding onto memory as one who nurtures a sickly child. She was familiar with every intimate crevice of nostalgia. In reverie; she would lose herself; no longer able to feel, nor caring that she could not, the lines between memory (of the way her eyelashes touched the soft belly of skin under her eyes), and longing (for the roughness of her seamstresses hands on the nape of her neck).

Maya pined from the tips of her fingers that moved over the stitches of the dreamcloth, the one Rochel gave in her parting, and there Maya was reminded how to breathe, this time, the warm dry air of a strange land. Her fingers dreamed, and she recalled all that had brought her joy. She played those memories, twisted them this way and that, coiled them, unfurled them, pressed her lips to them, until they were ragged with use. Like dreams, memories allow us to revisit what has long passed— God's meagre consolation when he takes things from us. We can live in our memories, when our bodies are malignant with pain.

Look to the future, her husband told her, berated her. But she was in love with the past.

*"Der goy iz tsum goles nit gevoynt,"** he reminded her. Jews knew from exile. She was behaving like a *goy*. And he would stare at her with angry eyes as he recited the *Ashit Chayil* each *Shabbat* evening. Was she a woman of valour or was she not? Between *Shacharit* prayers every morning at the synagogue as they wound their *tefillen* to put them away, his friend Moishie would shrug and say, "*Nu*? In a nice apple you sometimes find a worm."

In Yiddish, they say, 'No-one but a fool trips on what's behind him.' To Maya there were worse sins than foolishness. She was like Lot's wife, turned to a pillar of salt for looking back. Maya gagged at the taste of salt in her mouth as if she had tried to pickle her own tongue, or soak out the blood, as one does *kashering*† a leg of lamb for the *Shabbat cholent*.** Nostalgia became her sickness and she could not find her way back to health.

She remembered her promise to Rochel. How could she forget it? She held onto each blessed moment, and pressed it between the pages of her mind. But as the dry weeks in the African sun turned into parched months, and still she received no tangible evidence that the time she had shared with her seamstress had existed outside of her dream world—not even a letter, to remind her, to prick her back to consciousness, to peel away the papery coat of the onion—she began to doubt that it had happened at all. Perhaps it had been a figment of her imagination. A place she had written about, a story she had unfolded for herself in the quiet hours of her writing. In her dreams she revisited the places she had left behind, when the softest of mouths had pressed into her own, and she felt the warm brush of a tongue against her own. Words could not hold such memories. She, who had fallen in love with words, turned

* 'The Gentile is not used to exile', a Yiddish saying.
† making kosher.
** a slow-cooking roast eaten on the Sabbath.

away from language. For even *it* failed her, unable to hold the heart still.

In Kovno, there was so little of everything to go around that one was grateful, prayed before and after every meal, gave thanks for daylight and the flicker of warmth from a fire, the half pail of water for a warm broth, the body heat from a smaller sibling to thaw out numb toes beneath a blanket. Expectation was already an affluence; better to hope for nothing and give thanks for everything. A full belly, a book to read, a new pair of shoes—luxuries of which one dare not speak. So how to explain the happiness of the time with Rochel? Surely God could not have meant to bless such joy? She had seen good people suffer beyond endurance. Witnessed the stoic grief in mothers' faces as they buried a child—not for the first time. She had been kept awake at nights to the wails of children mothers could not feed or make well. Pain was the birthright of her people. So how to explain such happiness? Surely it had only been a dream.

★★★

"Depression," the doctor called it. This diagnosis he made by feeling her pulse, shining a small torch into her eyes and asking her a few questions about her eating and toilet habits. It was unlikely that she could be unclean for weeks and weeks on end, now wasn't it, Mrs Kaslowski? But how to explain the longing for the body to feel—something, anything? Alone in the bathroom, she would stare for hours at the bleakness of the white porcelain of the toilet bowl. She wondered how a splash of red might startle the senses. She could not remember when first she had thought to take the razor he used for trimming his beard, and hold it against the parts of her that ached for feeling. And then the welcome sting between her legs, sweeter than the numbness of feeling nothing. And how beautiful the bright crimson had looked in the white toilet bowl.

It did not feel like the breaking of a promise. For when Yankel climbed on top of her, that too was surely just a dream? Inside her paper skin, she was free of gravity (and did not feel the weight of him on her), and all that could feel remained safe, untouched.

"Pregnancy," the doctor called it. This diagnosis he made by making her put her hands on her distended belly and asking her when last she menstruated.

"I am still bleeding," she said.

"It's not possible, Mrs Kaslowski," the doctor laughed, with a wink at her.

The agony of childbirth was exquisite. All the pain inside her that she had held onto so tightly came pouring out in a gush of fluids and screams. She bellowed until Yankel begged her to stop, the baby was out. A boy. Mazeltov. What should they call him?

"Call who? What?"

"Our baby boy."

They handed her a nest of blankets from which a small swollen face peeked. She laughed out loud. What on earth was this?

"Post-natal depression," the doctor called it. An inability to bond with a baby. No desire to get out of bed and do the cooking or washing. Uncommunicative. Weepy. Very common, especially in new immigrants. Give her time. So time he gave her, for she had blessed him with a son. Eighteen months later she pushed out the second one, and it was as if she was awakening from the stupor in which she had arrived off the boat.

Joanne Fedler

When they handed her the new baby, swaddled in blankets, she smiled upon his face, for he looked so sad to have been born.

"Forgive me," she whispered to him. "For bringing you to this suffering."

Maya practiced remembering with scholarly dedication. She cast the line of her memory back to that bed, the space between Rochel's face and her own. And when her hook came back—as it often did—bare, she baited it once more, and recast. She knew the depths of the past held the golden tremors of her most precious life. She tried to remember the sound of her voice, the fall of her hair along her cheekbones, the twilight shadows in the irises of her eyes. Each morsel she recovered she savoured, feeding her insatiable hunger. But the bounty of her memory began to fail her, as the net of her recall turned up, time and time again, empty. On her eldest son's fourth birthday, she stood at the kitchen table watching him blow out his four candles on the sponge cake she had baked. And as the light of those candles extinguished, it hit her. Her memories of Rochel were dying. They were slipping from her fingers like water seeps through a cupped hand.

In the bathroom she retched into the toilet bowl. She could hear Yankel singing *Yom Holedet Sameach** to Shmooley in the kitchen. When she lifted her head from the toilet bowl, Israel was standing there looking at her.

"Mama sick?" he asked.

"*Oi mein kind*," she smiled through her tears. "*Meine oreme kind*."†

---

* 'Happy birthday' in Hebrew.
† 'My poor child,' in Yiddish.

The Ladies Section, Woolworths, Rosebank,
Johannesburg,
3 April 1994

"Let me buy it for you," Fran said. "I don't need it, Ma," Mia said. "It's not a question of need, Mia. I *want* to buy it for you."

Mia was standing with Fran in Woolworths at the ladies smart clothes section. Fran had held up a linen jacket against Mia's frame.

"You need some smart clothes."

"For what? When will I ever need them?"

"Even journalists can dress smartly. There's no rule about being a slob, just because you're a writer," Fran said. "Now is there?" She was already walking over to the cashier, holding the linen jacket in her hand.

Mia took a deep breath. This was a day out with her mother, godhelper. She had resisted so many invitations already. But why did her mother insist on taking her out—could it be that Fran actually enjoyed these times out with her? They were excruciating. Both of them teetering against the brink of the other's edge, hoping neither would push, neither would fall.

Mia watched as her mother paid for the jacket. She smiled at the cashier, a young black woman with 'Beauty' printed on her nametag.

"Here you are," Fran said, handing the Woolworths packet to Mia. Mia took it.

"Thanks, Ma," she said softly. "I'll try to wear it."

They walked side by side towards the car park, Fran strutting her victory.

"Let's go home for a lovely Greek salad, shall we?"

Mia looked at her watch. "Okay, just a quick lunch, I have to meet Henri later."

It was clear to Fran, the way suddenly letters on a page become meaningful as reading, that a kind of rhapsody awaited her. In her childhood (just as concentration could allow her to see holographic patterns behind her closed eyelids, if she became quiet and allowed the knowing to seep into her), Fran could feel the life inside her tiny as yet unripe ova taking root, growing sturdy, and reaching out into a dazzling mirage ahead. In the quiet of her secret knowledge, she ventured promises to herself, little outcrops on which to grab hold: "I shall travel to Europe and walk the streets of Rome"; "I shall buy myself an Italian handbag with money I have earned all on my own"; and "I shall make something beautiful all by myself."

In a life otherwise devoid of symbolic landmarks, Fran trusted roses. They were her only assurance of some kind of justice and order to the universe. She had stood by his side as his hand squeezed her neck, reaching for the softness between her shoulder blades. It had been such an innocent gesture, really. Bending to sniff his roses. The ones Uncle Max had planted himself. And then his yelp, which had turned to a growl and then to a red-faced frothing, before he buckled to his knees. It was a life-altering discovery: that bee stings could be fatal. And that watching someone die could be so unremarkable. She had stood alongside her mother at his graveside, unashamed of her cleavage, her wet eyes, easily mistaken for sadness—the Rabbi had even made a point of wishing her long-life on 'the tragic loss of her mother's brother'.

Fran's mother, Olive, had not wanted any more children. Fran was 'quite enough, thank you.' Her father Bertie, a dentist, had been a kind, ineffectual, effete-looking man, baffled by fatherhood and quite awkward in it. He kept a healthy distance from his daughter and spoke praisingly of her to others, unable ever to tell her that he thought she was 'quite marvellous', and 'rather wonderful to look at'. He was afraid that if he spoke the words, he might frighten her away. But she had taken his silence and distance as disinterest, spending long stretches of time with her cousin Desiree, when her mother went away on her six-weekly recuperation excursions to the Durban coast, 'for her lungs'. It was during one of these excursions that Uncle Max took the opportunity to become the bearer of secrets she did not want to keep, and she lay on her empty bed, sobbing for a mother who was always somewhere else. In her mother's bedside drawer, she discovered that 'her lungs' was really a man by the name of Archibald Turner, a successful Durban lawyer, in whose handwriting she first read the word 'fuck' in the same sentence as her mother's name, scrawled on a letter addressed to Olive, tucked away between pages 152 and 153 of Barbara Cartland's *Little White Doves of Love*.

Bertie died of a brain aneurysm when Fran was engaged to Issey, perhaps unable to bear to see his daughter enter the matrimonial system that had failed him so heartily. "Don't be too fussy," Olive had warned her daughter. "As long as he is decent to look at and can provide a roof over your head…" Well, Issey was decent to look at. He was perfectly okay.

Perhaps the happiest day of her life, looking back on it all, was the day she discovered herself pregnant.

"What is it?" Issey had asked, roused from his concentration on *One Flew Over the Cuckoo's Nest*.

She half-smiled. "I'm… carrying a baby," she had finally said. On that night, it is true to say that her tears and his tears were both joyous, shared.

The next evening he arrived home, laden with an

enormous bunch of red roses. And Fran had noted the roses, readjusted the dream. A glimmer of hope flared in the ash pit of her heart.

But she had not counted on hope's disloyalty. It is a long time—289 days—to hope and imagine and plan for the birth of a child. As her belly grew, her sense that the world held good things grew. But that time of preparation—for change, for a new person, a new routine, parenthood—suddenly became the wrong preparation. No-one in her prenatal classes, not one of her doctors, no other mother had ever warned her that you also needed to prepare for loss, for death. That day on the delivery table, the doors to her heart slammed shut.

"That's life," her mother Olive had said with head-mistress-like matter-of-factness. "These things happen. You just have to get on with it."

But this was anything but life. 'That's life' was a parking fine, a blocked toilet, a disastrous dinner party. Not the mingling of unbearable beauty (his face, his little lips searching for a nipple), and ugliness (the dent in his skull, the paralysis of his tiny arms) of a firstborn, unable to live despite how every atom of her body wailed for it to.

It was easier the second time around. She did not indulge hope nor think beyond the pregnancy. She would not plant her most tender buds in the cruellest of winters. She endured the weeks with impassive resignation, laboured as if a confession were being tortured from her, and when she awoke from her anaesthetic, she blinked several times. She was alive. The baby had survived. But, they were sorry to tell her, unfortunately things had not gone smoothly. They could not stop the bleeding. A hysterectomy. Radical. There was no other way. Very unfortunate. Never mind, at least she had a child. That was something to be grateful for, wasn't it? Her acrid laughter rattled through the maternity ward, mother's turned their babies away from it. No further proof was necessary—she could trust things going wrong for her. As for the baby, she made Issey happy. But to love this child, was to condemn her to Fran's inherent failure. So Fran pushed her away, it was her only chance for her own kind of happiness.

Fran took her mother's advice and got on with it. She executed her chores, managed the household, shopped and prepared for the passing of days. As for her rhapsody, perhaps that had all been a young girl's undiscerning error, mistaking hope for destiny. So she tended her garden, a place free of judgements, a corner of the world of predictable punctuality. A blossom does not ask your history, or refuse its beauty because you have made terrible mistakes. Plant a seed, water it. It will grow.

"Don't you want to know what I did all that time while I was away?" Mia asked Fran. They were sitting at the outdoor table on the patio overlooking the swimming pool and the garden. The roses were in full bloom. The brick wall that surrounded the house was now mostly obscured by plants that had grown tall during Mia's years of wandering. Hyacinths, daisies, but no trace of honeysuckle.

"What did you do?" Fran asked, dishing up some salad onto Mia's plate. She fished out three large chunks of feta cheese and some additional olives, and spooned them on top of the lettuce.

"I've been documenting world events. I was in Berlin when the Wall came down, and that was incredible, so moving. And I've just come from Bosnia. You know what's going on there?"

"That sounds very interesting," Fran said, folding her napkin onto her lap.

Mia felt a sinking inside, like going down too quickly in an elevator. Like one separated from a loved one by seas, she could not reach out, with the hands that were hers, and shrink the distance between her and her mother.

"Yes, it was, and… I learned so much—about myself and about humanity, really." She squirmed at how corny she sounded. Too much distance made language meaningless.

"That's good."

Mia ate silently for a while. She missed the honeysuckle. "It needs the fence," she had told Fran, her twelve-year-old face earnest and imploring. "It climbs and twists and holds on. That's why you can't tear it down."

"It's not safe anymore to have a wire fence, Mia," Fran had said.

Honeysuckle sweetness in the end of the flower on your tongue. The unexpected joy of the discovery. Honeysuckle can't climb on bricks.

"We need a brick wall. And we've got to put a stop to the constant stream of visitors that Sarafina gets. They're in and out of here like it's a station, at all hours of the day and night. We'll be able to control who comes and goes now."

Mia had gone down to the honeysuckle fence and leaned her face against it, breathing in the richness of the flowers' sweat. A brick wall—just like the third little pig had built. It was the only guarantee against being eaten by the Big Bad Wolf.

But she remembered now, sitting opposite her mother eating Greek salad with Fran's homemade dressing, as clearly as it happened, the leaden feeling in her belly as she sniffed the last days of the honeysuckle and caressed the silky flowers. How she had known—and wondered why no-one else could see it—that a brick wall would only keep the danger in.

"And Ma, I've been wanting to say, for a long time actually, thanks for sending me money—it was very welcome, since I didn't always earn very much."

Fran looked quizzically at Mia. "Um, I didn't—send any money." She said it almost apologetically.

"Oh come on, Ma. Can't you even accept a thank you?"

Fran paused. She stopped chewing. Was this Mia's way of exacting guilt? "No, Mia, seriously, I never sent you any money.

Joanne Fedler

I'm sorry… I would have, but things have been tight since, you know…"

There was a long silence. Fran speared a piece of cheese and then some lettuce onto her fork. She took a small bite of both.

"But my account was always topped up… every few months."

"That's strange," Fran said, "It wasn't me, sorry. You must have a benefactor. A secret admirer."

"Who?… Who?"

And then, like a kaleidoscope in motion, the pieces of the world tumbled in Mia's head. His words came back to her. "I 'ave always looked after you—to this day. I didn't 'urt you. I provided for you. I gave you all I 'ad."

"That bastard!" she said breathlessly.

Fran raised her eyebrows at Mia. "Who?"

She had ordered her life with fastidious intent. A place for everything and everything in its place. She had the husband, the child and a magnificent garden. It wasn't ecstasy. It was a trickle, even on its best days. But it was what she was given. And it was perfectly okay. But her discarded dreams, it turned out, were easily retrieved, the invitation to their revival, slight as it was.

He arrived on their doorstep—a rose in hand.

Had she invited him in? No, Issey had brought him in. Had she asked for the trembling in her throat? The flickering in her groin? She had asked for none of it. She had been minding her own business, as a goodenough wife, and then there he was. Life's promises to her finally met, though the timing of it was all wrong. But she was to blame—in her asking she had failed to be specific, she had just begged that it come to her, someday, not 'before it was all too late'. And despite the wrongness of time and place, warm water filtered into her bloodstream. There was life in her after all. In his eyes she read secret messages that made her heart stretch, was that with hope? The rhapsody engulfed her.

She watched for the words, '*Run away with me.*' It was coming, his asking. She had waited so long for it, the last shreds of patience were all she needed now. Caverns opened up inside her, a consuming hunger for lovemaking, for laughter— laughter!

He turned up one day, several weeks into his arrival, on Sarafina's day off, and stood at the doorway reaching for her throat with his fingers. She surrendered to his touch, kissed to life, as the cellophane was lifted from her skin. Longing scorched her body in blisters of desire. Every sensation before that moment had been half a feeling, half a living.

He came regularly after that. In the quiet of the day, when the streets were still and husbands were at work. Naked in her matrimonial bed, she would arch her back, and twist around his body like wet dough. When he first motioned for her to touch herself so that he might watch, she turned away from him in shame. But he insisted she put her fingers to the part of her that had been hushed into stillness with 'its just our little secret'. He watched as she allowed those fingers that brought the earth to life, to linger and slide and oil the origamied folds at the meeting of her thighs. In the reflections of his eyes, she saw herself, legs spread, aching, desperate, asking, and finally, at last, receiving.

Of love, he never spoke. Words were unnecessary. It was all understood between them—someday when they no longer had to keep their love a secret, their togetherness would happen, as things that are meant to do. Divorce, custody... she would cross all bridges when she came to them. And Mia would come to understand someday.

She had not doubted him, even after that awful business he seemed to be involved in. Shmooley was a gossip-monger. And Issey's rantings about his involvement with the government, Israeli nuclear weapons, was the beginning of his nervous breakdown.

But then he was gone. Her fingers grew stiff—her body cold. All the spaces that had opened, like petals to the sun, closed.

She always knew that someday he would come back for her.

She had waited for him.

She was still waiting for him.

Mia had stopped eating.

"Who?" her mother repeated.

Mia looked at her mother. "Someone I once knew who promised to always take care of me."

"Really? You should have married him," Fran said.

Mia narrowed her eyes. She looked at Fran all dressed up and nowhere to go. In looking at her mother, a middle-aged woman, sadness creased in every neat fold of her perfect attire, Mia wondered whether she had ever been happy.

"Didn't you want children, Ma?" Mia asked.

The delicate skin around her mother's perfect eyes crinkled, though her mouth did not stir. Her irises dilated, swallowing the ring of colour around them.

"Excuse me?"

"I mean, did you just not want to have kids—you can be honest with me, I'm beyond taking it personally."

Fran licked her lips, lifted the napkin and dabbed them.

"I did want children," she said evenly.

Mia exhaled and shook her head slowly. "Oh come on, Ma—be honest. We don't have forever. Just try it for a minute—you might actually find that it takes some of the pain away."

"I don't know what you are talking about," Fran said edgily.

Mia studied her mother's face, a face that had never bestowed comfort or paused to allow a child's needs to take hold. "It's true. You don't. You really don't have a clue…" she shook her head sadly. "Forget it, Ma."

There was a long silence in which mother and daughter sipped tea. Mia looked out across the sparkling expanse of the pool and felt the prickle of saltwater in her eyes. What words were there for this familiar disappointment? Of reaching a mirage of comfort, reaching out for it, and waking to emptiness.

After a time, Fran said, "I did want children, Mia. I did. It's just that it wasn't what I thought it would be… I'm sorry, Mia… I survived, though—that's something, isn't it?"

Mia swallowed. A lump of hardness in her throat would not go down. She had arrived, unwanted, like a disease in her mother's life. Fran had treated her like a condition that needed medication, regular check-ups, the changing of shamefully soiled linen. She was a hump on her mother's back, a degenerative illness of which one says, "I am doing fine, thank you," as one battles daily with the indignities, the disappointment of disability. "How was it supposed to be, Ma?"

Fran looked up at her bold daughter, with dark furious eyes, ablaze with intensity and passion. A jealousy surfaced. She had an iron-will more powerful than Fran could ever bend and a power to hurt more than she could ever survive if she exposed herself to its fury. Her jealousy subsided into grief, a sadness that had been handed down from mother to daughter generations back. In this moment of truth, this sadness, with an even greater love at its core, withheld her unspeakable confession: that she had wanted a daughter more than any other form of happiness, and also that her coming had struck a terror in her heart—the fear of loving too much and of losing what one cannot bear to live without. Every afternoon, while Mia was small, Fran had lain on her bed in a locked room and wept into her pillow, while Mia wailed and knocked on the door, each abandoned by the other. But now, with Mia sitting opposite her, there was no way to share that a withheld confession was the best way she knew of loving her daughter.

Joanne Fedler

Fran could not look up to meet those eyes, to share the unspeakable secrets of motherhood.

"A little easier, love, just a little easier…"

"You had Sarafina to help you, didn't you?"

"Yes, but still, it was very hard for me'"

"Harder for me."

"I'm sorry, love. I was such an unsatisfactory mother. I never had any tuition on how to do it well, and even if I had, I'm afraid it might not have helped me very much—like mathematics at school, I think I might always have found it very hard…"

Mia raked her hands through the tresses of her hair, "But it may have helped me."

"Yes, it may have. It's just as well you had your father. He did a better job of it all…"

Her father's invocation sat between them, between their plates of Greek salad, like a retrieved object, long forgotten, but utterly familiar. Mia remembered her father now. Softly. And the remembering between them grew until something somewhere in all that had past broke it and turned it to blame.

"Until your affair…" Mia said, looking directly at Fran.

Now Fran's eyes changed, the cold edge melted and a fire blazed in them. She looked mighty and exquisitely beautiful. But only for a moment. Her hand, clutching a serviette, clasped her mouth as if what had bubbled inside her, that rose to her throat, into her mouth might spill out.

"How *dare* you mention him?" she spluttered.

"Who? Asher? Asher? Can't you even say his name?"

"Don't! He… he… drove your father mad, he alienated you… he destroyed this family…"

"What do you care, Ma? You would have left us all for him."

Fran gasped for breath. "No, no, Mia…"

"Was it worth it, Ma? Was it worth it? I just buried him. Do you think he mentioned you in his dying words? Do you think he loved you? He just used you, like he did everyone, except me. Me, he loved—me, Ma. Not you. And you know what? You can have it—all his sick grim sadistic love. It's all yours."

Fran scrambled to her feet and stumbled towards the rosebushes. She did not trip, she did not fall, she sank to the grass at the verge of her rosebushes where the moisture and soil dirtied her knees through her stockings. Her hand still clasped to her mouth, she lowered her head, and love mingled with hatred for a daughter, a lost love, a buried husband. "Your affair..." was that all that the world would carry in remembrance of that immense passion that had taken her beyond her sadness, all those years ago? Was that what he had called it? Was that all that remained? The hot molten liquid inside her spilled over at her eyes. She felt her cheeks with alarm. They were wet. Her knees were stained. She was sinking. And the roses were in full bloom.

Sarafina's room at the back of the house,
February 1978

T he smell in the room was of mustiness and dampness
that has dried lingeringly without the sun's help. Mia
stood in the doorway of the tiny room and smelled
Sarafina. At first her eyes felt blind, and the room was just
darkness because eyes need time between outside and inside,
but as she stood at the threshhold of Sarafina's room the
shadows shifted and made space for light, and the room took
its shape.

There was a window the size of a shoebox above the bed,
which stood so high it was almost at window height. Little
stilts of four bricks were stacked like Lego under each leg of
the bed, because the *tokolosh* cannot reach that high.

When you are twelve, almost thirteen, they think they need
to call you and call you again to tell you Something.
Someone—maybe a mother—says, 'Sit down, there is
Something you need to know.' But even as you concentrate on
the block of wood in your hand, and make sure to carve *away*
from your body with the Swiss Army knife, you know that all
the pieces of all your days have been reshuffled. You know
when parts have been broken that cannot be fixed.

You know when you will need to start all over again with
'my name is so-and-so and I live at 48 Komatie Road,
Emmarentia, and Grace once was my best friend and she sang
to stop the nightmares. And my dad has had a nervous
breakdown but he's doing perfectly okay, thank you.' And
starting again maybe would not feel so bad if someone had
warned you that you were coming to the end of something.
So yesterday you watched her tie her *doek* while she fried fish

for dinner, but you didn't know that that was the last time and it was unfair not to know because maybe you would have asked her how old she was and what day her birthday was. And then there would be a pain in your belly like too much icecream, because who would tell Zolisa?

"Her family will be coming from Natal to pack her things, so don't touch anything," Fran had said, as Mia stood on the step of the laundry.

Fran had said 'no' when Mia asked whether she could keep Sarafina's ID book, which the policeman had brought to the house in a little plastic bag together with her snuff pouch. 'Sarafina Lena Senemela.' That was her full name. The name in her ID book. It was the first time Mia had thought about Sarafina as having anything more than one name. Suddenly she had three. It made Mia wonder about things you think are small that are actually big. Like places on maps. And the moon.

The ID book had a picture of Sarafina on the first page. She was young and her eyes were wide like it was a surprise to have a photograph taken of yourself. But Fina was smiling big, the way Mia had never seen her, as if the funniest thing just happened to her or she had just won at *faafi* and was finally going to dig that borehole for her family. She smiled so big you could see the space between her teeth where she had none.

As Mia stood in the doorway to Fina's room, she remembered voices from the kitchen a few days ago that had made her crouch low at the top of the stairs.

"Miss Fran, I need some money."

There was a pause. Mia imagined Fran with her hands on her hips. "Who died in your family this time?"

"Ja, my uncle she died. Taxi accident."

"Really? I'm sorry to hear that."

"I'ma need four hundred, and also one week to go home."

There was a clatter of pots. Fran must have been shaking her head.

"I'm sorry, Sarafina. We've already lent you two thousand rand

and you haven't paid it off yet, so we can't lend you any more money. Besides, we're not a bank. Money doesn't grow on trees. And as you know, Baas Issey has to be in hospital for a little while and that's going to cost us a lot of money."

"Pleeez Missie, I'ma need this money. I'ma need it now…" Sarafina's voice became a little child's wail and Mia hated how small Sarafina became.

"You can have Friday and Saturday off, okay? That means you can take off from tomorrow to Sunday—that should be long enough. I'm doing you a favour, okay? But until you pay back what you owe, it's no use asking for more money."

Mia knew Sarafina would be in a bad mood for at least a week and would break one or two of Fran's special dishes, maybe even a vase if her nerve did not fail her. She would make a racket in the kitchen, banging all the pots and pans during suppertime… But Fina did not. When Mia saw her later in the day sitting in the laundry, she grew afraid of the grey in Fina's eyes, and Fina did not laugh or talk. Every now and then she wiped her eyes with the back of her hand and shook her head. It was the saddest Fina she'd ever seen.

And then on Thursday morning after Fina left for the funeral, Fran had gone to the safe to get money to pay Two Boy his wages, and had thundered down the stairs to phone Uncle Shmooley. She shouted when she spoke. She used words like 'thief' and 'bitch', and Mia knew Fina was in big trouble. Uncle Shmooley came by soon after that and said not to worry he'd reported it to the police.

They were all just waiting for Fina to come back from the funeral on Sunday, and Uncle Shmooley said maybe she'd run away and decided not to come back. And then on Monday night the policeman arrived with his plastic bag and her ID.

Though Mia couldn't keep the ID, because Fran said it had to go to her family, she said she could keep Fina's snuff-pouch instead. "They won't miss that, it's not worth anything." Mia held the snuff pouch in her hand as she stood at the entrance to the little room. She opened it again. It was half-empty with dark bits that looked like little dried worms and smelled very bad. Mia shut it, and closed her fingers around it so it snuggled in her palm.

Bo Jangles brushed Mia's ankles with her tail and pawed her way into the room where little things stood patiently in darkness.

Mia followed her. The room's smell covered her like a shawl. Folded across the foot of the bed was a blanket of yellow and blue and white that Mia had watched Fina crochet last winter from the spare wool Fran had left over from her knitting. Fina's fingers had tugged and pulled at the wool and the blanket seemed to fold out from her lap in seconds. Mia had told her that if she could crochet, she could certainly write, because all writing was, was teaching your fingers shapes, but Fina just laughed and said, "I'm be too old now to learn."

The cupboard door was ajar and an old jersey of Fran's hung over it. At the foot of the bed were Sarafina's slippers. Brown Stokies from Jet Stores. Neatly, side by side, even though they were so old they could have been put in the jumble box.

On the small table was Fina's blue enamel mug because she wasn't allowed to drink from the good ones, a comb with small black curly hairs caught in its teeth, a box of Lion matches, a Coke bottle half full of seawater they had brought back from Umhlanga for Fina last July, an empty Nescafé Gold bottle filled with copper coins, a bottle of Meths, a tub of Vaseline Fina used to make her face shiny, a cracked piece of mirror, an old disposable razor—the kind her mother used to shave her armpits and legs, and a purple koki.

Mia picked up the koki. She took off the lid and looked around for something to write on. Under the table was a wire dustbin lined with old newspaper. Mia bent down and pulled it out of the bin. There was a photo of PW Botha. Underneath it was printed 'hands are clean in every respect'. Fran would like him, Mia thought. A pretty lady smiled next to a frozen turkey. "Pick 'n' Pay prime frozen turkeys only R1,32 per kilo," Mia read out loud. She then wrote an 'S' across PW Botha's face. The 's' smudged at the top where Mia pressed hard. She continued 'arafina Lena Senemela'. She then replaced the lid on the koki and put it back on the table next to the mirror. Then she picked up the razor and ran her index finger lightly over the blades. She pressed her finger onto the blade and held it up to the light. A small flap of skin had been neatly sliced away from her fingertip and a margin of blood was welling, but it did not feel sore.

Mia wondered what Sarafina had been doing in the backstreet and where the backstreet was. The young policeman whose feet had scrunched the autumn leaves as he walked up the driveway was handsome. He had brought her ID book with her full name and big smile. He had brown hair and blue eyes like tourmalines and a neat moustache.

"She was found too late. Collapsed in a bloody mess. But they won't learn—don't know the meaning of birth control. You know, it's like it's against their beliefs," he'd said.

Uncle Shmooley had to leave with the handsome policeman with the tourmaline eyes. He came back three hours later, very pale. They called for Mia. They called again. But she was carving a figure with broken wings, not caring that the blood on her hands from where the blade had slipped, was staining the wood.

'Sandringham Gardens',
Sandringham, Johannesburg,
13 April, 1994

"**Y**ou must go," Henri said. "I don't *must* do anything," Mia had said. "I don't want to see him. He can die and rot in hell—it will give me pleasure."

"He's an old man, you stubborn old *heks*.* Man, where's your respect?" Henri had shaken her head. The green Volksie was packed with pamphlets and flipcharts, and they were all ready to go. The phone in Henri's flat had rung just as they were locking to leave with Fran's voice, urgent. "Please go, Mia."

"I'll go see him another time," Mia had said. "Right now, I'm coming with you and you're gonna educate those voters and I am going to write a story."

Henri had grabbed her arm and with her other hand held Mia's face so that their eyes locked. "Listen here. Your ma said he needs to see you *now*. Going later might be too late. I'll drive you over there, you can run up to see him. African time, these voter education things always start late."

There was something in the way Henri had looked at her, a fever and an urgency that chilled her. What the fuck did Zaide Yankel, demented with old age, want with her now?

* Afrikaans for 'witch.'

She found him easily. An impatient nurse holding a full bedpan had told her 'the fourth door on the left on the sixth floor'. She entered his room silently. He was sitting with his back facing her, propped up in a chair looking out the window. He was a de-fleshed chicken of a man jiggling and pecking in full hospital regalia. The long tattered ribbons of his nightshirt hung down the back of the chair.

She did not know how to begin. Nausea began to well up in the place of a nameless hatred so old it had worn a well in the rocky crevices of her heart.

She stood in front of him. He nodded and squinted up at her. "Is that you, Mia?"

"Yes."

"Thanks God you have come. Sit down," he said, motioning to the other chair.

She sat. He wasted no time. "A man makes many mistakes in his lifetime. None so many as those he makes when he is an ignorant youth. A hungry younk man with many hopes and dreams. I always told my children—Shmooley, Issey, your beloved father, may his soul rest in peace—don't have regrets." He coughed and shook loudly, a rattly mucousy grumble. When he regained his composure, he continued. "Regrets is not good to have. I didn't think I was doing somethink wrong. It is not to pardon what I did, but I did not know a better way. Shame for me. It is a shame for an old man who can see the end of his life to have so many regrets as what I do."

Mia looked into his face, crinkled and folded in upon itself from a lifetime of days. She watched the rise and fall of his chest, like a bobbing ocean, exerting its last power, the hastened pace of one who can sense its destination.

"She wanted forgiveness from me, but I told her only *Hashem* forgives…"

He did not speak her name, but the way things were spoken lifted the edges from the darkness of ignorance and her ghost arched towards his voice, as the old man spoke to it directly.

"Such behaviour is a sin, I told her. And the rib, which *Hashem* had taken from man, made he a woman, and brought her unto the man. Genesis, chapter two, verse twenty-two. It is not my commandment. I didn't write the *Torah*. It is *Hashem's* word."

Mia felt her ghost spinning.

He continued. "I tried to get her out—her and the boy. But the law was bigger than me. They closed immigration to Jews. The government."

He paused. Lifted his knobbly hands to his eyes, wiped them.

"Maybe it suited me."

Mia did not move. She sat silent, witness to a confession.

"It was a tragedy. Nobody can deny it. I told her it was the behaviour of a *meshugennah*.* To kill oneself, how could such a think happen? But they loved one another. Of that I am certain."

Mia nodded and her lips wanted to form to say something, but stopped.

"I am not proud of everythink I did. I made mistakes. But she gave me two wonderful sons, and your father—may his dear soul rest in peace—was to me like Joseph was to Jacob. He was my favourite. And to bury a child, as I did, is my punishment. It is not the sons who bear the sins of the fathers as it is written in the *Torah*. It is the fathers' who bear their own sins. They have to sacrifice their sons. I was not so lucky as Abraham."

A black nurse put her head in at the door.

"Lunch, Mr Kaslow? We got macaroni cheese and jelly."

The old man waved her away. "I am not hunkry today."

"Sure? Supper is only at five thirty, remember?"

"Not today," he said roughly.

---

* 'a mad person,' in Yiddish.

"Suit yourself," she said, disappearing.

Mia crossed her legs and squeezed her hands together. Before long, he continued.

"I cared for her. I honoured her. I praised her. I put food on the table for her. Every Friday night before she died and even after she died, may her soul rest in peace, I said *Ayshet Chayil* for her. And when she was dyink, for the love of another, I nursed her. In my arms—no-one else's—she died. Her last breath I was there for. That," he said emphatically, waving the sickle of his forefinger, "is also love."

The old man turned his head away from her. His shaking had almost stopped. When he turned to look at her, his milky eyes, half blind from cataracts, seemed for a moment to see deeply, and the wetness that formed at their edges held fast before spilling into the furrows of his face. He reached for the drawer at his bedside table, found the knob, opened it. From it, he removed a brown envelope from which a small parcel of well-worn letters, tied together with a rubber band, fell into his lap.

Shakily, he pulled the rubber band from its hold and opened the first letter.

Mia strained to look at the writing, but it was indecipherable.

Without pausing for a breath, the old man read, translating from the Yiddish:

> *My beloved,*
> *This is the saddest love letter in the world. I want it*
> *to fill up the universe like the flood of Noah. I want*
> *it to break the hands of the postman, so heavy must*
> *it weigh. This is the map of my sadness. The letters I*
> *write, the words that reach out to you, leave me cold,*
> *empty-handed. What can you tell from afar? That the*
> *world is large, and we are small? My body curves*
> *towards you like a bow that arches for an arrow. To*
> *release this passion was a decision made by fools and*

angels. Just as we sensed eternity, they separated us.
With water. And earth. You gave me your dreams and
so I live on. You filled me to overflowing, you woke
everything in me that slept. You fed me and left me
hungry. I breathe still in the hope that someday I will
see you once more.
Maya

The words felt strange and familiar all at once, something half alive and half dead. *Touch the finger of a dead man.* Dejavu spun Mia's head in a spiral of giddy circles. She expelled a deep sigh.

"Who could help but hope that such words were meant for him?" Zaide Yankel said. He seemed to be looking through Mia.

"What is the difference between hope and despair?"

Mia sat very still. A bag of bones and heartache was all she could see. For years she had swirled restlessly from place to place, searching for what might make sense of it all. But right here, right in front of this old man, the rage that had coiled in her for decades slowly furled up, smaller and smaller winding into itself and making space for something new. She felt the gentle wash of its touch, softening all it traversed.

"One word. That is all that stood between me and my love. One word." Slowly he looked up at Mia, and said, "The letter begins, 'My beloved—Rochel.'"

He folded the letter, put it back in its envelope and tied the rubber band around the small wad. He leaned over and handed them to Mia.

"These are yours now."

Someone groaned from down the hall, a guttural, primal moan of agony. Nurses nattered outside the doorway. In the distance Mia heard the ping of the elevator as it arrived on the sixth floor. The riddle righted itself. The swirly twirl of a childhood dream, blood on her hands, a piercing shrill cry from a distant place, the knobbly texture of the dreamcloth, and something in her heart shifted, a small motion, like the rounding of a moon on its day of fullness, or the imperceptible flicker that sets the embryo's heart a-ticking, or the final gnaw of a mouse's tooth on a rope, and the world changed. Mia felt the unravelling of a lifetime's bondage as the umbilicus between her and her ghost spun in giddy spirals separating them to different times and places.

She shook her head to stop the giddiness, to hold everything in its rightful place. A hush descended. And as she reached out her hand to cover that of the old man's, she gagged. The taste of salt in her mouth was more than she could bear.

avek lozen:

to let go;
stop holding;
set someone free

The first shape Maya saw when she opened her eyes, still hazy with torment, was a gaping black hole in the centre of a head. Her husband, who had been at her bedside ever since she collapsed in a heap on the hard stone floor of the kitchen, a stark white letter in her hand, was deep in prayer, head hung low. The black circle of cloth on his crown was bowed in front of her and caused her to utter her first words in weeks, since her legs, her breath, her heartbeat were knocked out of her.

"Oiiiiii," she murmered.

Yankel raised his head, his eyes bloodshot from lack of sleep, his face grey with unshaven days, and smiled at her. "Maya? Maya, are you back?" He bent close to her, brushed the hair from her face, touched her cheek. She flinched at his touch.

"Oiiiiii, tell me it isn't so, Yankie, tell me." Her eyes, hazy like a newborn, stared loosely at him, a growing emptiness filling them, as his silence filled her with new grief.

"It's true. I'm sorry," he said finally.

The breath caught in her throat could find no place to go. "Oiiiii, it's better I should die," she moaned, turning away from him, and curling her knees up to her chest.

Yankel did not answer. In the long and silent days when she had lain in a state of terrifying slumber, in which the two small children had to be tended by curious but not unkind neighbours, who also brought him *kreplach** wrapped in clean towels and baked fresh bread for him to nibble on in between his prayers, he had decided that this was the final indignity she would be allowed to inflict on him. After everything he had done so that they could have a better life. He once believed the hardest times of his life had been left in Lithuania, that never again would he know the wrenching of separation as small siblings spluttered and were still. That days could not be longer than a twenty-mile march from Zager to Mitawa with a little boy's bundle on his back, his father's towering presence in front of him, explained only by the words 'Jewish expulsion'. His understanding of such things was modest—he was only a boy. And so he swallowed his questions and bartered knowledge for stamina to endure the uncertainty of shelter and the mixture of fear and exhaustion as he followed a father, widowed and broken, into an unknown future. Yankel believed, when he crossed the ocean, that he would never have to face that grip to his heart again.

After surviving smallpox, famine, civil war and the ravages of poverty, his uncle's offer to pay his passage to South Africa had come at a time when his hope had grown thin. Though it was a country full of natives, where there were no prospects of a job if one did not speak English or Afrikaans, it was perhaps a place to build a new life. The hand of God never left his shoulder when, crossing Latvia on route to London, the guard informed him that his transit visa had expired only the day before. And for a pious man, who in ordinary circumstances would not have dreamed of such things, it was only a miracle that he had the presence of mind to shove a handful of precious notes into the guard's hand and to have no more said about it.

And then for three years he was apart from his beloved wife who was a learned woman from a good family, a real *balebatishe*

---

* a sweet made from carrots, ginger and sugar.

Joanne Fedler

*tochter.** In this time he lived in a room the size of a cupboard in Randfontein, unable to find a job, wondering whether to become a fruit peddler or to make his way to Lichtenberg to the diamond diggings—not that he was complaining. And finally finding work as a carpenter, saving every cent he could to bring her to South Africa. Seven hundred and fifty two days in which he thought about nothing but her safety and well-being; in which he wrote her letters of devotion and courage, putting the scarcity of her responses down to the poor mailing system. And all the while she was comforting that young woman they had taken in after the fire started by Hirshke the pyromaniac destroyed her home.

He remembered how Maya had come home on a Thursday evening, Ladies Only wash night, tearful and imploring, a witness to the young woman's agony, as she scrounged around in the rubble for any remains of her meagre possessions which had been turned to burnt timber and ashes.

Maya had pleaded with him to open his heart and his home to the young widow with a small boy whose father had perished in the last smallpox epidemic. With such earnestness had she pleaded and persuaded him, in their one room, dark and smokey from the *pripetshok*, to make a small corner for these homeless Jews. So, he'd remembered the generosity of his forefathers as we learn in the *Torah* and the Ethics of the Fathers, and had cleared the corner where the goat sometimes lay when it was ill and it was too cold for it to remain outside. He'd hammered some nails into the wall, and hung up the *Shabbos* tablecloth he had inherited from his mother, so that the widow and her boy might have some privacy in such a small room with strangers.

Then he'd been glad that *Hashem* had given him the generosity of spirit to put a roof over their heads, for when it

* 'the daughter of a good family,' in Yiddish.

was time for him to leave for South Africa, his aching heart was relieved that Maya would have some company in those long dark nights, for the two women, who stood over the *pripetshok* and cooked, would sometimes lower their heads together and laugh gently—such friends they had become. She, whom he had only come to know as the Widow Stzupak, had nimble fingers, and was a superb seamstress, fixing his old jacket and trousers, and sewing him a new suit for his journey to South Africa. She had taken to teaching Maya to sew, with those hands, which could only write of pain and sorrow.

How could he have known what was going on behind his back? Who could have put such pieces together? Even when she wrote to tell him that she would stay in Kovno with the Widow until Yankel had enough money to bring them all over at once, he had not suspected. And when he wrote back to tell her that it would be many years before he had enough money to bring them, (the boy included), and she'd written that she'd decided to stay in Kovno and not to come South Africa, he had not imagined such goings on. He surmised that perhaps it was her fear of the ocean. Or a person's fear of what is new—such things happen. She had never seen a native before, let alone lived in a country full of them. He regretted the length of time for which they had been separated, for they had not had many months in which to consummate their marriage before he had to leave. A woman left so long alone might forget. And then he had promised he would find a way to bring her, the widow and her boy too, and suddenly, she changed her mind. She wrote to tell him that she would join him and he thanked *Hashem* that He had cleared her head of all illusions and distress.

When she finally arrived on the boat, all wrapped in new clothes sewn, no doubt, by the Widow for her journey, and he could barely hold back his years of waiting, she told him she was 'unclean'. He had restrained himself, prayed three times a day for courage to hold back. But after a week, two weeks, three weeks, and then a month, from one new moon to the next had passed and still she told him she was unclean, he began to suspect she was not being forthright with him, and sought the counsel of the Rabbi.

He had returned home, his convictions confirmed, not with self-righteousness, but with humility, for a falsehood between spouses is a serious concern, and he wished to put matters right between them so he might once again know the soft milky breadth of her thighs and belly. But when he asked her about the business of being unclean for a month, and told her that he had been to the Rabbi, who had confirmed that such a length of unclean days was either impossible or unhealthy, Maya had broken down and said that she wanted to see a doctor.

And so it was another two weeks until she had been taken to the doctor, who reported that Maya had shown him the wad of cloths she had worn between her legs that morning and that indeed it was blood-soaked. She had cried out in such pain when he so much as tried an internal examination that he had taken pity on her and not probed too deeply. The honourable doctor, a Doctor Kruger of Randfontein, had prescribed pain-killers for his sickly wife, and informed him that if the pain did not subside in four weeks, that it was his professional opinion that she should be hospitalised for further tests.

Yankel had nearly torn out the hair from his beard in handfuls—four weeks! And then he chastised himself for his selfishness, for his poor wife was in terrible pain, and here he was worrying about the itch in his groin that had become almost unbearable with her musky-smelling presence beside him in the bed.

That night, having made her tea and seen to it that she was comfortable, he had lain in the bed, his thoughts incoherent. All he could think of was the doctor's hands on his Maya's thighs, between her legs where the curls bunched, and before he knew whether he was awake or asleep, he was stroking the full-blown size of his circumcized malehood. It felt like moments, or was it hours, perhaps he had moved, or moaned, but at some moment when his relief was almost upon him, she had whipped around to face him and snapped on the bedside light. In her eyes and the yowl that followed, her horror was utter. And somewhere in the furious fuzzy jerks to the culmination, he knew that this was the end in many ways, but he could not stop. His brain told his hands to stop, his malehood to lie down, but the demon that had possessed him to begin held him to his destination, and Maya screeched, as he pumped his fist, and soiled himself, the linen and even her gown.

She had moved into the other bedroom after that. And spent all her hours, sometimes late into the night, sitting at the little table he had made especially for her, with maple wood he had travelled to Krugersdorp to buy. In his own bed, he sobbed, and could not bear to see his own nakedness that had cost him his wife's affection. He was plagued by dreams of wet swampy marshes, and of falling, sinking into them. Sometimes he woke with soiled sheets. Some nights he dreamed he went into Maya's room, and despite her cries and her pleas, lifted her nightgown and pushed into her, wretched and crazed. When he woke on those mornings, he was always ashamed of his dreams and went to the synagogue for *Shacharit** early to pray for courage.

So it surprised him when Maya announced to him one night, her lips tight and bitter, that she was pregnant. He thought that perhaps it was another one of her insanities, but sure enough, as the months passed, he watched her belly swell. He did not question but that he had fathered it, and though he did not dwell on the manner of its conception, he was pleased that at last they would be a family, something for which he had so wished, even in the days of Kovno.

* early morning prayers.

When Samuel was born, with Yankel's big ears and his large nose, his gratitude overtook his shame. He felt emboldened by the comingling of their selves, for he believed now, more strongly than ever, that she would not leave him and return to Kovno, to her beloved friend, as she had so often spoken of doing. After his son's *bris*, where he had watched eagerly as the Rabbi snipped the foreskin and mopped the blood with a cloth, and heard the hearty cries of his child, a sense of magnificent pride had worked its way into him. Maya sat in the kitchen drinking tea throughout the ritual, lost in some quietness that he dare not even approach with an offer to bring her some chopped herring on *kiechel*.* But he determined then that her distance was separate from his entitlement. Thereafter, he regularly had his dreams of opening doors, pulling back sheets and lifting up nightdresses, and he worried less about it in the mornings.

And his persistence paid off, for one night in his dreams, she had said in a voice he had not heard since they had first met, 'Gently Yankel', and so he had done it gently, she had let him kiss her on the mouth, he could hold her dark breasts to his bearded lips, and it seemed like a dream that lasted the whole night. And when he woke, he woke in her bed. She was already in the kitchen, but it was the happiest moment of his life. Never mind that he was alone.

Nine months later, their second son was born, and Maya had announced to him in the hospital, after her private parts had been torn and sewed back together, 'No more, Yankel. I'm tellink you, no more.'

When he had finally dreamed again of doors and sheets and nightdresses, he found her waiting for him, a terrible look in her eyes. She lay limp under his weight and when he tried to thrust into her, he found his passage blocked off. It could not

* a biscuit made with sugar on which chopped herring is traditionally eaten.

be. He thrust once more. But there was resistance where a yielding had always been. She winced in pain and let her tears flow soundlessly. And so he had bent his head to find the source of his delay. What he saw shook him from his nightmare, so that he found himself, his head between her legs, clasping his mouth to hold back the panic at the sight of his wife's lower lips, sewn together and bloodied from the rips he had caused with his passion.

From then on he had prayed five times a day and tended to his sons. He walked past her room twice a day and saw her, head bent, shaking empty matchboxes. He could no longer look at his wife with the same eyes. Her craziness had taken from him his innocence. He lost his capacity for arousal. He had become a wooden man, with a wooden leg. And all this he had tolerated. He had not kicked her out the house like his neighbour Shimon Tanchel urged him to do. He had provided for her, and though he could no longer say it to her, he loved her, still.

But now, he would be tough with her. She would have to pull herself together. There were children who needed her, a husband she had to care for. In only a matter of weeks it would be Passover. The house had to be spring cleaned and cleared of *chometz*.* There was an order to the universe, which had to be respected, and a way that things had to be.

When she had swooned into a faint which lasted many days after receiving the news of the Widow Stzupak's death, Yankel had taken the liberty of writing a letter to his sister Bilke back in Kovno, asking for 'certain details', for he wanted to be sure, once and for all, that the Widow Stzupak was buried and finished. Bilke—who was able to write only because their father had insisted that his daughters, all six of them, learn how to write a letter so that they could stay in touch if the family

---

* anything made with flour which is forbidden on Passover.

was separated—had answered his curiosities, telling him that their father, like all Jewish men in the community, was called upon to walk beside the coffin as a pallbearer, and had placed three spadefuls of sand onto the coffin. As he read these words, Yankel felt the thuds of earth on the wooden box, each bringing him relief and release from this crazy mad woman, this Trojan Horse he had invited into his home.

The letter went on to say that, since it was the first suicide in the community, it had caused great confusion, and a special plot had to be made for the Widow, away from the other graves. This had delayed the funeral by a couple of weeks. Further on in the letter, Bilke's words stirred in him the only wave of pity for the dead Widow that he felt, when she described how the son, a small boy, of nine or ten, still years away from his *barmitzvah*, who had found her body hanging from the rafter in the shed, his shed, above the barrel of herring, his barrel of herring, strangled by a scarf of many different colours, had lost his ability to speak. The effect of this was that he stood at the graveside, struck mute, whilst the Rabbi recited the *kaddish** on his behalf.

But the moment of pity that softened Yankel's heart soon passed and his anger took its place, for how selfish a woman could she have been to leave a young child, who had no father, without a parent in the world?

"Terrible thinks happen in the world, but we survive. Haven't Jews survived terrible tragedy?" he offered Maya some words of comfort.

"If we had brought her here, with us, she wouldn't be dead..."

"There was nothing I could do. They closed immigration

---

* Jewish prayer said by the bereaved.

here. Only family. She is not family. What could I do? What could I do?" he bellowed.

And then the wailing began. A piercing cry of one in physical torment, as Maya clutched her left breast in her hands and began a weeping that lasted eight full days. Her hand on her bosom had to be prised off by the *chevrah kedisha** when she finally joined her lover in rest.

* the Jewish burial service.

Part 6

To everything there is a season,
and a time to every purpose under the heaven;
A time to be born, and a time to die;
A time to plant, and a time to reap;
A time to kill and a time to heal;
A time to break down and a time to build up;
A time to weep and a time to laugh;
A time to mourn and a time to dance....
A time to love and a time to hate;
A time of war and a time of peace....

All go unto one place; all are of the dust,
And all turn to dust again....

Ecclesiastes, Chapter 3

★★★

i can say
one day the sky will weep
i can say one day
this flower
will stand in the bright sun
this flower will have no petals
one day

ah
africa
is this not your child come home
Mongane Wally Serote

★★★

A child's tears reach the heavens

Yiddish proverb

dybbuk:

haunt: to visit (a place) regularly;
(of spirit) to visit, appearing in a strange form;
to be always in the thoughts of (someone)

Old ghosts do not mean to hurt the living. They do not seek victims, only hosts. By accident, that is how it happens. Without forethought. A moment's lapsed attention. She had a premonition for some time that there would be a spill. For those years she was forced apart from Rochel, she was bloated with the tension of it, struggling with all her might to suppress, sublimate, forget. Some dust will not settle. An explosion is sometimes the only way out.

She was a poet. Not that that was an excuse. But the irresistible impulse, the same that pushed her to write, drove her to slide into someone else's life and make it her own. There was nothing sinister about it. Sad old ghosts, just like her, did it all the time. They took over other peoples' memory pockets, made them miserable and stricken with the past, heartachey for yesterday, its people and its ways. And that's when people fall into rummaging, the endless shuffling of photographs and letters and dreams—stuff so useless it would have been wormeaten if it were flesh, and fossil if it were bone.

Spirits got restless, especially around wailing season, and there was a panic in the stampede of souls passed on to claim the memories of the living—to hear the echo of their names in the *kaddish*. It was homesickness for human love, and she had held it at bay for longer than was ghostly possible. For her part, she grew sick on memory.

It was the passion that finally broke her; an urgent need to speak, to claim what she was forced to leave in Kovno. She thought dying was a way to find her again. But in death she was no closer to what she had lost. She died young. Old enough to birth two children and to live to see the eldest speak—in English no less. Even to watch her youngest boy pick up a pencil so knowingly that he too must have been possessed by some old phantom with a love that needed a human hand. But the pain in her chest folded her heart into itself too soon. And there was still so much that had to be written.

Metaphor does not melt away without a fight—it struggles in the face of extinction—unlike so many of the Jews, herded into gas chambers. Not made of that which returns to dust, it travels with the soul passed on, unshared, unvoiced. The wordache became, you could say, unbearable. Swirling in the eye of the storm that longs to break onto the white page, she was dizzy with the need to touch the living. This is why she had to haunt her.

Dogs mark their territory by lifting up a hind leg, and that's called natural. Even in Kovno, some of those stray hounds, with pinched bellies and the humming of fleas, would lift their legs leave their waste behind as a way of claiming, 'This is mine'. And so, how could she leave a trace? She knew not to mark flesh—that was for *goys*,* Hitlers, who scorched numbers on skin. Those branded ghosts still carried the smell of their numbers with them. Some ghosts leave black traces in fingernails, freckles in unexpected places, red patches—what the living call 'birthmarks'. She chose to leave a shaft of moonlight in her hair.

* non-Jews.

Joanne Fedler

Her first touch was too eager, too rough. She never intended to squeeze, so that its little skull caved in, and all was lost. The next time she left just a fingerprint.

When she breathed, poetry was how she understood living and dying. She read to Rochel while Rochel taught her cross-stitch, embroidery, double-stitch, and pricked her fingers like a queen who knows she must die in three red drops of blood.

We think that to die is to rest in the arms of our heavenly love. But they could not find each other here. Rochel heard her calling, her voice a-tremble in the elements, and she searched, cast her eyes over oceans.

Rochel chose oblivion over life without Maya, even leaving her child. But this loneliness in death is far worse than that in life.

The unfulfilled hopes of the dying, when time has run out and the flesh must be boxed, are called deathwishes. And Maya left life brimful of them. Watchful as a duckling's mother, she brooded, wept, waited with restless resolve. She left her young husband, a fresh immigrant in a foreign land, with a coffer full of her words. Not written for him. And with the dutifulness of the obedient mourner, nightly, when his children were tucked into their motherless sleep, he would slide the chest from under the wooden bed and read himself into a teary slumber, taking her words of love carved in the image of another, and remoulding them in his own.

Between them they left enough people bereaved, speechless and mad with loss. But it is a mistake to believe that it is only the dead who haunt the living. Those who have stopped living and yet still breathe are deadlier than old ghosts with shattered hearts.

***

Asher Stzupak woke up one day in the prime of his youth, his stutter almost completely cured at the age of twenty-one, and the daily erection that marked his awakening like a flag in his belly swamped him with a flood of memories.

An image of his mother, her glorious face, copper hair, filled his mind. It had been so long ago. He had been so young. He always needed a photograph to remind him of her broad forehead, her rich hair, as if the substance of her face evaporated like turpentine. But now her unreminded image was clear, in colour, unlike the black and white of the photograph. She was bending close to him, and as she bent the shadow between her breasts seemed to dip towards him, and his right hand moved to grasp the shaft of his penis, and began rhythmically to rub the flesh. He did not resist his mother's smile, the curve of her cleavage—she was dead after all. Her smile was glorious, shy, and her parted lips, the glisten of saliva on the lower one, increased the tempo of his movements, his pelvis arching on the bed.

He could smell her, the oily sweetness of sweat and soap, and old clothes hugged to bodies, and the greediness of a child's need overtook him. He tried to get her to lower those lips, to take him in her mouth, to suck the hardness, the bursting ache inside him, more desperate than he had ever felt for any of the scores of women he had taken in this bed, but she would not. He doubled the efforts of making her do his will, making a mother's mouth only for a son's pleasure, but she did not take him, as if she, and not he, was controlling this fantasy. He masturbated more roughly now. "Suck it," he uttered. "Suck it Mama,"—a command, an injunction. It was *his* fantasy, goddamit. But she slowly turned away from him. Her back to him, he could no longer see the bulge of her breasts, her parted lips. She was smiling

Joanne Fedler

in profile, but not for him. There was someone else hovering at the margin of his memory.

Suddenly, his penis shrank, it was as long and as thick as his baby finger, but was still hard and swollen in his hand. He felt something soft, like draped linen against his forehead. He reached out to pull it aside. And his eyes and little penis were astonished.

His mother's naked body was covered by the naked body of another woman. There was hair everywhere and the hands moved over bodies drawing spirals and circles. The sounds from his mother's throat were sharp and her breathing was broken. Every time she moaned, like she did in the weeks after his father's burial, when the organ leaned against the wall, collecting dust, his little heart galloped, but she was so far away, beyond his grasp, which grasped at his groin.

He wanted his mama too, but his mama wanted the other woman. The woman's hair fell over his mama's thighs like a shawl. His mama was gasping as if she could not breathe, but it was Asher who could not breathe, as twenty-one years of repressed memories threw him into a convulsion and his body released everything held back.

At first he had stood there, mesmerized, as if in a dream. Watching her. Was Mama flying? Playing? The gallop in his chest made him unstable, so skinny were his legs, but he stood there for a while watching. "Mama? Mama?" Eventually he had touched her foot in its shoe. She did not blink open her eyes and say, "Tricked you". She did not answer him.

On an errand to collect the bucket from the barn, he had made the discovery, not intended for his eyes. The limp body of his mother hung from the rafter like a bag of potatoes.

He had not run to call Mrs Tevik. He had walked. One foot in front of the other across the snow, his feet crunching into its crackly surface. He had even paused, looked back to admire the straightness of his line of footprints, a game he and his mama always played. He had pushed open the door and stood in the doorway. She was standing at the *pripetshok*, peeling onions.

"Asher?" she had smiled. "Come in and close the door. It is icy."

He had not moved.

"Come in, child. Close the door."

He did not speak. An instinct overtook her.

She left the onions and approached him, ready to scold, but stopped when she saw his eyes.

"What is it, child?"

He turned and walked out the door. Mrs Tevik stopped to pull on her coat before trailing him.

"What is the matter? Talk, talk."

But Asher did not talk. He walked, retracing his footprints, putting toe into the heel of each of his freshly pressed shoe prints in the snow. Mrs Tevik followed. And when he nudged open the door of the barn, it was she, not he, who screamed a cry that roused the whole village, as she pulled his face into the folds of her skirt to protect him from a sight from which God in his mercy would have spared a child's heart.

Strangers' hands offer no comfort even as they provide necessities—a blanket, a warm bowl of broth, a handed-down jacket from a child too big. Even kindness— the bulwark against starvation and destitution—has its limits. Strangers' hands were all Asher could remember. He was passed around like a hat at the synagogue on the occasion of a tragedy—a home burned down, a business gone bad, a child who needed burying—into which everyone dropped a *matbeye** or two, whatever could be spared after provision had been made for

* 'coin' in Yiddish.

one's own. Some whispered his name, *Rachmonis,** in kind tones, others with a look on their faces such as one might get in smelling a herring several days unfit to eat. Some whispered his mother's name with voices brittle and unmerciful. His memories of his mama passed down to him from the voices of strangers: a seamstress like none other, a redhead, a selfish woman... He held onto these descriptions, the tatters of his past, for they were all that remained entirely his own.

He had known from the first stirrings of consciousness that his birth was a burden. Like a crooked spine, a withered polio-spoilt limb. His hungry belly, the ache in his chest, were accusations, and his mother always hung her head in shameful confession.

At her grave, he stood silent, his mouth a stranger to his face, his voice an empty box, overturned of all it had held and learned. And so his eyes became his voice, for the eyes need no language, only light and shadow, and in this way, people came to know when he was hungry or tired: the only two needs strangers could read. He grew sturdy from the comfortless alms of strangers. His body hardened, became lithe and lean. It did not betray him. Never did it hurt. He taught his hands to work, to speak for him, and in this way, he became useful and earned his right to be a person amongst people.

The Teviks took pity on him, fuelled more by anger at his mother's pitiless actions than by the boy's abandonment. It was not natural, a sin of unforgivable magnitude, to leave a child, to desert him to the wolves. Such things he heard from neighbours' mouths, hushed though often they were, for his ears had sharpened when his mouth had closed.

Malke, their daughter, with a honey-filled heart and an exaggerated bosom, tucked him in blankets and sang softly to

* 'Pitiful one,' or 'Poor thing,' in Yiddish.

him, inviting words back into his mouth. But his ears drank, while his mouth remained locked. For three years they thought he was mute—the Teviks' older boy, Zalman, reluctantly read his barmitzvah *parsha** on his behalf, and was rewarded with a new pair of trousers. And when the Teviks got passage to America, they raised money for his ticket too by putting him to work, for he was as strong as a small ox and could carry heavy loads. He worked with the gratitude of a lone survivor, never heeding physical pain, nor relenting in the face of a challenge to his strength. When finally they told him the good news that he would accompany them, something in his heart fluttered open, and he said his first words, 'Sud Afrika?'

The Israeli army had suited him. He had thanked the Teviks for their kindness, put his arms around Malke, who had grown wide and pinguid with thwarted romance, and joined the recruit to make *aliyah*† a year after the State of Israel was created. At last, a new start, a place welcoming the homeless.

He trusted the harsh commands of his superiors, the merciless regimen of becoming a soldier. He rose in the ranks. Without a heart, a good brain can be trusted with many secrets. He had nothing to lose in pitting every ounce of his life against the forces of Middle Eastern conflict. Only small pockets of memory remained for him, like the sound of his mother's voice in her lullaby to him, "Sud Afrika", she reminded him. "Soon, we will be in Sud Afrika." She had wrapped his fingers in a dreamcloth to keep them from the cold.

When the Israeli army was recruiting to train people to go to South Africa, Asher had been first to volunteer. Arms trade.

---

* passage from the Bible that boys on their barmitzvah read in synagogue.
† 'to go to Israel,' in Hebrew.

A barren childhood and twenty-five years in the Israeli army had hardened his masculinity into an allure women mistook for mystique. Malke, his adopted sister, grateful for the shield of his muteness, had shown him what to do with his early morning erections, by lifting her skirt and squeaking in a voice soft and afraid. Though he could not speak, she taught him other things to be done with the tongue. Language came back to him. His penis grew thick with the years, and his understanding grew firm—women were his manna from heaven, they gave themselves without his asking, and each day there were more. His ejaculations left him rigid, fuelled with a hormone as hardy as battery acid. Of sinew, cynicism, and sinister resolve, he blasted his path through life, with the soft space between a woman's legs as his target. He never grew tired of the chase or the kill, only the disposal of the corpses, for how women hung on, begging. They were pliable, weak, full of talk. 'Don't you love me?' 'Please stay the night,' 'I though you cared,' 'Why do you hurt me?' His cruelty stoked their desire (what kind of creatures were they?) and he feasted on them, a starving castaway.

But he knew their secret: that despite their lies, their penetrable design, they desired one another. Their deceit thrilled him at first, until he had emptied his aching rage into them. Then all he desired was oblivion.

It had been easy. Much easier than he had thought.

He was a tracker. An assassin, if such were his orders. A happy little family, just waiting to be imploded. The father was a pushover, a limp-cocked artist with a naïve trust of people. His wife practically unzipped herself for him. Even the black one did as she was told for two rand. Revenge would be easy. Child's play.

But he had not counted on the child.

Children were an irritation. Shrunken dependent creatures,

easily hurt, vulnerable. So when she first beheld him, he feigned his smile. But she did not smile back. He had tried other tactics. But she surveyed him knowingly, with eyes like spies. Her gaze was full of questions, suggesting that all he said slipped too easily out of his mouth. He had been given a second chance with speech, having lost it once before. She hovered around his words, a tilt to her head, as if she knew they had come from the dead.

Suddenly, in her presence, the feeling of being half-alive grew dimmer. Parts of him revived. He could not explain the warmth in his blood, which had always flowed with reptilian silence. He found new ways of talking, as bits of, no, not happiness, but something other than bitterness, crept from his lips. Around her, he felt a pounding, unlike the sexual throb of conquest. Something in him melted, seeping through his chest into cavities brittle and empty, filling the desolate dungeons that had emptied the day he found his mother's body hanging from the rafters.

The Emmarentia Dam,
June 1994,

The dam was ruddy with weeds and the water browner than she remembered. She walked alongside her companion, whom the years had not entirely disgraced. She had grown like a clump of untended brambles, like a spot at the end of a garden, into a slightly overweight woman of medium height. No visible scars. No adornments of jangling silver necklaces with crystal pieces. No makeup. The prettiness that was once bestowed there by the hand of Nature had been slowly eroded over time. A large gold Star of David nestled in the dent of her throat. Her legs seemed tied up in the folds of the long brown skirt she wore.

"Who is it?" a black woman's voice had come over the intercom. Mia had paused, uncertain that her intrusion into the present would be welcomed.

"Mia Kaslow, an old friend of… Grace, um… the madam," she said awkwardly.

"Please hold on."

There was a long pause and then, "Hello, who is it?" in a white woman's voice.

"Mia Kaslow."

There was a momentary silence. "*Baruch Hashem,*[*] it's you Mia!" The buzzer clicked the gate open and Mia stepped into a small paved garden to the little Glenhazel house.

The woman who opened the door wore a large brown wig and was bloated either with the aftermath or the beginnings of

---

[*] 'Thank God,' in Hebrew.

a pregnancy. Beyond the doorway, Mia could see the unruliness of a home ordered with Jewish values. A *menorah*[*] stood on a bookshelf, and other than a picture of a religious man with a white beard and a black hat, there were no pictures on the walls.

She was invited in. Shown around. Introduced as "an old friend of mine from school, when I was a little girl", to Selina, the nanny; Shlomo, who was three, with a nose caked with dried mucus, *tzitizit*[†] hanging out of his jumper and a lopsided yarmulka; and Yossi, who was eighteen months, holding a wooden spoon and a bunch of keys, without the *tzitzit*, but also yarmulked. The house smelled nauseatingly of fish. "*Gefilte*[**] fish", Grace had said apologetically. For the coming *Shabbat* lunch—sixteen people were expected.

Mia had nodded. "Grace, I'm sorry for this intrusion..."

Grace had smiled. "Gila—I go by my Hebrew name now."

"Gila..."

The years stood still between them, lining up to be counted, in silent awe. A window in Mia's heart opened, recalling a singing voice to hush the aching. But there was no singing in that house. "How wonderful to see you again—after all this time," Grace said.

"Really?" Mia smiled.

The years averted their gaze, sidled on the fringes of time, unsure of who was who and what still mattered.

"Do you remember our spot?" Mia asked.

"Oh ja, it's a little further along," Grace said. Her face seemed so much smaller under the *sheitel*[††] she wore, which

---

[*] a candelabra with seven candle-holders.
[†] Fringes on the corners of a small garment worn under clothes by religious men and boys.
[**] Jewish fish balls made from minced fish.
[††] a wig traditionally worn by married Jewish women when in the presence of men other than their husbands.

Joanne Fedler

plastered itself down over her scalp. She had hesitated, but only for a moment, when Mia had suggested they take a drive to the dam. Selina could stay to watch the kids. They had driven in the green Volksie, Henri's generous loan for the afternoon. A group of black kids was throwing stones into the dam and shouting. Some crouched at the water's edge.

"So, Gila, when did this—when did you become religious?" Mia asked, pulling her linen jacket closer to her body.

"About five years ago," Grace said.

"And before that?"

Grace was thoughtful. "I went through a bad patch as a teenager. Things at home weren't great… I developed a bit of an eating disorder, spent some time in Tara, but I met a really amazing guy there, who was coming off drugs. He got into Judaism and invited me to come to these lectures by a Rabbi, and there I met my husband who was studying to become a Rabbi himself. We only went out on three dates…"

"Wow…." Mia said. "No wasting of time, hey?"

"Not really," Grace said, "but that's about average for the religious community. We don't really believe in dating too long and all the stuff that goes with that… You know pretty much immediately if you are compatible with someone. Long courtships just dilute your common purpose—which is to settle down and have a family."

Mia nodded. "Uh, so how's it going?" Mia asked.

"Great. I'm busy, though. There's lots to organize—kosher meals, Passover, constant visitors, two maids... It's hectic, but at least I know what's what." She scratched her wig, and it moved. She adjusted it to fit properly again. "I don't expect you to understand..."

"I'm glad it works for you," Mia said. "Everyone deserves to be happy."

"How about you? Do you still have nightmares?"

Mia turned to look at her with wonder. "Yes, yes, I still do.

You remember... It's been a long time since anyone sang me songs to take them away. But I'm working on it. My ghost has been, sort of, tortured out of me, if you get what I mean..."

Grace did not answer. Both sat still, struggling in memories. One of the black kids was crying. Something had been lost in the bulrushes and no-one was helping him to find it.

"I'm not so sure it's such a healthy thing..." Grace paused, "...to be forced to remember everything," she finished eventually. She coughed uneasily, put her hand to her lips. "Some things are best forgotten."

The Passover night had had songs sung in it. The sweet red wine had flushed all cheeks and there was laughter and remembering. Asher felt victory close at hand. He was regarded by this family as one of them, invited to share with this family their Passover Seder. Eggs bobbed in saltwater. He knew what it meant to accept the kindness of strangers. His miserable life was worth only the sum of the charitable gestures of others. He surveyed his options. Tonight was a night for freedom. And the past welled up against the dam of hurt and anger he had built.

The child, how she had outwitted his heart, giggled with her companion, touched her face with delight. Two girls on the brink of womanhood, oblivious to all else. That streak of white hair admonished him, held him to a sacred core of something untainted, in an age beyond the assassin he had become, to a little boy's need so unmet, so denied.

The children left the table to find the missing matza, a game he had played with his foster family in America, where he changed his name from Stzupak to Trubik. He strolled outside for a cigarillo, inhaled the night air. A commotion was coming from indoors. A little thief had been caught. So much for a night of freedom. He turned to step inside. No-one but the old fool of a man at the table. All were congregated in the entrance hall, a small black boy at the centre. Asher walked down the hallway and stepped into the toilet room. Sitting on the toilet was the friend. She protested, but no-one heard, and he put his finger to his lips. "Shhhhhhh," he said. Locking the door behind him, he moved to where she now stood, pulling her panties up to cover her nakedness. "But…" she said, and again, he commanded, "Shut up."

Releasing the belt from his trousers, he revealed a sight that made her cry out, "No, no," but that was soon stifled by a muffled retching as Asher snuffed out the voice that sang to take nightmares away.

"Ja, I know what you mean," Mia nodded.

"It's a good thing we grow out of childhood, isn't it?"

"I think we grow into our childhoods as we get older…" Mia mumbled. "As a child, you're so ignorant, but as you grow up, you can make sense of everything that felt so scary back then."

"Not me," Grace said quickly. "I left my childhood behind me. I just put my life in G-d's hands. It saves me a lot of worrying."

"You put a lot of trust in someone with a really bad track record," Mia laughed.

"I'd rather put my trust in G-d than in people," Grace said.

Their spot was still in the same place. They sat on the bench overlooking the water. And in the distance it looked like there was a family of ducks circling one another. On the other side of the dam, the ice cream man rang his bell. The sound carried all the way across the water. But what can you really tell from afar? The road can look wet, but up close it's just the way the sunlight falls on the tar. Can you tell from afar whether someone is waving or drowning? Up close the earth looks flat, but from afar, we know it's a curved ball. What can you really tell from afar?

"There's your mom," Grace had said.

Mia had looked up from where she sat doing her homework on the grassy bank where she sat on the picnic blanket under the weeping willow. Mia was working on Pythagoras's theory where the sum of the squares of the two sides is equal to the square on the hypotenuse.

"Where?"

"There," Grace had said pointing across the water. Mia squinted her eyes, looking into the sun. A woman was walking next to a man. They were holding hands. One might easily mistake it for Fran. She was also wearing a blue chiffon scarf. But it could not be anyone she knew because they were walking close, the woman snuggling into the man's neck, and they were headed for the clump of bushes called the Glade, where Grace's brothers said everyone went to 'do it'.

"Naah, it's not her," Mia had said, looking back at the page teeming with numbers and pointing triangle darts.

"Mia, she's holding hands with someone," Grace had said, shielding her eyes.

"Why don't you just shut up and do your homework?" Mia had snapped.

"They've gone into the Glade," Grace had said. "Should we follow them?"

"It's *not* her, okay?" Mia had shouted.

"Well if it's not her, then why don't you just come with me and we'll spy on them anyway."

"'Cos I've got better things to do than watch people have sex. I'm not a slut like you, okay?" she had said, the pitch in her voice rising.

Grace's eyes glazed over, their pinpricks of light snuffed out in the sting of Mia's words.

"I'm not a slut," she said quietly.

"I'm going home," Mia said, collecting her homework into a pile. "I don't need to sit around here and listen to you."

Grace didn't say anything. She watched Mia pack in a fury.

"You gonna walk all the way?" Grace asked.

"All the way," Mia said. She put her books in her satchel, closed the flaps, put it on her back and stood up, dusting the grass from her skirt. She turned and left Grace staring into the distance.

It was a ten-minute walk home. Up the hill she trudged, breathing hard and furious, hating Grace. What could you see from so far anyway? Her mother would be at home in the garden fiddling with her roses, or knitting in the sunroom, or ordering Sarafina about in the kitchen. She huffed her way, not feeling the books on her back or the heat of the afternoon. Grace was not a friend to have, making up stories. The man with that woman had silver hair. Now, did her father have silver hair? No. So how could it have been her mother? That's what she wanted to know. She waited impatiently for the traffic to pass on Clovelly Road. She crossed the road and began to run, for it was not far now. Just a few more blocks and she'd be home and then this whole business would be cleared up. Grace and her lies. What could you really tell from afar?

When she got nearer the house, she picked up speed and began to run, only two more houses, 44, 46 and into the driveway, all the way to the top. When she saw Fran's car parked in the driveway, a wave of relief washed over her. See? There it was, her mother was at home, where she should be. She rang the doorbell and waited. She would throw her arms around her mother—just hug her for being at home when she needed her to be there.

No-one answered. Mia rang again. Maybe her mom was in the garden. "Moooom," she called. "Open up."

The doorknob began to turn from the inside. In the open frame of the door stood Sarafina.

"Fina? Where's mom?" she asked breathlessly.

"Out."

"Out where? With who?"

"She go help the master."

"Which master, Fina?"

"Mista Troobeek."

The next day in school there was an envelope waiting for Mia on her desk. It had a small note in Grace's neat handwriting:

'Dear ex-friend. I didn't find any magic stones at the dam, but I did find this. But your mother doesn't smoke, does she?'

Lolling in the seam of the envelope, was the stub of a small cigarillo.

"So, what are your plans?" Mia asked.

"Well, after the baby is born, we're probably going to make *aliyah* to Israel. Chaim doesn't think South Africa is a place for Jews. Who knows what's going to happen here? With the ANC in power there's going to be civil war. Africa just has a history of things going wrong. Maybe the blacks aren't ready for democracy. They're tribal, you know. And they don't like Jews. We'll always be blamed, no matter what. Africa's not a place for Jews. It's just not our struggle. I want to be among my own kind. Ja, we'll probably go to Israel...." Mia let her speak, and her words spiralled higher and higher, until they were just specks in the sky.

"Israel... now that's a lot of history to inherit..."

"Ja, but at least it's *our* history..."

Mia nodded. "I've got a bit of my own history here to work through," she said. "I just need to figure out what's mine, and what's not..."

The afternoon huddled around them, herding them to a place of gentler times, when blue dragonflies hummed.

"You know what I remember?" Grace said suddenly, smiling.

"What?"

Grace started giggling. "I remember how I gave you

silkworms when I first met you in Grade One, and how you took them home..."

"Stop, I can't bear to think of it..." Mia said, a smile gathering.

"And how you laid them out on your pillow..."

"Don't..." Mia said, shaking her head.

"And how you woke up the next morning, and there were green smears all over your pillow..."

"I don't know what I was thinking," Mia said.

"And how you cried at school the next day..."

"I had killed them all. I just wanted them to sleep next to me... I was devastated when I woke up... My mother was so cross with me, for ruining the linen... Sarafina—you remember her? My nanny?"

Grace nodded.

"She laughed and laughed 'til the tears poured down her face. But she comforted me, she always knew how to comfort me..."

"Where's she now? Do you know?"

Mia's laughter shrunk. "She died... unnecessarily, horribly... a botched abortion."

"Shame, hey."

"Ja... a lot went wrong that could so easily have been prevented... You know, in retrospect."

Grace nodded.

"You know what I remember?" Mia said.

"What?"

"Aunty Rinky baring her tits on the Zoo Lake..."

Grace shook her head. "It's even embarrassing to think about it now."

"How is she?"

"She died of breast cancer a few years ago."

Mia shrugged, remembering a wide gap in a smile, the shimmering of some kindness that held her close, nudged her towards a gentle love for her own kind. "Now there was a fabulous woman, if ever I met one."

"She certainly was unconventional," Grace laughed.

"She was a looney."

"A goofball."

"Did you ever find out why she ate that shongolulu?"

Grace shook her head. "I don't think she even knew why. I think it was just to see me laugh."

Mia bent down to pick up a stone, felt it in her hand. Its cold earthiness held her steady, anchored her to this place.

"I can't think of a better reason," Mia said. And then, "There's something I want you to have," putting her hand inside her shirt and removing a folded rag.

She opened it up in the sunlight. It winked, even in old age.

"It's beautiful," Grace said. "What is it?"

"A bit of history… that needs a good home."

Grace took the cloth in her fingers and ran them lightly over the beaded stubble.

"I inherited it from my dad, he got it from his mother, and she got it from someone who loved her greatly."

Silence shifted between them as Grace lay the cloth over the hillock of her knee, her fingers moving over the patterns, the labyrinth of loops and stitches, the ridges of buttons, the Braille of lace. She began to smile.

Mia watched her. Grace shifted her weight, crossed her legs, dusted an ant off her stockings. She seemed to be nodding, but it could have been the wind bobbing her wig, which had hidden her head from sunlight for many years now. A silver-haired man walking his dog bent down to tie his shoelace. A helicopter passed overhead. The dam was smaller, certainly smaller than it was before.

"Make up a poem for me, Mia," Grace said, turning to look at her.

"God, I haven't done one of those 'on the spot' ones for ages."

"Please."

"Only if you sing, *Somewhere Over the Rainbow.*"

Grace laughed. "I don't even remember the words."

"Start with the chorus and work your way backwards. It'll come back to you."

Acknowledgements

Part 1

'He wishes for the cloths of Heaven,' by WB Yeats in *W.B. Yeats Collected Poems*, Macmillan, 1933.

Part 3

'Love is so short…' comes from 'Tonight I can write….' by Pablo Neruda in *Neruda: Selected Poems*, Houghton Mifflin, 1970.

Part 6

'I can say….' comes from *No Baby Must Weep* by Mongane Wally Serote, AD. Donker, Johannesburg, 1975.